8/10/96

The American Student

Jo Martin,

I miss seeing you. We need to have pancakes again someday.

Sam

The American Student

Samuel A. Berkman

iUniverse, Inc.
New York Lincoln Shanghai

The American Student

Copyright © 2006 by Samuel A. Berkman, MD

All rights reserved. No part of this book may be used or reproduced by any means, graphic, electronic, or mechanical, including photocopying, recording, taping or by any information storage retrieval system without the written permission of the publisher except in the case of brief quotations embodied in critical articles and reviews.

iUniverse books may be ordered through booksellers or by contacting:

iUniverse
2021 Pine Lake Road, Suite 100
Lincoln, NE 68512
www.iuniverse.com
1-800-Authors (1-800-288-4677)

This is a work of fiction. All of the characters, names, incidents, organizations and dialogue in this novel are either the products of the author's imagination or are used fictitiously.

ISBN-13: 978-0-595-36104-5 (pbk)
ISBN-13: 978-0-595-67332-2 (cloth)
ISBN-13: 978-0-595-80550-1 (ebk)
ISBN-10: 0-595-36104-8 (pbk)
ISBN-10: 0-595-67332-5 (cloth)
ISBN-10: 0-595-80550-7 (ebk)

Printed in the United States of America

The book is dedicated to the memory of Kenneth B. Schwartz

Acknowledgements

The author would like to acknowledge the help of the following people: Simon Wiesenthal, Allan A Ryan, John O. Koehler, Louise O'Hanley, Winfried Staar, General Charles Sweeney, Bernd Rother, Jacqueline Berkman, Michele Berkman, Joel Swerdlow, Lauren Berkman, Howard N Allen, Gerald Bender, Jon McWilliams, George Ulmer, Daniel Lidman, Philip Zakowski, Stacy Fusaro, James J Kenneally, Robert O Paxton, Roy O'Hanley, Eddie Doyle, Andreas Aebi, Catherine Parker, Brian Beam, Will McDonough, Hope Harrison, Harold Hurwitz, Laurie R Morris, Theodore C Sorensen, John E Walsh, Father Ronald Siciliano, Shirley Doyle, Dr Thomas Connolly, Helen O'Hanley, George and Anne Druke, Risa Potters, Agnes Hoepker, Larry Bachman, Larry Ramin, Margaret Collins Weitz, Sidney Kaplan, John Kurkjian, Laurence Dworet, Ian Sanders, John Lewis Gaddis, Rosemarie Austraat.

PROLOGUE

▼

Saturday, July 17,1999

I planned to take the Métro to the symposium, but the staccato buzzing of the telephone beckoned me back into my small hotel room. My wife, Sarah, pleaded with me to travel around Paris only by taxi.

"I don't need you getting involved in one of those 'at-tent-tats,'" my night-owl wife said, making fun of how I pronounced French words. But why was she calling me at four in the morning, her time? She wasn't an alarmist.

I told her she should be sleeping. "Those terrorist attacks were four years ago," I said.

She said I could accommodate her in that one small way. After all, how many women let their husbands travel to Paris alone?

I looked around the dark room in the hotel, with its narrow corridors and unfamiliar odors, and wished out loud that she had come along.

"You know that neither of us liked the idea of the kids coming home to an empty house, and they can't be missing school. So how could I?" she asked.

I hung up and rang the concierge to call me a cab. He told me to come down in ten minutes. I turned on CNN and gasped at the wide expanse of ocean around Martha's Vineyard, as the news anchor described the situation.

A plane had gone down, but it wasn't a commercial jet. It was a private aircraft that belonged to John F. Kennedy Jr., the son of the former president of the United States.

I must have become mesmerized by the story, but the flashing of the local time on the television screen jolted me. I sprinted out of my hotel—my presentation was scheduled to begin in twenty minutes. The cab driver shot onto the Champs-Elysées, eliciting a cacophony of car horns to complement the preexisting noise. The wide boulevard surged like a raging river from the Arc de Triomphe down to La Place de la Concorde, where it flowed into several tributaries.

It was a clear, warm Saturday morning, and Parisians and tourists packed the broad sidewalks, which were as wide as most avenues back home. People poured into the stores and restaurants as though the merchandise were free.

I arrived ten minutes late at the hotel, on Rue de Rivoli, for my lecture. By the time I located the conference room, the coordinator of the meeting was pacing in the hallway. He let me know I'd delayed the meeting fifteen minutes.

After apologizing, which almost killed me, I gave my presentation and sat down to listen to the next two speakers, intending to leave at the break and spend the rest of the afternoon at the nearby Louvre.

After the two talks, I helped myself to an oversized lemon meringue pastry, whose moist, creamy, white topping overwhelmed my resolve to lose those two pounds on my trip. I had almost reached the exit when a burly, middle-aged man with a short haircut, whose arms were folded in front of him, obstructed my path like a sentry. He appeared to be about my age.

"Dr. Harrison, *vous souvenez-vous de moi?*" he asked sheepishly. My presentation had been in English. How did he know I could speak his language?

He had asked if I remembered him. While he appeared vaguely familiar, I couldn't place him. He stuttered, and at first I couldn't understand him, but it wasn't long before I knew him. It had been thirty-seven years; we had not been friends, and that was an understatement.

"I'm very sorry for what happened between us," he said. "I'm now a doctor in Versailles. I read one of your publications a few years ago."

I folded my arms in front of my chest and said nothing as he unfolded his. I looked at the Tuillerie gardens through the large casement window behind him.

"When I heard you would be in Paris, I decided to attend this symposium, so we could talk," he said.

"What became of your father?" I asked, not moving my arms.

"He died five years ago," he said. I glanced at the large picture of Napoleon on the sidewall. In the portrait, he held a sword in front of his waist.

I asked whether his father had gone to prison as I munched on the remainder of my pastry.

"My mother would be shocked to know you are this famous doctor. She always thought you were an idiot," he said. His features lightened as he said it.

As recently as five years ago, I'd have bristled at the unpleasant reminder wrapped in a compliment; it was progress. I had never liked this guy, but our history together had been so compelling, I had to take advantage of this meeting.

"Your mother wasn't the greatest judge of character. I could picture her married to your father's boss, Klaus Barbie," I shot back. Maybe I hadn't made as much improvement as I'd thought.

That was when he let me know all the details about Barbie's escape from Europe, made possible only through the help of the United States government. It was as though he had the story all stored up for me in case I mentioned his father. What made it creepy was that I knew he was right about Barbie's escape to South America, and he would know the real story.

We walked across Rue de Rivoli to the Tuillerie gardens and, after speaking for over an hour about the heroes of the French resistance and the monsters of the gestapo, he suggested we visit the Jean Moulin museum. I told him I was unaware such a place existed.

He said the traffic was crazy on Saturday afternoons, so we took the Métro to the Montparnasse railroad station, on the left bank. Sarah would have to understand my disobeying her wishes, because she knew how I felt about Jean Moulin. The loud trains shot through the crowded stations like missiles, which caused me to hover around the dirty graffiti- and advertisement-covered subway wall, well away from the tracks.

We emerged from the Métro, which was located under the Montparnasse railroad station on the other side of the river, not far from Ernest Hemingway's old haunts. The museum was above *Voie Une,* my companion commented as he guided me to a well-concealed staircase above railroad track number one.

On top of Gare Montparnasse hid a tiny museum full of pictures, etchings, letters, and other treasures with which I was so familiar. We sat down, and turned on a video of Klaus Barbie, head of the German police in Lyon during the occupation, interrogating Moulin in a prison. The footage showed Moulin responding to the German's ravings by drawing a caricature of his scary facial expression. I knew Moulin died from that torture. The museum curator came up behind us and commented that Moulin never gave Barbie one morsel of information, but the video showed that, and we both had known it anyway. As we left, my companion told me Moulin was buried at the Panthéon. His ashes were moved there in 1964.

We rode the Métro to the Panthéon, and I paid for our entry tickets with my American express card. The cashier nodded his approval as he viewed the issue of *Le Monde,* a French newspaper, folded under my arm. We descended the spiral staircase, down two floors, into the subterranean crypts. As noisy as the underground Métro had been, it was silent here. The crypts were cold and gray, and neither of us spoke a word; we could have been the only people in the building.

After we passed the memorial to Victor Hugo, we found our way through the wide, dim corridor. All I needed was to see Moulin's name on the stone memorial; once I did, I couldn't budge.

I glanced at my companion, who stood silently with his brown suit jacket folded in his arms. His face had become very red, just as I remembered it. I remained at the grave site for at least half an hour, and I know that he would have waited much longer. I can't think of any other human being who would have.

We took the Métro back to the Louvre.

"I'm a different person now," he said, extending his hand. He obviously felt that I had something to do with it. It was early evening, but the sun was still high in the sky. After we spoke quite a while longer, we said good-bye, and I crossed La Place de la Concorde.

My mind was entrenched in the early 1960s, when my companion had been a major part of my life.

THE BLOODY NOSE

November 12, 1961

The weeks that preceded our move to France remained a blur. Mostly I remembered a feeling of intense loneliness, despite being surrounded by friends. I would sit in the crowded cafeteria at lunchtime, but felt as though I were eating alone in an empty, dimly lit restaurant. Maybe it would have been easier if I'd had a brother or sister who was in the same predicament. It was my first lesson that loneliness had more to do with one's internal situation than it did with literally being alone. But the day of the bloody nose sticks out in my memory, not because of the injury, but because it fell on my mom's birthday, which I had forgotten. I was fifteen at the time. She would have been forty-five years old.

It was an exceptionally warm day for November in suburban Boston, but blusters of wind doused us with leaves. I sat on the five-foot brick wall across the street from the high school gymnasium with my cross-country teammate Mickey Lehigreo. We had just completed a grueling three-mile run. The gusts finally caused us to seek refuge in the locker room. The trees were in the final stages of shedding their multicolored leaves, which crinkled under our feet as we walked to the gym.

"I'm moving to France next month," I announced as we crossed the parking lot.

Mickey looked as if he hadn't heard me, and for a second I thought he hadn't, but I was wrong. "What the hell are you going to do that for?" he mocked.

My classmates viewed me as somewhat eccentric, I guessed. I didn't always know what to say to them, and I got nervous sometimes when I tried to be social.

So I made up strange nicknames for other people. I may have engaged in a few odd social antics, but nobody thought I was a liar. I always followed through on what I said I would do, no matter what.

I told Mickey my dad's Air Force Reserve unit had gotten activated. "I'm dreading going," I said. I couldn't imagine being on a deserted Air Force base halfway around the world in a foreign country. It was hard enough making friends here at home. Mickey was one of the few guys I was comfortable with, and I was so shy that most girls terrified me.

Mickey looked at me again, and his eyes showed his growing belief that I really was going. He shoved open the locker-room door. "Hey, man, why don't you just tell your dad you don't want to go?" he asked.

"I did," I said as I looked at the two football helmets on the floor. Whoever wore them would be able to stand up to their fathers.

Mickey placed his hand on my sweaty uniform and recommended that I tell my father that other parents would let their kids stay with a relative or friend.

"He'd say he's not other people. That's one of his stock lines," I said.

Mickey leaned against the locker and smirked a bit as he said, "You know, your dad is a real smart guy and all that, but that doesn't mean he can't also be an asshole at times."

I just opened my locker without saying anything else. I wasn't about to tell my teammate what my father thought of him. My father had repeatedly told me Mickey was an insolent punk. In fact he had even discouraged me from associating with him at all. Mickey wouldn't be able to hear this without making one of his glib remarks.

The room, usually crowded and noisy with the football team present, was atypically tranquil. The team was still outside on the field, practicing. I didn't bother wrapping the white gym towel around my waist. Mickey snuck three hits on a cigarette before following me to the shower.

I relaxed under the soothing, hot water. It was a luxury not to have to rush. At home my dad would tell me to get out after ten minutes, just as he limited my phone calls. I really didn't think it was about money, since he always asked me if I had enough cash and gave me more than I said I needed. Maybe he didn't really understand how to be a single parent. Then again, maybe he just liked to boss me around.

In this shower, the city footed the bill. I was taking advantage of a rare opportunity; normally the football players monopolized the showers as if they owned the place. But who was I kidding? The football players did own the locker room in a way, and everyone knew it, especially them. They were bigger and louder than the cross-country guys—and much greater in number. Furthermore they received all the attention from our schoolmates, the faculty, cheerleaders, and the school newspaper. Once a year, the *Gazette* ran an article about the courage of cross-country runners, who endured those long, painful distances. But it was only during the last minute of the fall pep rally—and on a cue from the principal—that the football coach finally admitted that cross-country was an important part of the fall athletic program.

I hoisted my textbooks onto my hip for the twenty-minute trek home. Some of the students drove, but I enjoyed the brisk walk to my house, as long as it wasn't during one of our damned New England blizzards. The cars did help attract girls…but usually the athletes, rich kids, and student leaders were the ones to catch a girl's eye. I was ordinary, and everyone else thought so too.

I was about to walk out of the locker room when the swinging door smacked into my face. I fell backward against one of the benches, banging my back. I wasn't knocked out or anything, but it took me a minute to get my bearings. Though I'd passed through that door, with its Caution: Door Swings In sign countless times, this time I didn't see it. I guess I didn't realize at the time just how much my mother's birthday was affecting me. Two football players in cleats and pads stomped in. They saw what they did to me and joked about cross-country being a contact sport after all.

I pulled myself up off the floor.

"You have a bloody nose," Mickey said.

I reached into my pocket for some Kleenex, but only came up with seventy-five cents, my house key, my wallet, some bubble gum, and a ticket to the Thanksgiving Day football game, which I didn't think I'd use. I felt sad about needing the key—it was a reminder that no one would be home to let me in.

Mickey pushed a brown paper towel against my nose, which was throbbing like crazy. This hurt more than the smack and did little to stop the bleeding. Two more football players strode through and saw me sitting on the floor with my back against a locker, as Mickey tried to stop the bleeding.

"It's an unusual running injury," they said, grinning.

My nose hurt too much for the taunting to bother me. Still, I cheered myself with the certainty that I would become a famous sports announcer, like Mel Allen, while these guys would never make it past high school football.

After two towels had soaked through, Mickey said he'd call his mom and have her drive me to his dad's office. But I wanted to go to Dr. Clayton. He was my doctor and a friend of my family. Also my dad had told me Mickey's dad, Dr. Lehigreo, was connected to the Mafia.

"OK," Mickey said, as he marched into the football coach's open office, leaving me behind. Later he would recount to me what happened when he grabbed the coach's telephone, intending to interrupt his mother's afternoon bridge game.

A broad-shouldered man in a blue windbreaker appeared at the office door. "What the hell do you think you're doing?" he asked Mickey.

"I'm calling my mother," Mickey said.

"Who said you could use my phone?" The voice was gruff and insistent.

"My friend has a nosebleed, and I was calling my mom," Mickey said. The football players tiptoed and whispered around Coach Prescott, but I'm sure Mickey figured cross-country runners weren't responsible to him.

Mickey led Coach Prescott out into the locker room, where I lay on the floor, my upper back arched against a gray, dirt-streaked locker. I gripped the blood-soaked towel against my throbbing nose.

The coach bent over and asked me what happened, and if I'd swallowed much blood.

I explained what took place and added that I was becoming nauseated.

"Sooner or later, this was bound to happen. We should've changed that swinging door a long time ago to one with a handle where you pull it back," the coach said.

He sent Mickey into his office to fetch an ice pack, then pressed it against my nose. Mickey got more towels. "I think I'm going to puke," I said as I turned my head to the side.

The coach took off his hat, squatted on his haunches, and told me he thought I should go to the hospital to get the blood vessels in my nose cauterized. He was going to call an ambulance. "Do you want me to call your mom?" he asked.

Neither of us said anything for a minute, then Mickey whispered to the coach, "Roy's mom is dead."

"I'm sorry," Coach Prescott said. "How about your dad?"

"He's on active duty at the Air Force base at Logan Airport and can't be disturbed," I said. "You can call my doctor."

Dr. Clayton told Coach Prescott to bring me right over. Unbeknownst to Coach Prescott, I could hear Dr. Clayton's explanation coming out of the earpiece: "The ambulance and the emergency room will just scare the crap out of him," Dr. Clayton said.

The coach guided me to his car. Mickey continued to press the ice pack to my nose as we treaded across the green-topped parking lot. There was no room for Mickey in the coach's 1957 baby blue Impala; playbooks, footballs, shoulder pads, a tennis racket, thermos bottles, football action pictures, bottles of salt tablets, and other miscellaneous athletic equipment stuffed the back of the car. A large, gift-wrapped package and flowers, along with a few children's toys, sat on the backseat. The coach removed a toy football for a small child from the front passenger seat and placed it in his trunk. Mickey helped me into the front of the car. I thanked him for his help, but he just waved me off. He didn't believe in thank-yous.

"Don't worry about the blood," the coach said.

I held the ice pack against my nose and leaned forward. I retched but didn't throw up.

The coach switched the music from rock and roll to Frank Sinatra, as though he were trying to cover up some kind of double life. He overtook a few cars as I looked out the window at the homes we passed. I preferred the Victorians and colonials on the other side of town to the flashy, new ranch houses, with all their glass, that bordered the high school.

"How did your mother die?" the coach asked.

"Breast cancer," I said. I stared straight ahead at the middle of the street. There was silence for a few minutes—that awkward pause I wished I could get used to.

Then he turned to me and said in a soft voice, "My older brother was just diagnosed with lung cancer. I'd been trying to get him to stop smoking for years. They took his right lung out." I didn't say anything, but I looked down and nodded. Then he asked me, "How old were you when your mom got cancer?"

"It was six years ago, when I was nine," I said.

"I bet you spent a lot of time in the hospital then," he said as the Chevrolet entered Newton Centre, a village with several shops and churches, and a park. None of the buildings were more than two stories high.

I must have grunted some vague response. I remembered the two weeks at my pal's house, when I hadn't thought about why my mother had to be in the hospital. Living at my friend's house gave me the brothers and sisters I'd always wanted. That was when I developed the habit of rapping on the walls eight times at night before going to sleep. I still did it, so nothing bad would happen to me while I was asleep and couldn't defend myself. My friend who was lying in the other bed would ask me why I was pounding on the wall but I would just give some vague response.

We arrived at Dr. Clayton's office. It was in a two-story, red-brick building.

There was no ordinary waiting room or secretary, just a large central area where the doctor could be seen talking to the kids and their parents with a few examining rooms in the back. As usual Dr. Clayton was in the middle of the large room, talking to a boy my age and his mother. The woman's hair was up in curlers, and she was shouting over her transistor radio, which was playing the "Bristol Stomp."

"I'll be right there, Roy," the doctor said.

"You can go, Coach," I said. "Dr. Clayton can drive me home."

"I'll stay until he comes over," the coach said. He continued to press the fire-engine red ice pack against my nose. I almost cried at this point; I could handle the pain but wasn't used to tenderness from a tough-acting, adult man.

We sat in two scratched wooden chairs near the door. Pictures drawn by children papered the walls. Toys and dolls of every variety lay scattered on the floor. A mural with Donald Duck, Mickey Mouse, Goofy, and Snow White and the seven dwarfs covered the far wall. Dr. Clayton wore a lab coat, which came down to his ankles and was as white as Doc's beard in the seven dwarfs mural.

Dr. Clayton was as large as Coach Prescott, and his hands were even bigger. He came over smiling, with a handshake for the coach and me. The doctor reminisced about the two years his oldest son played for the coach as he escorted me into one of the treatment rooms. The coach smiled for the first time. "That was a long time ago," Coach Prescott said.

Coach Prescott shook my hand and left. I wiggled my wrist to let the feeling return and took a deep breath, as I settled into the chair.

"Put your head back and your nose up," the doctor said, as a serious look appeared in his brown eyes. I retched again.

The doctor took a washcloth and wiped the blood off my face as he shone a blinding light at my nose. He took a stainless steel nasal speculum, which shimmered in the light like a sword, inserted it into my bleeding left nostril, and held it in place with his left hand. The confidence in his hands relaxed me. He soaked two cotton balls in some fluid and placed them into my nostril with tweezers, then removed them.

He packed gauze into the nostril, like a magician stuffing rabbits into a hat long after the hat was full. "Are you swallowing any more blood?" he asked me.

"No, not anymore. I'm OK…I think."

"Just sit here a minute," he said, as he went to finish with the other two people in the office. The woman in curlers kept staring at me from across the big room, so I looked back at her. She sure was different from the way my mom looked.

I got up and went to the mural with Snow White. In the picture, she was sweeping the ground outside a small house as the dwarfs gathered around her. Her black hair was perfectly combed, and her red lips suppressed a smile. She wore a modest, brown skirt and blue blouse. The dwarfs seemed so happy to have her there. They knew she would take care of them. She looked a lot more like my mom than the woman in curlers who was continuing to blast her radio.

The doctor said good-bye to the woman and her son, and came back and stood next to me. He put his hand on my shoulder, and we both looked at the mural. "Those parties your parents used to have at your house were the best," he sighed. I shrugged and said nothing; I mean, what the hell was I supposed to say? He probably brought up the parties because the mural reminded him of my mother too.

Before we left his office, he edged me onto the scale and checked my height and weight.

"Is it the cross country running or has your pop been starving you?" he asked, as he fiddled with the sliding weights on the scale.

"I'm the cook at home," I defended my father, but my voice broke when he measured my height.

"I don't want to stay five—six forever," I muttered.

He smiled at me like I was a cute little boy and said, "I'm sure you'll grow another four inches or so if you stop living off Oreos."

He turned out the lights, and we walked out to his white Cadillac behind the office. We drove in silence for a few minutes as it became dark.

He lit up a Newport and opened the car ashtray, which was overflowing with butts and ashes. "Your mother was one of the strongest people I ever met," he said.

I stared at the road ahead. "What do you mean?" I asked.

"Her arm was so swollen after her surgery. She never complained."

I said nothing. That arm had been puffed up when I'd returned home from my friend's house, and it had stayed swollen until she died, four years later. She had to wear those special clothes and that big stocking on her left arm, but no one ever mentioned it. She did all the housework with her arm like that, never asking for help, except from a cleaning lady who came once a week. Some of her female friends from the synagogue offered to do grocery shopping for her, but she wouldn't hear of it.

"Your mom told me that she never worried about anything before her sister died. What happened to her sister?" Dr. Clayton asked.

I told him my mom's younger sister died of pneumonia when she was nineteen and my mom was twenty-five. "They lived nineteen years together in the same room," I said.

"I've never seen any pictures of her in your house," Dr. Clayton said, as he flicked his ash out the window. I told him we didn't have any; I didn't even know what she looked like.

"My mother told me my aunt died in six days. It was just before they discovered antibiotics," I said. Mom had never wanted to talk about her sister. I think the only reason I knew about her was from overhearing Mom mention Rose's name to my grandmother. I'd asked who Rose was.

There was silence the rest of the way to my house. Just before we arrived home, Dr. Clayton asked me, "Hey, Roy, how'd you like to announce an inning of a Red Sox–Yankee game for me?"

"Sorry, but I guess I don't really feel much like doing any sports announcing right now," I told him. I felt a little guilty though, since he'd stopped my bloody nose and was going out of his way to drive me home. Also, he seemed so enthusiastic about wanting me to do it…but I just didn't have it in me.

"That nose must really be hurting you," Dr. Clayton said.

He pulled up outside my house. He opened the passenger door and walked me to the side door. "Don't run cross-country for two days," he said. I watched as his car pulled away in the dusk.

My home was a two-story Cape Cod, painted white with red shutters. It stood on a large, wooded corner lot on an acre of land. My favorite room was the kitchen, a cozy and warm place. It was the room where my mom and our golden cocker spaniel, Taffy, would always greet me when I returned from wherever I'd been. The copper pots and pans hung next to the sink. Our neighbor had remodeled the room three years ago, and its oak walls still looked freshly varnished.

I thought I smelled chocolate chip cookies baking in the kitchen, but that was impossible. No one was home, as usual; it must have been a memory—or something was wrong with my nose from all the gauze the doctor had stuck in there. I used to smell chocolate chip cookies when my mom was alive. She would always have a snack for me when I got home from school. She would be in the kitchen with her apron on. My taffy-colored cocker spaniel, who once jumped up on me to greet me, had bitten the mailman and was also gone. The man didn't sue us, but we had to get rid of the dog.

I walked through the kitchen and dining room, across the foyer, in front of the stairs, and into the living room. I rarely walked into that room, and I wondered why I'd done so now. It was surely because today was my mother's birthday, but I didn't realize it at the time. I closed my eyes and remembered seeing my father sitting at the beige wooden desk in the far corner, answering condolence notes in his impeccable handwriting with his fountain pen. I guess his way of keeping going after Mom died was to make it look as if he were always in control. Now the room seemed very empty. The silence weighed on me, but I was used to it. Despite the gauze in my nose, at least I could still smell the familiar aroma of autumn as my neighbor took advantage of the Indian summer, ridding her property of its remaining fallen leaves.

It was 4:45. I returned to the kitchen and yanked the roast out of the refrigerator, scowling because I'd almost forgotten to remove it from the freezer that morning. My dad was difficult enough without my making mistakes with dinner. He should have felt proud of my transformation from a kitchen bench sitter into a skilled cook since my mom died, but the only comments I received about my cooking were critical.

I placed the roast on a rack, shoved three garlic cloves into the meat with a fork, and stuffed it into the oven, which I had preheated to 350 degrees. I chopped vegetables on a wooden board next to the sink with a large, serrated, black-handled knife. I never opened the closet to take out my mother's aprons.

I stood next to one of the windows and stared at my neighbor, Tom Courtney's brown wooden house across our large backyard, where three massive, leafless trees cast their shadows against the leaf-covered earth. For company I turned on the plastic General Electric radio on the kitchen counter. Bobby Vee was singing "Take Good Care of My Baby."

DINNER WITH DAD

The day of the nosebleed was the first afternoon my dad took a break from Logan and went to his law office since starting active duty on October 1. We never talked much without my mom there to sort of jump-start the conversation, as she used to. But he told me a little about his day at dinner that night. He didn't go into any detail, though. I think he figured that I lived in my own little dream world; maybe I thought the same about him. I found out more about what happened to my father that day later on, because I couldn't help but overhear him and one of our neighbors Larry Roberts discussing the day. Their voices interrupted my concentration while I was studying in the kitchen that evening. Also my father spent half an hour on the phone with his sister, going over every detail of the afternoon.

Normally I didn't find his phone conversations all that interesting, but when I heard my father telling his sister that his boss, Mr. Shatten, claimed he needed to get laid, I focused on the discussion. Certain familiar images of what Dad and Mr. Shatten looked like when they were talking to each other came to my mind then, so I could imagine the entire scene and what led up to it.

I can picture my father speeding through the Sumner Tunnel, under Boston Harbor, around four. He probably pulled a few of the chalky pills he was always taking for his nervous stomach out of his shirt pocket and chewed them. Maybe the upcoming move stressed him out. I'd noticed that, since October 1, he'd tripled his intake of these tablets, which often left a whitish film around his mouth. If my mom were still alive, she would have taken care of all of the details of our move to France.

My father must have driven into the parking structure and taken the elevator to the penthouse of his office building. He snuck into his law office, Slater and Shatten, which occupied the entire floor. At this point in his story, my father complained to his sister on the phone that when he cleaned off his gold-rimmed glasses in the men's room with his handkerchief and washed his face, he noticed his hair was now almost half gray, and his stomach was slightly more prominent than he remembered. He then strode into his office, with its panoramic view of Boston Harbor and downtown Boston.

In minutes his workplace became crowded with attorneys of every age, sex, size, shape, and demeanor—and all of their secretaries. They spread depositions and files across my father's desk, the table by the window, the floor, and the couch, bringing up details from at least ten pending trials, continually interrupting one another. It was an hour and a half before he was able to disentangle himself. He'd always been the one to answer all the complicated questions at the firm. They thought he had unlimited patience, but it was all he could do to keep from screaming. They were like his relatives and friends who called him at home for free legal advice, kept him on the line for hours, then thanked him by calling him a saint.

Finally everyone cleared out, and Dad checked his desk drawers to make sure he hadn't misplaced any important papers. As he turned, he saw Dale Shatten standing in his office doorway, a cigarette in his mouth. He wore a gray, pin-striped suit with a red and white striped tie. His stomach protruded over his belt. He could fill up a whole doorway with his short frame.

"We're terribly concerned that the number of cases on the docket is becoming unwieldy," Mr. Shatten said.

"Don't worry. The guys will be able to handle them. I've told them what to do." My dad smiled as he placed both his hands on his sturdy, reddish brown desk. However, he felt burning in the pit of his stomach. He needed more pills, and maybe an Alka-Seltzer. My father told Larry Roberts, that he knew damned well the firm would be handicapped by his absence, but had no plans to share this with Mr. Shatten.

"Don't tell me not to worry. I get paid to worry. Most of these kids are just out of law school," Mr. Shatten said. "I know, because I picked them," he added.

"Most of these cases will settle anyway." My dad folded his arms in front of his chest.

"I'm not worried about those. It's the ones with complications…the difficult judges, and the intimidating opposing attorneys," Mr. Shatten said. "There's no substitute for experience." He sat down in one of the two brown, leather armchairs and placed his bulging briefcase on my father's desk. He shifted his legs in the chair and spilled some ashes from his cigarette on the beige carpet.

"I don't see anything bad happening, Dale," my dad said as he unfolded his arms and sat back in his swivel chair.

"I wish you'd gotten the hell out of that National Guard. It isn't right to put us in this position. We owe more to our clients." Mr. Shatten squished out his cigarette. "What do you need that extra crap for anyway? We pay you a great salary."

"I have an obligation to my country…your country. You don't want Berlin to get taken by the Russians, do you?" my dad asked.

"I never understand any of that military posturing. The politicians never tell you the truth anyway. And you're going to miss my daughter's wedding." Mr. Shatten smiled for the first time.

"I'm the loser on that one," my father said, as he shook his head from side to side.

Dale Shatten stood up. "Anyway, Steve, would you like to go to the Celtics game tonight? I've got two tickets in the first row. We can go to the Union Oyster House first. You won't be getting much clam chowder for the next six months."

My father took a deep breath. "I'd love to, but I've got to start packing and get my kid ready for this trip. Every night is arm wrestling between us."

"When was the last time you got laid?" Mr. Shatten asked. "That sexy attorney from Gilbert and Sanders throws herself all over you."

"I'm not ready. Getting laid is not what I need," my father said.

Mr. Shatten pulled out his pack of Camels and said, "I miss your wife, Ellen…such a sensible woman. She tried to get you out of the Guard, but you'd never listen to her. She knew something like this would happen." He put his hand on the door, tapped it, and was gone. My dad turned and took another look at the harbor. He walked to his other window and glimpsed the sun, descending behind the Charles River. He popped two more pills, took an Alka-Seltzer from his pocket, and got a glass of water.

He walked to the parking garage, started up his blue Ford Fairline, and drove along the Charles. He turned on a classical music station, and his breathing slowed after five minutes of Mozart.

Dad was used to Mom having dinner ready the minute he walked in the door. He ate the food I made, but he never seemed to acknowledge that making it took any effort. I didn't feel as if he had much faith in my ability to keep the household going. I guess maybe he had as much trouble saying what he thought and talking to me as I did to him in those days. In later years, he told me he had always thought it was even money whether I would have his dinner ready each night, even though it was always served up and eaten, again and again. Somehow he just hadn't noticed that I never messed up.

I heard the turning of the front-door latch. Even though it had been six weeks, my father's Guard uniform still jolted me. My father perused his mail, walked into the kitchen, poured a bourbon and ginger, and, without speaking a word to me, walked back into the living room to finish reading his letters. I could have been the kitchen table. I thought to myself that I would never choose a profession that required an hour and two drinks to calm down enough to talk to my relatives.

We sat down in the wood-paneled kitchen. The lights from our neighbor's house reflected on the kitchen windows, making them feel close. This soothed me, because I got comfort from a nestled-in feeling.

My dad announced, "We'll be leaving for France in the beginning of December."

I took the decanter of salad dressing that I'd prepared by mixing oil, vinegar, and a packet of dressing mix. My father never would try my dressing. He opened the bottled Roquefort dressing he bought at the supermarket on Saturdays.

Although he'd never mention it, I could tell he was enjoying his salad from the way he ate with gusto and smacked his lips a little bit from the tangy dressing. "We'll only be there a few months, depending on how soon this thing can be resolved," he said.

I had tried to put this trip out of my mind and live my life as normally as possible. But every night he'd remind me of this impending tidal wave. It was like getting flailed with the same whip over and over. I wasn't that happy about my life at the time as it was, in terms of having lots of friends and doing great in school. But I was getting by, day to day, so the idea of dropping the whole business and starting over from scratch in a foreign country with kids and teachers who didn't even speak English was very scary.

"What am I going to do about school?" I asked. I stopped eating and put my knife down loudly on the table. It was rude and uncharacteristic of me, but a tidal wave called for drastic measures.

"I'm going to enroll you in the *lycée* in the town where the base is. Otherwise I'll have to send you to the American military school in Verdun, and I don't want you to live that far away," he said, motioning for me not to bang the knife again.

"I can't see myself bored in a classroom halfway around the world, listening to a language that I don't understand, for eight hours a day," I said.

"You'll be there with me. I'll take care of you," he said. He threw his hands up in the air, as if this would persuade me.

I wasn't quite sure what that was supposed to mean. He supposedly took care of me at home as well, yet I found myself alone most of the time. But I couldn't say that. It would just make my father angry. I felt panicked at the idea of being trapped far from home. I probably looked and sounded desperate as I asked him, "But, Dad, you don't understand. I mean, what would I do there?" I knew my voice went up an octave, but I couldn't help it. I would surely pay the price.

He looked stricken for a second but quickly gained his usual control over himself. "Honestly, Roy. Just stop whining. You never have trouble finding things to do. You're better than you think at making friends. Besides, on long weekends, we can go places together…Paris, Rome, Berlin, and London. Look at it from this point of view: You're lucky. Most people don't see these places until they are adults, if then," he concluded.

"I don't want to do those things until I'm an adult," I said. "I want to go to parties and hang out with my friends." I felt slightly better, but had no delusions it would convince him of anything.

I got up, took two hot pads, and slid the roast out of the oven. It was medium rare, with reddish juice oozing out of the meat. I decanted the gravy into a pitcher, which my dad poured over the large, steaming baked potato I placed on his plate. The steam clouded his glasses, but he didn't take them off to clean them.

"That's the problem with you kids. You don't know what's really important," he said.

"You don't respect my opinions or my feelings, let alone my wishes. When Mom was dying, you wouldn't even let me visit her in the hospital."

My dad's face turned white. "From where did you pull your dear mother into this conversation?" he asked. That's when he reminded me it was her birthday. I was shocked—I wondered if I would have gotten the bloody nose if it weren't her birthday. Maybe I was thinking about her without realizing it when that door slammed into my face. I calmed down a little after that…but not much.

"The only reason that I didn't let you visit her in the hospital was that I wanted you to remember her as she was…young and beautiful," he said. He coughed a few times and stopped eating. He went to the sink and gulped some water. He coughed awhile longer and sat down. I waited until my dad's color returned.

"How about what I wanted, Dad? It would've been nice if I could've said good-bye," I said as I looked at the floor.

"Take it from me: you wouldn't have enjoyed it. Your mother was no longer herself. Her mind had been affected by the pain medications. The last week she was alive, she introduced me to her nurse as her brother." He wiped his eyes and replaced his spectacles.

"Enjoyed it? No. I wouldn't have enjoyed saying good-bye. But I would have liked to have had the chance."

He took off his glasses again and cleaned them; they were as clouded as before, but there was no steam from the potato. "You and I are at different stages, Roy. You've still got your whole life ahead of you. You'll understand better when you're my age. Someday you'll get married and have your own family. I'm fifty. I can't imagine getting married again," he said.

I'd never seen my father upset in this way. He'd been angry, but not distressed like this. Maybe I'd finally gotten through to him. I felt I should say something comforting. "I need you to be there for me," I said.

"I know." He smiled. "That's why I want you to be with me in France."

For the first time, he looked right at me, and his eyebrows lifted in surprise. "What's wrong with your nose, Roy? Why have you got a piece of gauze in your nostril?" I'd forgotten it myself, but still I wondered how he could have missed it all through dinner. Dr. Clayton had stuffed enough up there to fill a cannon. At least my father finally did notice and seemed to want to know what happened to me. So I explained the afternoon's episode, and Dad said he would call Dr. Clayton and thank him.

We continued our meal in silence until I said, "Sometimes I don't think you see me."

THE BERLIN LECTURE

Two evenings later, I put the dishes in the dishwasher and sat at the table. Dad was in the living room reading. The bright kitchen soothed me and made me feel less isolated. A reassuring glance at the line of canisters on the countertop or the familiar sight of the toaster seemed to help me start my homework and pay attention to the complex history documents I had to read. But later in the evening, when I'd developed momentum, I got a different comfort from my own room, where I did my math. My parents had given me the largest bedroom, which stretched from the front to the back of the house. There was room for the modern desk that our neighbor built, a bed, and a piano, with enough space left over for me to lose myself in imaginary basketball games using a tennis ball and toy basketball net.

As I sat in the kitchen reading my history textbook, the washing machine made a continuous humming noise that kept me company. But the pounding on the back door jolted me, and before I could react, Larry Roberts entered our kitchen. He nodded without breaking step as he strode through the dining room into the living room. The nod signified an unusually generous measure of greeting from our next-door neighbor to the west, who would march into our house at any hour when he needed something from my father. I wonder how Larry would have handled this Berlin wall my father was always talking about if there were something he needed on the other side.

I returned to my work, but within ten seconds, the two men had apparently finished their business, and my dad was showing him out. Before he left, Larry turned and faced me. "Are you looking forward to the trip?" he asked.

I looked at Larry and rolled my eyes.

"What's the matter, kid? I remember how you couldn't sleep before those Babe Ruth League games. What's happened to all that scrappiness and enthusiasm?" he asked.

"These aren't baseball games I'm going to be playing over there, Larry," I said.

"You'd be welcome to stay at my house when your dad leaves," Larry said.

I shrugged noncommittally and mumbled, "Uh-huh."

Dad looked down, sort of embarrassed, and softly muttered, "Appreciate the offer, Larry." Then neither of us said or did anything else. We just waited.

I knew from the look on his face and his silence that my father wanted Larry gone, but he couldn't tell him so. Even if he did, Larry wouldn't really hear it. That was the sort of guy our neighbor was. While my father rarely had a clue what I was thinking, I knew what was going through my dad's brain 90 percent of the time. My mother could read him the same way; I must have inherited her gene for that ability. I certainly didn't get that skill from my father.

Larry looked at me with a gleam of excitement in his eyes. "Hey, Roy, the next time you're doing some of your sports announcing, how about putting me into a Celtics game in place of Sam Jones in the last minute against the Lakers?" he pleaded. He looked as if he were dying to score some points; he was as excited as if he were expecting to get into a bona fide basketball game. He wanted me to create a basketball game out of my imagination right there, featuring him as the hero. It always amazed me how adults would feel as though it were real when I inserted them into one of my make-believe games, transforming them into the hero who scored the winning basket in the last minute to defeat the Lakers. It didn't register how much power they were giving me. They actually looked as if they believed they'd stolen the ball from Jerry West.

"I don't want to announce any games right now, Larry," I said. I returned to my history homework, and Larry finally went out the back door, across our yard, and back to his home, but not before needling my father by saying Dad should have left the National Guard reserves to the goyim years ago. My father grimaced and said, "Larry changed his last name from Rubinstein to Roberts years ago so it wouldn't sound so Jewish; now he chides me for working with Christians in the Guard."

Unfortunately, my dad stayed in the room. I wanted him to leave as much as he wanted Larry gone. It wasn't so much to finish my work as to just feel by myself, out from under pressure and comfortable again. But Dad started fiddling with my French textbook, which had a picture of the Eiffel Tower on its cover. I wondered how long this would go on.

"You'll be number one in French when you get back next year," he said, interrupting my thoughts.

I gave a vague response and returned to *Jackson v. Biddle*. My father asked next, "Why is it you're having trouble getting good marks?" He went berserk every time I brought home those report cards punctuated with Cs and a few Bs.

I slammed my book shut. My lack of success was as much an enigma to me as to him. I studied hard every night and believed my problem was bad luck. Two of my teachers could have given me Bs but had decided on Cs. The school was full of teachers trying to feel superior at the expense of young students.

Years later, after completing college and a year of medical school, on a visit to the high school, I told my physics teacher, whom I had nicknamed "the Golden Vector," that his class was the hardest I'd ever taken. He snickered and rattled off a few sentences that were no more understandable to me than his class in high school. The Vector was a subtle showoff who spoke to the slide-rule guys rather than to all of us. As a high school student, I didn't know there were different kinds of showoffs. When I finally became a doctor and taught some courses at the medical school, I made things simple for my students.

"With grades like these, when your buddies are in college, you'll be sweeping floors in some luncheonette," my father said.

"Why do you call them my buddies? No one uses that stupid word anymore," I said, glaring at him. Why couldn't he see how unhelpful those comments were? But I couldn't say that, because he didn't respect opinions from people under the age of thirty. So instead I complained about the word "buddy," even though I didn't care whether he said "pals," "friends," or whatever. I had known my father would make these unhelpful, critical comments, which was why I'd hoped he would retreat to the living room.

He told me I was going to have a unique experience in France. "There's no substitute for experience," he parroted Mr Shatten's words with an earnest look, as though he were arguing in front of a jury.

"There's no substitute for fun either, and it doesn't look like I'm going to have much for a long time," I said, turning my back. It was hard enough to swallow these grades without his badgering.

"You may be surprised," he said as, fortunately for me, he left at last to stretch out on the easy chair and ottoman to read Moses Maimonides's *Guide for the Perplexed*. It was a book he needed to read.

My father was accustomed to rising at six thirty by the alarm and making a cup of coffee. He'd toast an English muffin and read the *Boston Globe*. By the time I made it downstairs, he'd be gone. But he never left without coming up to say good-bye, and to make sure I was up and dressed. I was never sure which of those two things was more important to him. He would check my clothes as though he were conducting a military inspection. Women were supposed to be fussier about these things, but my mom had never bugged me.

The next morning was cold, and the ground frozen. I had already walked down the driveway and crossed the street when I remembered I hadn't locked the deadbolt. I sighed and returned to reluctantly insert the key I'd been carrying for two years, since my mom died.

The trees, whose leaves joined together in the middle of the street during spring, summer, and fall, were bare. As I crossed the brook on the way to my school, I saw an ever-increasing number of students walking. I was one among so many, and people didn't realize I would soon be gone. It was bad enough to be mediocre, but to be superfluous was even worse. To top it off, my nose began to burn from the nostril that had been injured earlier in the week.

Three tall boys with athletic letters sewed onto their white sweaters stood chatting in the school lobby.

"How're you doing?" Tom D'Andrea asked me.

"How're you, Apostrophe?" I responded. Even then the apostrophe was my favorite punctuation mark. Maybe it was because it linked things rather than separating them.

"He's called me that name since little league," Tom told the others, as if he were bragging. They laughed as they looked at me. Tom was the captain of the hockey team. Although we didn't travel in the same circles any longer, I knew he liked the name.

"Do you call anyone by their right name?" Tom asked.

"Nobody I like," I answered and walked away.

I put my coat in my locker and walked into my homeroom. My homeroom teacher, Mrs. Bartlett, told me how nice my new sweater looked. Even though I'd bought it over a month ago, this was my first day wearing it. It always took me awhile to get used to new things. While I was proud of the sweater, it reminded me of the man who stole a woman's purse and ran right past Mickey and me outside Mr. Louis's clothing store the day I bought it. Neither of us tried to stop him. Mickey said we weren't cops, but that didn't satisfy me. Later that day, I had gone into my backyard and twisted myself into about twenty contortions pretending to tackle the villain or give him a cross-body block. I got my clothes filthy and spent the afternoon getting them clean.

I heard another of my names used as I sat in my seat, waiting for the morning's announcements. Epithets I gave people were widely used. They caught on, and even teachers and coaches used them. The nicknames just came to me. I never pressured myself to think them up. It was a weird side circuit in the wiring of my brain.

The popularity of my nicknames didn't translate into respect or acknowledgment for me, however—at least not enough to make a difference in my social status. People liked my names, so they adopted them. Some people viewed me as a tad eccentric, because on the rare occasion when someone would reject one of my names, I acted like an artist whose gift had been refused, and either pouted or kept using it.

My epithets were more of a problem with adults. I remembered a phrase from *Romeo and Juliet* from freshman year where Mercutio, when asked the time, responded that the lusty hand of the clock was on the prick of noon. I applied this idea to Mrs. Garber, the school librarian, who closed the library religiously as the second hand closed in on noon. The library would remain closed until one thirty. There had been many times when I was frustrated that she would make me leave so precisely at noon. So I named her Merc, short for Mercutio. Once I made up a name, I used it everywhere. My marketing was the secret to my success, more than the names being so clever. Soon many students referred to the librarian by that name.

Mrs. Garber discovered the name when two members of the English department called her that. When she found out where the name originated and what it meant, she complained to the principal. When Dr. Downs ignored her protest, she disturbed my dad in his office. He had been less than pleased, but it wasn't the first time he'd heard from an adult about my antics. He cornered me in the kitchen that evening, and even before checking his mail or pouring his drink, predicted my future as a janitor. However, years later his secretary told me at a wedding that he had a howl over the whole thing with his law partners.

As my classmates asked questions of our teacher in English class, I gazed out the window, watching a truck driver attach a cable to a blue Ford Skyliner in the student parking lot and tow it away. As he hauled the car, it became detached from the line and went twenty feet onto the grass. Three dogs scampered after it. It would have been great to be that runaway car, which attracted such a following.

As I watched the Skyliner take off, in my mind I was running away too, heading to Yankee Stadium in a taxi to broadcast the first game of the World Series between the Yankees and the Dodgers; the game couldn't start until my arrival. My cab was between the Hotel Commodore and the stadium, but the game never started, because the bell rang and shocked me back to reality. Class was over. I walked to the library.

"Mrs. Garber, do you mind if I stay here until about twelve fifteen?" I asked, hoping she might make an exception to the library's closing time. It was too painful to go to the cafeteria and see everyone together. None of them realized how lucky they were.

"You must want to stay pretty badly if you used my right name," the librarian said with a look of relief. Normally the color drained from her face whenever she saw me; today she had a healthy flush to her cheeks. I decided that was a no and turned and headed to the cafeteria.

"I'll miss you," she said, and I turned to see her smiling with two other librarians, who stood beside her. I sensed that she was sincere enough in her remark right then, but that she might also be just as glad to see me gone in the long run. So I decided I had no choice but to go to the cafeteria.

I was almost to the lunchroom when I saw her. My heart beat so loud that I was sure she and the two pretty girls she was sitting with in a cove outside the cafeteria would hear it thumping. It always made me nervous to see a group of young women in a position to observe me, but with Julie there, it was more than I could handle. Every time I saw her, I would have this reaction, and I was terrified she could see the effect she had on me. I sped up, so I could get by quickly, and turned my head away toward the outside glass wall.

But she got up and walked over to me. "Hi, Roy, how's it going? Break any windows lately?" she asked, as she always did—with a big, enthusiastic smile.

I just met her by coincidence. She was a friend of our other next-door neighbor Dave Courtney's daughter. One afternoon several of my friends were playing a game of Goodman in my huge, unkempt backyard. It was a game I invented: The pitcher threw a tennis ball as fast as possible, and the batter, who stood in front of the back of my house, hit the ball. The pitcher had the discretion of saying whether it was an out or a base hit. Dave Courtney's house made up the left and left center field walls. A ball that hit Dave's roof was equivalent to a ball over the green monster in Fenway.

Anyway, Tex Callahan, who was batting left-handed, hit a line drive right through the window in the left center field wall. It put a permanent end to the Goodman game which I had named after Red Sox second baseman leadoff batter,

Billy Dale Goodman. It was the third and final broken window Dave Courtney was willing to tolerate. But the loss was more than compensated for by my brush with Julie, who was in their house when it happened. She came outside with Dave and one of his daughters. We didn't exactly get introduced in all the excitement and lecturing by Dave who had come running out of the house, and the commotion caused by my friends, who were disputing who was going to pay for the window. We couldn't ask Tex to pay, because he was the best athlete in the city, and nobody ever asked him to pay for anything. But after that day, whenever Julie saw me in school, she smiled and waved. Although I knew she just thought I was a nice, younger kid, my realization didn't put any brakes on my overactive fantasy world.

She was about five feet five, with a natural beauty that I always found very appealing in the opposite sex. No amount of makeup, however skillfully applied, could reproduce the natural glow of her skin, although some women did somersaults trying to achieve just that.

"I saw you outside the gym yesterday," Julie said. I dropped my book with the Thomas Jefferson cover and fumbled it again. It squirmed to the other side of the corridor. Finding my grip I returned it to its original position.

"Are you going to run indoor track this winter?" she continued. She seemed to really want to know about me, for whatever reason.

I told her I couldn't because of our planned departure in two weeks. Now with another reason to regret this move, I cursed my father for the tenth time that day and it was barely noon.

She asked me how long I was going to be gone.

"The rest of the year at least," I said, convinced that every syllable of this conversation would replay itself in my mind the rest of the day and awaken me at exactly 2:00 AM.

Despite their beauty, I filtered out the other girls. Their confused expressions told me they shared my bewilderment about what their friend found intriguing about me. It was a rare occasion for me full of the excitement of being in the minute: I could delude myself that Julie was within my grasp. It felt like a heroine injection must to an addict—thrilling, but with the meter running.

Julie asked if I would actually see the wall in Berlin, but before I could answer, a high-pitched voice intruded into my playground.

"If Germany's where the problem is, why aren't you going there?" The disturbance from Jane, the girl on Julie's right, was like someone pulling at my sleeve, telling me I was late on my way to Hebrew school or my grandmother's house.

I told them my dad's base was in Alsace-Lorraine and forced myself to look at Jane, who peered at me through her Ben Franklin glasses. Her skirt ended well above her knees, teasing me. She was sexy, but the look on her face wasn't friendly. Barbara, Julie's other friend, chimed in that Alsace was part of Germany, as though she knew more about this than anyone else.

I had become so absorbed in this conversation that I hadn't realized there were seven people standing nearby, listening to us.

"It used to belong to Germany," I said, "but since World War II, it's been part of France."

A tall boy with a Hopalong Cassidy lunch box said he thought it was a backward area. He looked as if the last topic he'd be interested in would be Alsace-Lorraine.

"I really don't know," I said, shuddering at the thought that he might be right.

"Why are we sending forces over there?" asked a girl wearing a tight dress, whose mouth was smeared with dark lipstick. I was shocked to find the crowd had increased to over ten people. I parroted my father's words.

"Because the Russians built a wall in August separating the city into East and West Berlin."

A girl holding a brown folder across her chest asked why America hadn't given Germany to the Russians. "My uncle and aunt were in a concentration camp in Poland," she said. She looked angry and frowned at me, as though I were the architect of our country's pro-Germany policy. I felt flattered she would think I was so powerful.

There was silence. They expected me to answer. I repeated what my father had told me a dozen times, although I didn't understand it.

"We hate the Germans as much as the Russians. We support the Germans to keep Communism at bay. A strong Germany prevents the extension of Communism into Western Europe." Barbara and Jane stared as though they were seeing me for the first time. My palms were moist, my mouth was dry, and my heart pounded. But now I could view myself differently, because they did.

I was the center of attention and liked it. Maybe it wasn't necessary to be a famous sports announcer. I didn't need to hide in the library. I threw my shoulders back, abandoning my typical slouch, and found I was taller than these girls. The conversation continued for twenty minutes, and I must have answered ten more questions. The bell rang; my lunch period had passed, and I hadn't gotten to eat. It didn't matter, because I wasn't hungry.

That evening I was at the kitchen table with my United States history book open, forging my way through a passage in the Dred Scott decision, when the phone rang.

It was Gordon Kramer, the president of the Current Events Club. He wondered if I would be willing to give a lecture next Wednesday at 3:00 PM. "I heard you're an expert on Berlin, and you're leaving soon," he said.

"How about if my father gives the lecture? He knows much more than I do," I said, amazed the idea came so quickly.

Gordon sounded stunned that my dad might be available.

"I'll ask him and let you know in the morning," I said.

I inched into the living room, where the "Prime Minister" reclined in the easy chair with his legs stretched on the ottoman, sitting under a picture of my mom. He was reading one of his religious books.

"Dad," I began a little hesitantly, "there's a Current Events Club at school, and the president said they need someone to give a talk next week about Berlin. I know that you know a lot about the situation there, with the wall and all that…and I was wondering if maybe you could come to my school and give them a real professional lecture."

"Well, Roy, an invitation to give a lecture like this is an opportunity, but maybe it's too much with everything going on. I think I can do it, but I'll need to rearrange some details," he said. I let out a deep breath and glided back to the kitchen suppressing the urge to call Gordon at home.

* * * *

In my year and a half at the school, I'd never heard of the Current Events Club. The loudspeaker announced that my father's lecture had been moved from a small classroom to the much larger cafeteria, where two hundred and fifty people, including twenty teachers, were already milling around. Where had all these students come from? Nobody I knew talked about Berlin.

Over the past few days, I had heard my dad's name over the public-address system. I had even taken home one of the club announcement posters in the hallways and put it up in my bedroom.

There were a million conversations going on, so I found a spot away from everyone. Nonetheless, some senior found me and said, "Gordon wants to know if you'd like to introduce your father."

"No, that's OK. Gordon should do it, since he's the president of the club." I was never very comfortable standing up in front of a group of people, so I shook my head and moved to an even more remote seat. But within ten minutes, all the chairs around me had filled. Just after three, the principal marched into the cafeteria with my dad and two of the housemasters.

I could never have given the lecture myself. What if someone asked a question I couldn't answer, and then someone in the audience could? A radio sports announcer had to speak to the people who were listening to the game, but that was different. I wasn't afraid of speaking; it was being watched while I spoke that scared me. People might see my nervousness and remember I was an awkward, skinny kid with too many freckles. And what if I fainted or something embarrassing happened?

Gordon introduced my father as Lieutenant Colonel Harrison, an Air Force reservist activated by Kennedy because of Berlin. Loud applause filled the room, slowly died down, then gave way to silence while Dad stood behind a microphone on a wooden stand, which showed an orange lion, our school's logo. His blue uniform displayed his medals on his lapels.

He stood behind the lectern and said nothing. He looked to his left and right, then straight ahead, coughed a few times, and remained silent. He didn't seem nervous. He must have been waiting for something…but what?

After twenty seconds, people fidgeted and leaned forward. Had my father forgotten his speech? I wouldn't be able to look any of my classmates in the face. I would have to switch to the other high school, even though it involved a special permit, waking up half an hour earlier, and taking two buses. No more invitations to friends to come to my home either. I would have loved to trade places with the yellow ladybug that crawled under the chair in front of me.

Suddenly my father came to life, as though someone remembered to plug him in. He stood straight as a rod, up to his full height of six feet, and spoke slowly in a soft, intense voice.

He mentioned how World War I led to World War II and said something about a conference in Yalta where Roosevelt made way too many concessions to the Russians, leaving them in control of all of Eastern Europe. He said Roosevelt did it because he was very sick the last year of his life and wasn't thinking correctly. Roosevelt died a month after that meeting. His giving the Communists all that power led to our current problem with them.

Then he mentioned another meeting six months afterward, in Potsdam, outside of Berlin, in a large palace, where all of Germany and the city of Berlin were divided up among the Allies. The Russians received East Germany and East Berlin, and the United States, Britain, and France got West Germany and West Berlin. My father used the slide projector to show a picture of Germany and Berlin, and mentioned Cuba and the Bay of Pigs. I wasn't really sure what that meant, except that our government invaded Cuba earlier that year to disrupt their government, which made the Russians very angry. Russia's resentment caused them to put up the wall in Germany. He also mentioned the U2 incident involving our spy plane being discovered over Russia as contributing to the present crisis.

As I looked around the room, nobody was fidgeting, yawning, or staring at the floor, and there were no side conversations, as there were when teachers or the principal spoke in the auditorium.

My dad spoke without cards. Our teachers always looked down at their notes and often read their speeches. Many of them stuttered and said "uh" a hundred times, but Dad didn't do any of those things. He spoke as though he were having a conversation with the audience.

When he finished, everyone clapped for a long time. My father took off his hat. Gordon Kramer came up and led a question-and-answer session for twenty minutes. My father rocked back and forth during a few of the questions. I could tell he thought they were stupid, but he answered them courteously, much more so than he would if I had asked him the same questions in our kitchen.

My history teacher, who spoke as if he were the world's authority on everything, almost whispered a question about whether my father thought Kennedy would use nuclear weapons. My father said he didn't know and dropped his eyes. The room was silent for what seemed like an eternity until another teacher commented that my dad had been a bit rough on Roosevelt, since FDR had led the U.S. as president for twelve years, which was much longer than anyone else ever had. "Roosevelt was a great president," my father said. "He just lost his health the last year of his life. He was in heart failure at the time of the Yalta meeting."

I breathed a sigh of relief as my father stepped down from the stage and received a second ovation. Several people approached him with more questions, which they probably hadn't wanted to ask in front of the crowd.

On the way out of the cafeteria, Julie and Barbara came up to me. Julie squeezed my arm; fortunately I was holding my books under my other arm.

I introduced the girls to my father and told him they had been responsible for his invitation.

My father shook hands with them. He acted aloof, as he usually did with all my friends. If the girls had been adults, I think that he would have been friendlier. I guess a person needed an identification card with a birthday before a certain date to earn my father's respect.

The only exception to this rule was my friend Jordan. "Jordan is a real friend," Dad always said. He liked Jordan, because Jordan sent me letters every day I was down at Cape Cod, when Dad's reserve unit used to go there every summer. Letters in the mail seemed to Dad like more of an adult way to communicate than a kid way, I guess. He said Jordan was loyal, and that was a rare and praiseworthy quality. He talked to Jordan as he did to his own friends and to my uncles. Jordan said my dad was a great guy; adults said that about him too.

Julie linked her arm into mine and commented about my freckles being cute. I didn't know what to do and must have looked awkward. "Don't you think you could leave him here?" she asked my father.

"Sorry, but I need him. He's my right-hand man." He finally smiled.

"Roy, you've got your dad's smile," she said as the girls walked away.

"Watch out for that one," my dad said, his smile gone.

"What do you mean?" I asked.

"The way she shook my hand. She's been around. How well do you know her?"

"I just met her."

"People who come on strong like that usually disappear just as fast," he said.

"I don't know what you're talking about," I said.

"That's what I'm afraid of, Roy. You don't understand what I'm getting at, because you're still so young and inexperienced. You don't recognize traits in people who might disappoint or hurt you." I guess he wanted to protect me, but it was still pretty hard to take right then.

So I said, "Maybe you're right about me, Dad, but wrong about Julie. Hey, maybe she really likes me and wouldn't disappear so fast after all."

In the car on the way home, I told him how much he'd impressed everyone. His only response was, "It was no big deal, Roy. After all, I earn my living in a courtroom. If I couldn't speak under pressure, I wouldn't be much good as a lawyer." Then he looked straight ahead and didn't glance at me the rest of the time I was talking to him.

"You didn't think all those questions were good, did you?" I asked.

"You don't want to come across as being arrogant. When you give a presentation, you want to put your best foot forward," he said.

I couldn't imagine ever putting his advice to use about appearing haughty; seeming conceited was the least of my worries.

"What do you think of the answer I gave that teacher about Roosevelt?" he asked.

"You're asking me? How would I know?"

"Roy, Roosevelt was a great president, because he had vision. He knew we would have to get into the war, even though 90 percent of the country wanted to avoid it. He just shouldn't have run for a fourth term; he was too sick."

"What do you think of Kennedy as a president?" I asked him.

"The jury is still out, but don't quote me on that; you can't say anything about him in this state," he answered. "There have been very few excellent presidents…no more than five. I would include Franklin Roosevelt, Abraham Lincoln, Thomas Jefferson…and maybe Harry Truman and Teddy Roosevelt. The problem with most presidents is that they lack vision. The British leader, Winston Churchill, would be another man who would qualify as a great president."

*   *   *   *

About a week after the lecture, we went to Aunt Joyce's for Thanksgiving. After a strained relationship during their childhood, my dad and aunt were on better terms, but not really close, according to him. Joyce and her husband, Mitty, had been frequent guests at our house before temple for Friday-night dinner prior to my mom's illness.

We sat in the large living room of their brick, two-story colonial house, which looked onto Commonwealth Avenue, a broad, leafy avenue. People used the wide, grassy center strip for jogging, running, and walking their dogs. From the lengthy couch, I saw several houses with large front lawns and oak trees, now bare. The rain pounded the roof, and moisture clouded the windows like steam. A squirrel ran up one of the trees in the front yard. My cousin played "The Lion Sleeps Tonight" upstairs on his phonograph.

"Are you excited about the trip?" Mitty asked as he sat in his easy chair and sipped apple cider. All adults asked me the same question; it was easier to answer it than create another conversation. But I couldn't say how I really felt; I'd sound like an irritable teenager.

I looked at the floor and muttered, "I guess."

Joyce asked if we needed help with moving and packing.

"The government is sending packers and movers," my father said, sipping his drink while looking at the pictures of landscapes on the walls.

Mitty asked if I enjoyed the Thanksgiving high school football game. He couldn't stand silence. My father told me Mitty was good at what adults called "small talk." It was what made him rich—and such a good golfer.

"Yes, I was there." I clasped my hands and worried about the future lifespan of a new pimple, which I felt surfacing smack in the middle of my forehead.

"It was a great game, wasn't it?" Mitty asked.

"Yeah, but I left after the first half," I said. It was hard to sit there in the stands with everyone having such a good time and having such a sense of togetherness. I felt like such an outsider.

My dad used the word "obtuse" in reference to Mitty, but in those days, I thought obtuse was strictly a geometry term. "The reason he jabbers on is because he wants everyone to have a good time," my dad said.

"Steve, why does your unit have to go, rather than one from somewhere else in the country?" Mitty shifted in his chair and lit a cigar.

"Since we didn't go to Korea, it's our turn now. We've been on top of the list for years," my dad said.

Mitty had a look of resignation on his face. "Well, if I had to go somewhere, I'd rather go to France than Korea," he said.

"If we'd knocked that damned wall down the day the Russians put it up, none of this would be necessary," my father said. It was the first time I had any inkling he didn't want to go either. But he'd never tell me that, not even later.

Joyce and Mitty looked at each other in disbelief.

"It'd be better if Ellen were going," said Joyce.

My father went to the window and stared into the distance. He was wondering why on earth Joyce thought that was a helpful comment. When it came to the topic of my mom, people didn't know what to say.

"You know, Steve," Joyce continued, "I've always wondered about something Ellen told me. She said that she woke up alone in the recovery room after her operation, and it was dark in there."

He put his hands into his pockets and continued to gaze out the window. Despite my skills at reading his body language at this point, I had no clue what he was thinking. Finally he said, "They told her if all they needed was a biopsy, she'd wake up, and there would be light in the room…but if the breast had to come off, it'd be dark."

No one said a word.

I asked if I could watch television with Claire and Jonathan.

Joyce nodded, and I darted upstairs.

After dinner my cousins and I left the table to go back upstairs to watch television again. However, we could hear the conversation in the dining room after Joyce served coffee to Mitty and my father.

"Stephen, I'm wondering if it's a good idea for you to be taking Roy," she said. She never called my dad Stephen unless she wanted something. Maybe

Joyce would do what my mother had sometimes done: break Dad's stubborn streak.

My hopes were short-lived. "It's the best thing that could ever happen to him," my father said.

"We've got plenty of room," I heard Joyce say. I could imagine her leaning forward, peering into his eyes.

"A year in Europe will change him in ways this place can't," my father said. He probably took off his glasses and wiped them with a handkerchief. I'm sure he was wondering whether it had been a mistake to come over here so close to our departure, but he'd seen no way out—it was Thanksgiving, after all.

"Think how lonely it'll be for him. Why can't you see it from his point of view?" Joyce asked.

"Why can't anyone see it from mine, goddammit!" I heard a loud thump, and I knew my father had pounded the table with his fist—which had surely caused Joyce and Mitty to flinch. "Besides," he added, "all changes are difficult."

Later, my father told me that his fist had vibrated a pitcher on the glass tabletop, and some water had spilled. Mitty coughed several times, and Joyce went to get a sponge. My father went out the back door and must have felt the cold rain pelt the back of his neck and freeze his hands. He rummaged in his pockets for a cigarette, but there were none. He had quit three years ago, but years later he told me he'd have smoked that Thanksgiving if he'd found one.

Mitty had remarked wryly, "There goes Steve's infamous temper." Joyce probably just waved him off, as usual.

THE OTHER SIDE OF THE OCEAN

We were scheduled to leave for France on the first Tuesday in December. The alarm clock clanged in the predawn cold and awakened me at five. I dressed in brown corduroy pants, a blue oxford shirt, and a brown sweater. I pulled my thick, gray, woolen socks as high as they would go and tied my high-top, black sneakers with double knots. My father promised it would be at least as cold in France as it was here in Boston.

I ran downstairs to look at my mother's picture. I really wanted to see it one more time before we left. She would have known how to manage this change. That soft, optimistic expression told me she could handle anything.

I remembered what she told me that one time that Dad had given in and allowed me to visit her in the hospital. She hugged me and told me, "Roy, my darling, I want you to remember that, even though my spirit will be flying away someday soon now, I will always be with you."

I tried not to cry as I said, "I know, Mom, but it's not the same. I will miss you so much…I won't know what to do."

"You'll know what to do, Roy. Your life will go on, and you'll grow up to be a fine man. Just think of me once in a while."

"I will, Mom," I promised her that day. And I did think of her, so very often…but the phrase "once in a while" stayed with me for some reason, maybe I thought she wanted me to move on but that thought was too sad. So I just remembered the phrase. Dad wouldn't let me go back to the hospital after that. I wished I could have been there at the end to open that window by her bed and help her fly away.

I boiled water and poured it into a brown mug, then stirred in chocolate powder. I wished I could be excited about this trip and see it as an adventure, as some other guys at my school might have, but I just couldn't.

We drove to the airport in the freezing darkness; the limousine sped through the empty streets. As we passed under Boston Harbor, a monotonous procession of bright yellow lights lit up the Callahan Tunnel. When would I go through that same tunnel called the Sumner Tunnel in the opposite direction? It might be six months or even a year, maybe more. Who knew?

We arrived at the air base as a glimmer of pinkish, dawn light peeked over the ocean. An Air Force plane waited on the airstrip to carry my father and forty other reservists to France. The small military plane would stop for refueling first in Labrador, then in Scotland. I would be traveling separately on a commercial flight to Paris. Then I'd change planes for the short flight east to Strasbourg, where Dad would meet me.

Before boarding the military plane, the men passed the time in a large waiting room furnished only with blue chairs arranged in horizontal rows and a few pictures of outdated airplanes on the walls. Children screamed; it would have been hard to hear myself think, if I'd wanted to.

"Nice to see you, Roy," said the ever-smiley Dave McDermott, a member of my dad's reserve unit whom my father especially liked. I knew Mr. McDermott from Cape Cod summers. Except now, he didn't look at me with that carefree grin, the way he had when he was drinking beer on the beach at Falmouth. He introduced me to his son, and then he walked away.

I shook hands with a boy my age who wore a blue Boston Red Sox cap. I wondered why I'd never met him down the Cape all those summers. I guess I figured all kids spent those summer weeks wherever their dads' reserve units were training.

"Are you coming to France?" I asked him, hoping he was. It wasn't so much that I wanted to be friends with him, particularly since I didn't know anything at all about him. But I was encouraged by the idea that at least someone else my age should have to suffer through this same uprooting with me.

"No, I have to go to school," he answered. When I heard that, I looked at my father, but he was talking to three other people.

A red-faced man with a handlebar mustache told another man he'd be depending on his brother to run his business. He looked worried as he twirled his mustache.

His friend told the mustached man that his bosses resented holding his job for him. He'd love to be taking his family, but they had their own lives. His shrug conveyed his resignation.

My father introduced me to Lieutenant Grayson.

His teenage daughter smiled at me. "Are you going to Europe?" she asked, looking excited to find out.

"Yes," I said, my mood suddenly changing. Maybe it wouldn't be so bad after all. "Are you?" I asked.

"No, there's no way I could go to France right now. You see, I'm the lead in my school play. I have to rehearse every day," she said.

I felt the blood drain from my face. I walked into the bathroom and stared at the mirror. I kicked the stained, white wall and sat down on the toilet seat. I wished I could have had those other parents, who had the sense to let their families stay home and get on with their lives. Some kids had parents who didn't expect them to just pick up and move into a whole new situation, a new school, a new country, a new language. What if I didn't fit in over there any better than I did here? Or even worse, maybe? What if I ended up a big disappointment to the one parent I still had? Why did I get stuck with someone as rigid and unyielding as my father? Our lives were better when Mom was there to work it all out between us, but that was past history. I cursed my lot and the trap in which I found myself.

Maybe I could run away. After all, what could my father do? He'd be on a plane bound for Europe, and my aunt wouldn't kick me out. I had my life savings of seventy-five dollars in my pocket. That would easily cover cab fare to Aunt Joyce's. But I'd be back at the airport in two days. It was like the time I skipped Hebrew school, because I hated it so much, and my mother tracked me down by the brook. It was the only time I ever saw her cry. Since she'd never gotten her driver's license because she hated the idea of driving, she called my aunt, who came right over and drove me to the school and made me walk into that boring class forty-five minutes late.

After two minutes, I took some water from the sink, cleaned my eyes, and returned to the chaotic room.

The military rules didn't allow me to travel on the plane with my father, since I was a civilian. As the men boarded the plane, the families and friends left. One toddler put his arms around his daddy's knees and tried to tackle him.

The man picked his little boy up. "I'll be home before you know it, Joshua. Just take care of your mom," he said. I couldn't remember Dad ever lifting me up like that.

Because my father's flight left midmorning at 10:15 AM, and mine didn't depart until early evening, I had to deal with the hours in between. I felt emptiness in my stomach and remembered the day my aunt came to my junior high school, and the principal interrupted my class. The principal and my aunt pulled me into an empty classroom. They looked nervous, and I knew right away that something was wrong. Then they told me Mom had died that morning at 6:21.

That empty, alone feeling hit me in the stomach hard that day. I was thirteen years old, and my mom was gone forever. I didn't know what to think or what to say to them, so I just stood there, staring at the drooping American flag. I had known my mother was sick, but I hadn't thought she would die so soon. It was so different having her gone—so hard to grasp, so hard to accept. During those days when she was in the hospital, although I didn't see her at all, I somehow always thought she would get well and come back after a while. I had been living in a dream world, I guessed.

My dad had told me to bring books to the airport to deal with the boredom, but I was too agitated to concentrate on the text. The television barely worked, and game shows didn't interest me, so I studied the harbor. Formations of birds, which made high-pitched, squawking noises, flew in every ten minutes and landed on the runway near the water, remained ten minutes, then continued on their way. Large boats entered and left the waterfront, which appeared green at times, at other times gray, still others blue. Nothing stayed the same for more than ten minutes.

Airplanes sped into the airport, barely avoiding the water before landing. Their engine noise was deafening.

A large barge entered the harbor in the afternoon. Initially a speck on the horizon, the boat produced large amounts of black, thick smoke from its smokestack. It dominated the harbor for half an hour until it came to port. My appetite came back as the lobster catchers came in with their nets full of shellfish.

My mind went back and forth between the wharf and a basketball game I created between the Celtics and Lakers. It was the seventh game of the NBA championship, and Bob Cousy and Jerry West were exchanging baskets in the fourth quarter before a frenzied crowd at the Boston Garden. As the announcer, it was hard to stay impartial, but that was my job. When there was a time-out, I handled the Ballantine beer commercial as Mel Allen, the famous sports announcer, would have; he was the man I wanted to be.

The game went into overtime. My hands were cold as popsicles when an older woman, at least fifty, in an Air Force uniform touched my back and offered me something to eat. She handed me a sandwich, but it had butter and lettuce on it, neither of which I could stand. Instead I ate the tuna sandwich Dad had told me to make the night before. I got a Coke out of one of the machines, and a piece of candy. He'd warned me about the food at the air base; he knew I was fussy.

Just after five o'clock in the evening, everything became dark suddenly. The military bus took me to the commercial section of Logan. I felt even more alone in this miserable, little shuttle bus than I had in the deserted lounge where I'd spent most of the day. My heart pounded as I prepared to board the jet to France.

"Will you be traveling by yourself?" the middle-aged woman behind the ticketing desk asked.

"Yes, ma'am."

"Will someone be there to pick you up in Paris to help you find your connecting flight to Strasbourg?"

"No. My father will pick me up in Strasbourg."

The woman looked concerned as she issued my ticket, but I felt the warmth of her smile after she'd finished and wished me good luck. Maybe she was lonely too.

There were no teenagers or children on the plane; the passengers were mostly French. The people spoke rapidly; I couldn't understand them, despite my year and a half of studying. Many of them read the *Boston Globe*, even though they spoke to one another in French.

I sat near the front of the plane. The airplane taxied onto the runway and shot over the harbor, above the Atlantic. There was a black, cloudless sky above, an infinite, inky black ocean below, and an unknown continent waiting for me. But the plane's interior was bright and warm, and the pretty flight attendants smiled, although they spoke with funny accents. The hot chocolate warmed my stomach.

I couldn't sleep. I closed my eyes, but all I heard was the jarring sound of people chattering in a foreign language. It was anything but restful. I thought I'd have to fly all night before it became light, but after four hours, I got my first glimpse of the morning. At first it was a glimmer of pink across the black sky. The clouds below looked like icebergs. The gleam became larger and brighter, until a quarter, and then a half, of the sky was light. The blue ocean shimmered in the early morning light through white clouds.

I pictured Julie and all the people back home reading the article in the school newspaper about the Berlin wall that I would write. I then realized I might be able to handle what the world had in store for me. The next thing I knew, the flight attendant was shaking my shoulder gently as the plane descended into Orly airport, in Paris. Dad's military flight would have stopped twice for refueling, but this big, commercial plane went nonstop.

The weather was freezing, and I was grateful for the heavy coat and scarf my father had told me to wear. I followed the other passengers into the baggage area and went through customs, feeling like a newborn baby expelled from the womb. I looked in every direction for something familiar, shoving my hand into my pocket every five minutes to feel my passport.

The people at the airport wore berets with scarves and heavy coats. There were loud announcements every few seconds in French, and the person who made them spoke too rapidly for me to understand more than a few words. I was on my own getting from Paris to Strasbourg, the city in Alsace-Lorraine where Dad was supposed to pick me up. What if my father was late at the Strasbourg airport? My stomach burned every time that thought came to my mind. I changed my money into the French currency, francs, but the only food at the airport was coffee and rolls. I'd never tasted coffee, and it was bitter, but the crisp baguette with blueberry jam was great and settled my stomach.

I knew the French language and culture would be different, but the reality of a completely different world overwhelmed my flimsy preparations. Occasionally people would blurt a translation in accented English, but all the signs were in French. I pulled out my pocket dictionary and learned three new words in my first five minutes in France. *Chomage, amertume,* and *huis clos* were in the headlines of *Le Monde*. I stood in the corner and looked them up in my pocket dictionary.

Posters advertising restaurants and plays lined the walls. Finally I caught sight of a picture of Maurice Chevalier, whom I recognized from the Ed Sullivan show. I knew he spoke English and always was friendly. If only he were here to welcome me. I stood next to his picture for five minutes, touching my back to his image.

I left the international section and arrived at the domestic terminal an hour before my flight east. I walked up to the officials every ten minutes to ask if the flight to Strasbourg would be on time. After the third time, the woman at the counter scolded me and ordered me to sit. Couldn't she see how scared I was? Maybe French people were mean. The tilt of her nose told me she didn't like to speak English and thought I should know her language.

When it was time to go, the airline officials told me I was with the fourth boarding group and made me wait until almost everyone was on the plane. What if there weren't any seats left? My dad would never find me if I were left behind.

I felt that sick feeling in my stomach. "Please get me on the plane," I said to the woman collecting tickets.

"We won't leave without you," she said and smirked to her colleague.

I finally got aboard and found my window seat. No one sat next to me, so I put my foot on the next seat, until the flight attendant ordered me to keep it on the floor. It was impossible to sleep; my mind was whirling. Christopher Columbus must have been uncomfortable on his expeditions, wondering whether he would propel himself off the end of the world.

I remember almost nothing of that hour-long flight, but we arrived in Strasbourg on schedule. I looked all over the airport, scanning for that familiar face. But there was no doubt about it: my nightmare had come true. I was all alone. My father was nowhere to be seen. Everyone else from my plane had already met up with their families or friends and moved very purposefully through the lounge, carrying their small bags, paying no attention to me. I had no idea where to go—or even what to ask anyone.

The Strasbourg airport was much smaller than Orly, with signs in three languages. There was no place to sit down in the lounge. Looking out the windows, I saw only desolate farmland in every direction. I walked over to the pay phones and tried to figure out how they worked. The phone required French change, for starters, and I soon realized that phoning would have been an overwhelming challenge for me. Besides, speaking to the operator would have been an impossibility, even if I knew where to call.

Everything was so confusing for me. I was tired, because it was the first time I hadn't slept in a bed at night. I was starting to feel scared; I tried not to panic. I took a deep breath and decided I'd just wait a few minutes, then try to ask one of the ticket agents in English to help me phone the American military base.

Meanwhile I tried to calm myself by leaning against the wall of the lounge and tapping on it with my knuckle, as I did every night to help me fall asleep.

Waiting in that small, empty airport lounge, I felt the same emptiness as I had sitting at our house on the day my mother died. All my relatives had come to our house, but they ignored me, like the people passing by me in the airport now. I had been so confused—I hadn't known what to think or what to say, or even where to go in my own home. So I went and sat on the back porch by myself for an hour while they ate and joked as if they were attending a gala get-together. They might as well have been speaking another language. No one came out to keep me company. When I finally walked inside, people patted me on the head and kissed me, but they didn't talk to me. That was what I needed—couldn't they tell? I wondered how I survived that day.

Suddenly a firm, but friendly, hand pressed my shoulder. My father grinned. "Funny running into you here," he said, as he gave me a rare hug. I couldn't ever remember a time when I had been so happy to see him.

The blue Peugeot 403 drove smoothly as we approached the center of Strasbourg, within ten minutes of leaving the airport. "I'm taking you into Strasbourg. It's on the way to the base," he said.

I looked out at the endless farmland. "If we were from South Dakota, we'd be right at home," I observed. I wasn't big on museums or theaters and didn't consider myself a real city person, but this place was all monotonous, flat, rural land.

"This region is the site of the most significant battles of both world wars," my father said.

"Why is it so important?" I asked, only half wanting to know.

My father didn't need much incentive to launch into one of his history lectures: "Because we're at the border of France and Germany, and the two countries have been fighting over this area since at least the middle of the nineteenth century. It is finally back in France now, but it was a part of Germany between 1870 and World War I, and then again during World War II. But Alsace-Lorraine has always been a complex place, because of geography, war, and the mix of cultures and languages."

"Is that why all the signs are both in French and in German?" I asked.

"The people here speak both languages," he said. Dad accelerated around a curve where I would have jammed the brakes, if I were allowed to drive.

It occurred to me that in addition to French, I would have to learn German at the school where he planned to send me and I voiced this concern.

He told me to calm down, and that I didn't need to shriek. "Do you see those spires on the buildings?" he asked.

I told him I wished we were in Boston; this place looked as if it were out of the past century. "It gives me the creeps," I said.

"Well, those spires are Gothic architecture," he said.

"I couldn't care less," I said. He never seemed to hear what I was saying; I didn't know why I even tried.

We reached downtown Strasbourg, if you wanted to call it that. It looked nothing like any downtown that I'd ever seen. Everything was different from the cities I'd been in at home. Old, red-brick buildings lined the narrow streets, which were paved with cobblestones. The buildings were all attached to one another, which seemed weird to me. There were no skyscrapers, as there had been in Boston. In fact the highest building was only four stories. Many of the structures had strange, triangular points on their tops, and some resembled gingerbread houses. It was foreign and upsetting; I wanted to get back on the plane and be with my friends. The funny thing was, I hadn't been all that happy most of the time at home either. I didn't have a lot of friends at school, and sometimes I didn't know how to act around other kids. Maybe if I had been more sure of myself all around, I wouldn't have felt so overwhelmed in this strange place.

We went to a restaurant, Le Petit Moulin, which was located on Place Kleber, a large, cobblestone square with a monument of a famous French general. The restaurant was dark, and the waiters dressed in tuxedos. We had soup and meats, but I didn't eat much. My appetite, which had come back at the Paris airport, now vanished with the stark reality of what my life would be like for the next months. After lunch we drove to the base, which was on the way to our cottage.

Dad accelerated the blue sedan along the country road, shifting gears as though it were second nature, even though his car at home had an automatic transmission.

"We'll be going past your school in five minutes," he said.

"Great," I said with mock enthusiasm.

"It doesn't look like your school in Newton," he warned me. He was good at giving warnings; he would have made a good Paul Revere.

As we drove through the small town, my father pointed to a large, gray building with a high, dirty, black wall. I couldn't take my eyes off the barricade, which occupied an entire block.

The place didn't resemble anything close to any school I had seen before—or any school I could imagine, for that matter. There wasn't a chance that I'd know how to fit in there. Besides, to me, it seemed more like a jail than a school, with its high, dark wall and lack of landscaping. It was even more foreign, in my mind, than the town buildings had been. Seeing my new school just added to my feelings of misery and upset. "I don't think this is going to work out," I said, and it came out in a low wail.

"It'll be the best thing that you could've hoped for," he said.

I begged to go home and stay at Joyce's. I told him my friend Jordan would be happy to have me too. If we hadn't been in a car, I would have gotten on my knees.

"I suppose you'd like to move in with Mickey's family," he said as he banged the palm of his right hand against the steering wheel.

I told him I wouldn't have asked to live with Mickey, but Joyce was different. "She's your sister," I said.

My father continued to look straight ahead at the country road without speaking. Finally he told me I wasn't the only one who had to make adjustments. He accelerated the car, and I fell back hard against the seat, but my feelings hurt more than my head.

I wasn't about to give up. I told him I met lots of kids at Logan, and none of them came to France with their fathers.

"You're going to be here for the year, and you're going to get used to it. It's the chance of a lifetime, and not all opportunities come with ribbons wrapped around them," he said.

Years later I came to recognize the wisdom of this comment, and would profit from it many times. However, at that moment, I needed my mother to reassure me, not my father's stern commentary. But she was no more available to me than on the day she died. It was frustrating that I couldn't will her into being, so she could tell me everything was going to be all right. I needed someone to do that, because this place was so unfamiliar. I never realized how comforting it had been to just see the same, boring things every day.

On the day that Mom died, my father came to the porch with tears behind his glasses and told me that everything was going to be all right—that we were going to stick together. Then he disappeared to be with the guests. I survived that afternoon by believing my mother would come back. I continued to tell myself that for at least a year. I remembered my uncle commenting that afternoon that I had my mother's eyes, even though I had the same color eyes as my father. People didn't see me; they didn't want to.

The rest of the way to the base, Dad and I were silent. An armed guard saluted my father as he pulled up to the entrance. We moved inside and drove around the flat, gray area, which was dotted with one-story, brown, concrete buildings.

We walked into the prefabricated building where my dad's office was. White plaster peeled off the walls, and paint rollers sat on the floor. Packages of supplies sat unopened on desks. Mops and brooms stood lined up on the back wall, as if at attention. The desks had been shoehorned into the front area of the room. But the room was clean—not a speck of dirt on the concrete floor.

My father introduced me to the ten men sitting at their desks. Most of them had been there for two weeks; they laughed as though they were at baseball camp.

Dad told them he would be heading to his cottage, as both he and his son had been traveling all night. After five minutes, we returned to our car for the ten-minute ride to our cottage.

Our new home was a development of two hundred red-brick cottages in a community called Cité Perkins, named after an American general. The furniture was typical of a government office building, with a couple of pictures of country scenes on the living room wall. The two bedrooms were furnished with queen-size beds and nightstands. The walls in my room were bare as a shower stall, as the hospital-room walls had been when I was there for my hernia operation. My mother had decorated that space within an hour; she would've known how to fix this place up and make it feel like home. I lay down on the bed and fell asleep within seconds…but not before my father gently placed two warm blankets over me and turned off the light.

THE LYCÉE

The next morning, I awoke at seven thirty. Back home it would have been light for over an hour. What kind of a crazy place was this? I rolled over to go back to sleep, but my father barged in and ordered me to get going. I stumbled into the tiny bathroom and washed my face. I took the soap and fired it into the bathtub, making a loud thud, which caused Dad to run into the room.

"What happened?" he asked.

I told him I was getting ready to go to his stupid frog school. My father took the soap out of the tub and placed it back in the soap dish.

"Get moving. You can't be late on your first day," he said.

We climbed in the car to drive to the *lycée*. The unexpected darkness outside made the experience even more foreign and nightmarish.

"What time does it get light in this foolish place?" I asked my father, as I took in the rural scene.

He looked at his watch and said, "At about half past eight."

On our way to the school, we stopped at the base to get breakfast at the canteen. We walked into a large, bright room with American servicemen sitting at scattered tables. The voices of Dion and the Belmonts singing "I Wonder Why" filled the room. Pictures of Ted Williams, Mickey Mantle, Wilt Chamberlain, Bob Cousy, and other athletes, along with American actors and politicians, covered the walls. Copies of the *Stars and Stripes*, the armed forces newspaper, were everywhere.

I sat down to two pancakes with maple syrup and read about the Celtics clobbering the New York Knicks, with Bob Cousy scoring twenty-five points. This was more like it. "He'll probably retire at the end of this season," I said and felt relieved there still was a Bob Cousy. I would have loved to stay there talking to the men, reading, eating, and listening to the music. My father said he'd bring me back after school.

We got into the Peugeot and drove seven miles down the hill. It was now light. We passed miles of farmland dotted with fences, tractors, horses, and cows.

"This place not only isn't much of a city…it's also in the middle of nowhere. It looks as if we've gone back to the nineteenth century," I said, as I took in the scene of uninterrupted countryside. There wasn't a house or sign of civilized habitation in sight.

My dad looked over at me and touched my shoulder, but I withdrew.

He told me he hoped I would have a nice first day as we drove down the hill and entered the small village where the school was.

I sat biting my lip, my fists clenched.

"Why don't you stop being such a crabby Abby?" my father asked. "No one likes being around a grump."

"If you feel guilty for forcing me to be here, then that's your problem," I said. Thinking of it later, I was always amazed I came up with such a psychological statement, because it was uncharacteristic of me then.

We'd no sooner descended the hill and entered the village when we faced the concrete wall of the school. It stood there like a barrier to be vaulted. Its darkness and eerie appearance was more apparent in the light and gave it a medieval feel.

Before we entered the building, we heard students shouting on the other side of the wall. As we passed through the courtyard, we saw boys and girls dressed in gray, heavy coats to protect them from the cold, damp, penetrating weather.

We walked up to the middle-aged woman at the front desk, who told us the *proviseur*'s office was on the second floor. The odor of cabbage cooking reminded me of visits to my grandmother's tenement, where I would sit for hours in her antiquated living room, listening to my mother argue with her about everything from the rising price of toilet paper to Eisenhower versus Stevenson. The receptionist escorted us upstairs to meet Monsieur Guérin, *le proviseur*. She tripped once on the stairs and again outside the principal's office.

M. Guérin was an older man with disheveled, white hair, an unkempt beard, and a red nose. He didn't speak to us in English. His assistant, the *censeur*, a middle-aged woman dressed in black with dark hair tied into a bun, translated.

He sat behind his old, brown desk, which creaked when he stood. There was a high, narrow window to the left of his desk. Books were strewn around the small room. There was a French flag along one of the walls.

"I'm skeptical he'll be able to follow," M. Guérin stated through his translator.

"It'll be a priceless experience just to spend time in your school," my father said.

The principal told us he would place me in the second class, or *classe de seconde*, with the sixteen-year-old students. "If he can do the work and is here next year, he will go to *classe de première*," the *proviseur* said.

"He'll do the work," my father said in his best lieutenant-colonel voice, as I contained the grimace I craved to show.

They told us my class would be *seconde moderne*, because I would be taking modern language, rather than classical. English would be my primary foreign language. M. Guérin said I should do well with that, but I would also have to study German. How was I supposed to study German in French? And why was the *proviseur* talking about next year? I assumed I was going home at the end of this year no matter what. I wasn't a soldier, despite my father's wishes.

I tried my French by asking the date of the last day of school. My hands were trembling, and I stuttered on the words.

"*Le vingt-sept juin*," the *proviseur* answered. He didn't seem impressed with the question and almost certainly guessed what motivated it, judging by the terseness of his reply.

It seemed like an eternity until June 27.

Both of the school officials wanted to end the interview. Neither offered to shake hands with us. As we prepared to leave, the *proviseur* mentioned we could buy textbooks in Sarrebourg or Saverne, two nearby towns, and gave us the names of the bookstores. What a waste to buy books. I wouldn't be able to read them, but I didn't bother telling my father that.

The same woman who had escorted us to the principal's office guided us to the front door. She told me something neither of the school officials had.

"There's another American student in the school, a teenage girl, who will be in your class. She is excited about meeting you," she said while pulling at my shirt. It was my first clue there were human beings I could relate to in the gray building.

We walked out the front door onto the narrow Rue de College. I again asked if I could go home. I told Dad I wouldn't be able to understand anything they said in this place.

"You may feel that at first, but give it a chance," he said.

"The people don't want me here…I can tell by the expressions on their faces," I pleaded.

"French people aren't the warmest. Just let yourself get used to the place," he said.

I told him my friends were getting ready for college. "I'm going to be wasting my time and falling behind," I said.

He said a year in this school would put me so far ahead of them for college and everything else, they'd never catch up.

My father opened the car door. "All you have to do is show up. I don't care about your grades," he said.

As if it were so easy to just show up. Dad worked at the base, where everyone spoke English. Everyone knew each other from their summers at the Cape, when they did their two-week training at Otis Air Force Base. They could joke about the Red Sox and go to the office's club for drinks, but I had to attend this strange school where I knew no one and was unwelcome—and where the air reeked of garlic and cabbage. Dad had no idea what I was feeling, and I couldn't reach him. It was like being locked in a prison and rapping on a window, but the guard walking by doesn't want to hear the desperation of your knocks. My father placed his hand on my shoulder, which I pushed away. If I'd had a clue of how pivotal it was in one's life just to show up regularly, I might have reacted differently.

The next morning, I arrived at the *lycée* in the predawn cold. I carried seven books and a sweat suit with sneakers, and wore my new brown French shoes, which had a zipper on the top. After we bought the books the previous day, my father had taken me to a store, Chausettes Michel, and bought me the shoes.

"They'll make you fit in better," he said.

"It'll take more than shoes," I snapped. Still the shoes were the most comfortable I've worn.

The students formed a circle around me in the courtyard. They didn't ask questions; they just stared. They looked different from the kids back home. It went beyond their berets, scarves, and pointed shoes; it had more to do with the expressions on their faces, as well as some of their features, but I was too disoriented to notice what the exact differences were. I should have enjoyed the attention, because at home my classmates ignored the foreign exchange students. My friends were mainly interested in fast cars, clothes, beer, and sex.

At my old school, I had felt bad for foreign students in America, because they were far from home and must have been lonely. Little had I known just how soon I would be one of them. But here I faced the opposite problem: I wasn't lonely enough! I walked to a chair along the wall, sat down, and placed my books on the bench next to me. They followed me and stood in front of where I was sitting. I felt like asking if they wanted a picture, so they could look at that instead. It would last longer and take the pressure off me. However, I didn't know how to suggest it, and if I could have, one of them probably would have gone for a camera.

One of the boys said, "*Tu n'as pas besoin de porter tous tes livres.*" Most of the classes met only twice a week. I could leave some of my books at home.

"*Viens voir,*" one of the boys said, as he seized me by the arm and towed me across the courtyard to a locker room. He grabbed three of my books and shoved them in his locker.

When we returned to the courtyard, the *censeur* was standing with a dark-skinned boy named Abdelak Bonnini. He had a wide smile and dark, curly hair. "*Il sera votre guide,*" she said as she introduced me to the boy who had been assigned to show me around. She clapped her hands, and everyone gathered their books and lined up in seven different lines. She clapped a second time, and we marched to class.

I followed my guide to physics class. The boy turned and talked as we moved through the courtyard. He said the word "*Algérie*" six times, which was all I could understand. I wondered if I would ever see those books again—they were in the locker of a classmate whose name I didn't know and whose face I couldn't identify. My classmates were one big bunch of scarves and berets that first day.

The physics teacher was six feet five and almost completely bald, and spoke in a booming voice. I found out later he'd been a fighter pilot in the war, and explosions had made him almost totally deaf. Sitting in his class meant enduring constant, deafening sound, but the others didn't seem to mind. Maybe to them, it was just loud language.

The next class was English. The teacher announced, "We have our second American student in our class, and I'm certain you'll all learn a lot from him." Despite her small size, the English teacher had a firm grip on the class, much more so than the physics professor, who had seemed scarier at first due to his size and loud voice.

After English I approached the other American student in the courtyard.

"I'm Roy Harrison," I said with more pride than I could remember. She was a few inches shorter than me. Her brown hair, the same color as mine, bounced up and down on her shoulders. She was wearing gray slacks and a brown sweater, which matched her eyes. She had a scarf much like the ones the French students wore. Her expression revealed interest but not friendliness. Although she looked very demure otherwise, I took two steps back when I saw a wildness in her eyes that I would expect more in a blonde or redhead.

"I'm Cheryl Dexter. I heard that you would be coming," she said. She stood there with two books in her arms, which were folded in front of her chest. Her breasts caused her sweater to bulge. It was hard not to stare at them, so I turned my eyes away, but I knew she had seen me, and now she probably felt they held power over me. "My father is a pilot from the Syracuse unit," she said. She pronounced Syracuse "ser a cuse," like Red Grange when he announced the football games on Saturdays.

One of the surveillants who supervised the courtyard, a young man in his early twenties, interrupted us. He told us not to speak English. The point of Americans being at the *lycée* was that we speak French. If we were caught again, we would get *deux mauvais points* apiece. The man walked away and took the Gitane cigarette out of his mouth. If I had to work in that place, I thought then, I'd be a chain-smoker too.

The boys in my class went into the small locker room off the courtyard and changed into shorts and sweatshirts. The floor was scuffed, and there were no toilets—and, surprisingly, no showers. The mirror was dirty, but it hid my skin blemishes. Since my mood fluctuated in proportion to the clearness of my skin, I would use it when I needed a psychological boost.

It was a seven-minute walk through the harsh winter air, and I was freezing by the time we reached the stadium. Although I had a sweat suit, I didn't put on the pants, because everyone else was wearing shorts, and I didn't want to look different from the other kids.

The class was divided into two teams, and we played soccer, which they called *futball*. I knew about soccer, but nobody played it back home. Despite my cross-country training, I became winded after ten minutes. In contrast my classmates sped up and down the hundred-meter field without difficulty. Many of them smacked the firm ball with the tops or fronts of their heads and could kick the ball fifty yards while running.

After fifteen minutes, I finally got the ball, but an opponent kicked it away. The coach looked upset; he yelled at me not to dribble but to pass the ball. It was as though he were the high school football coach at an important scrimmage. The second time the boy kicked the ball away from me, he stepped on my foot and hurt my ankle. I yelped in pain, limped a few times, and fell to the ground.

The French boy jumped up and down, waved his arms over his head, and screamed at me to get up. "*Les Américains sont laches,*" he yelled out. Even that first day, I knew what he meant, but didn't understand why he felt so strongly that we were weak. He was a red-faced, stocky boy with dirty-blond hair in a crew cut. He looked mean, and I saw he would be a problem for me. The coach blew the whistle.

Within five seconds, Abdelak Bonnini came up to the boy and hollered words I couldn't understand. The stocky boy grabbed Abdelak by the shirt and made a comment about "*Arabes.*" The two had to be separated by the teacher.

Another tall classmate, with dark brown hair, screamed, "*Ta gueule,* LePerrier." The stocky boy, whose name apparently was LePerrier, tried to grab him also, but two others held him back.

The pain, which shot up my foot like an electric shock, began to subside after I hopped on my other foot for ten seconds. Two other boys went into the grandstand to sit. They looked as though this episode were something they were prepared for. Everyone else milled around, and no one returned to the game.

"*Quatre mauvais points pour* LePerrier *et la même chose for* Bonnini," the coach said.

"What's a *mauvais point?*" I asked a sweating classmate, remembering what the surveillant said about Cheryl and me speaking English.

"It's when you get into trouble and have to go to extra study hall," he said.

The teacher paced back and forth, moving his hands wildly. The game never resumed, and we returned to school. As we walked back, I focused on the narrow cobblestone streets. All the buildings were two or three stories. Villagers wore berets, scarves, and heavy coats and carried long baguettes and packages of pastries. None of them looked at me. I don't know what I expected, but my sweatshirt said Newton South High School in bold, orange letters. It was as though the locals saw people with that insignia every day. Maybe they weren't curious or interested.

We toweled off in the locker room and marched into the massive dining room. We filled the chairs at the rectangular tables within seconds. The noise of all the furniture moving at once was deafening and gave way to the din of thirty simultaneous conversations. Wooden baskets full of crisp French bread were waiting for us on the table. The students alternated as waiters, and those serving today brought out fresh vegetables.

Fifteen minutes later, beefsteak and french fries appeared on the table. The fries were the crunchiest I'd ever tasted. The waiters placed pitchers of cider in front of every fourth student. My first full day in France, I had pancakes for breakfast and steak for lunch. I couldn't complain about the food, but I wouldn't admit that to my father.

A picture of Charles de Gaulle hung in a conspicuous location on the wall opposite my seat. There was also a picture of Napoleon Bonaparte on one of the sidewalls. I saw three unfamiliar flags in the front of the school through one of the two large casement windows in the front of the room.

Six classmates came over to me during the hour and fifteen minutes we spent in the dining hall.

"Do you know Ray Charles?" one boy asked, pronouncing the singer's name "Sharl." He wore dark brown corduroy pants and a tan coat unzipped in the front.

"I know who he is, but I don't know him," I answered.

"What about Gene Vahnsaw?" His eyes sparkled with curiosity under his black beret.

I told him I didn't know who that was, but he wasn't satisfied and repeated the question. He looked impatient and serious.

"'Be bop a lula,' *tu ne connais pas?*" he persisted.

"Oh, Gene Vincent. Yeah, I like his record," I said.

A girl wearing a beige skirt and brown kneesocks stood next to the boys on the other side of the table. All of them leaned forward, waiting for my answers. She smiled at me and asked, "*Tu connais* Johnny Hallyday?" I was surprised that she, like the boys, used the familiar form *tu*, but that was how students talked to each other. I later made a mistake by using *tu* to address one of the teachers, and he got really angry and corrected me immediately.

"That's one I never heard of," I said. I liked these questions and hoped they would ask more. I was the expert again, as I had been outside the cafeteria with Julie and her friends…except these were easy questions, and I didn't need to miss lunch.

She continued, "He's our big star. If you listen to the radio, you will hear 'Samedi Soir' and 'Retiens la Nuit.'"

"What about Edith Piaf?" I asked, as I thought back to the summers on the Cape when my mother played "La Vie en Rose" as the ocean air wafted through the windows of our cabin near Falmouth.

"She's for the older folks," she said. A few of them laughed, but I didn't mind.

Another boy sat down next to me. His hands fidgeted, and he spoke quickly, but I understood. He had a slide rule in his belt, lodged like a revolver in a holster, and looked more serious than the others.

"You need to be careful about Robert LePerrier," the boy warned. "I was sitting at his table, and he was saying awful things about Americans. They're making fun of you."

From the other table came a raucous chorus from three boys. They were singing, "Hit the Road, Jack" as they danced around their table. Two surveillants came over, and they sat down.

The boy with the slide rule said, "*Fais attention, s'il te plaît.*"

The afternoon began with geography. I'd never heard of geography as a subject of classroom study. It had to do with maps and finding out where places were, and that was it. But they made a big deal out of it here and even had a textbook. On the red cover, it said *Classe de Seconde Géographie*. I spent the hour leafing through the textbook and was shocked at the number of topics—climate, volcanoes, tornadoes, hurricanes, and astronomy—that made up the course. I only picked up an occasional word of what the teacher said. It was a waste of time.

Understanding in class was more challenging than conversing with my classmates; it was like watching the news on television at the Paris airport. I came to realize that one wasn't fluent in a foreign language until he could understand the news. I didn't know how foreign students did so well in our country.

The last class was biology, which was called *sciences naturelles*. I understood nothing and alternated between daydreaming and being angry with my father. The biology teacher, a young woman with jet black hair, shot a few irritated glances my way. What did she expect me to do?

The school day was over at 3:30 PM, and I walked out the front door, then through the large gate underneath the three unfamiliar flags. Dad was waiting for me.

"How do you like this buggy?" he grinned, pointing to the new, burgundy Peugeot 404 on the street. "I bought it in Strasbourg this morning." It was bigger than the blue rental car he'd picked me up in at the airport.

"How about driving me to the airport in it?" I said.

He ignored the suggestion. "How was your first day?"

"It was different."

"How do you mean, different?" he asked.

"I have to take geography. I didn't even know it was a subject. And in physical education, they play soccer every day. I hate that game."

"Would you like to go to the bakery in the town square and get a pastry?"

"It's going to take more than one of those stupid croissants to make me like this place," I said.

The afternoon was chilly, and I pulled my thick, gray scarf tight around my neck. The gray clouds surged across the sky. They never moved that fast back home.

We left the car on Rue de College and walked through the square, which was called *"Centre ville."* The city square was large, with a cobblestone plaza in the middle and many shops on each side. A game of *futball* had sprung up among the younger students on the cobblestone square. The boys were dressed in sweatshirts and didn't seem troubled by the chill.

There were only two tables in the *patisserie*, as most of the business was take-out. My father ordered a lemon meringue pastry on a flaky crust, and I had an apple tart with whipped cream. When I asked the woman for extra whipped cream, she looked annoyed and gestured that she had given me the standard amount. So I took the whipped cream off the hot chocolate I ordered and transferred it to the tart. She could have told me to do that.

I turned to my father and told him I didn't think the *censeur* or *proviseur* appreciated having Americans at their school. He repeated that French people are slow to warm up, and I should give them a chance.

"The students seem fine, but there is this crazy guy in my class who hates Americans," I said.

"How do you know that?" he asked me.

"He deliberately stepped on my foot during the soccer game, and he and his friends were making fun of me in the dining room."

My father told me I was too sensitive.

"This other guy told me to watch out for him," I said as I pounded my fist on the table. My dad was impervious to anything I would tell him that indicated I was in pain.

He said the French liked having us there to protect them, but they'd never admit it, because they were embarrassed that they had needed us to rescue them during the last world war. He also said much of the negative feeling toward Americans originated with de Gaulle, who hated Roosevelt.

"You mean it's because de Gaulle and Roosevelt couldn't get along that I almost got my foot busted?" I asked as I put down my hot chocolate.

My father explained how President Roosevelt feared that de Gaulle, as the symbol of the French resistance, might become a dictator, and so Roosevelt never recognized him as the real leader of France until after the end of the occupation, when the Germans were kicked out of France, in 1944. He said de Gaulle harbored anti-American feelings, which filtered down to the people. "Don't they teach you kids European history?" he chuckled, placing his hand on my shoulder, which I dislodged.

"Well, never mind," he said. "Let me tell you about the Vichy government."

"What was that?" I asked and immediately wished I hadn't.

Dad explained how Germany stormed into France in June of 1940 and took over the country in six weeks. They divided it into two parts. The Germans ran the northern part directly, but a puppet French government totally controlled by the Germans, called the Vichy government, directed the southern part. Charles de Gaulle, a veteran of World War I and a brigadier general in Alsace at the beginning of World War II, became the leader of the Free French movement, so he had to flee and set up an exile government, first in London and then in Algeria.

"I'm not interested," I said, taking a big drink of my hot chocolate. Actually it was kind of interesting, but I couldn't give my father the satisfaction of knowing that. He would think I wanted to know more about France and was beginning to accept being here. But of course I still harbored hopes of leaving. Although I couldn't cover my ears with the mug, I could cover my face. "I've had enough education for one day," I said.

But he persisted and told me the United States government not only supported this Vichy government, but also granted it diplomatic recognition and sent a prestigious ambassador, Admiral William Leahy.

"What does this have to do with Charles de Gaulle?" I asked. The general's picture, which was comfortably ensconced in the center of the cafeteria, indicated to me he was doing fine.

"De Gaulle fled the country. The Vichy government tried to destroy him."

I had to be missing something. I didn't know much about history, but I was sure the United States and France had been allies during both world wars. "And we supported them," I said.

"We did back them," my father said. "So our country isn't as loved around the world as your history teachers tell you, and as you learned firsthand today."

"They tell us that we're always on the right side," I said.

"I think that's true, but the rest of the world doesn't view us with affection…except the Germans."

That was another one I didn't understand. We beat the Germans in the war, so why should they like us? History was such a confusing subject. I had received a C the first semester back home. The textbook was OK, but I spent hours reading the complicated documents over and over. Then the teacher would invariably show I missed the point. I knew my problems in history weren't just bad luck, like in the other classes.

My father bit into his pastry. "Germans are into fighting and obedience and authority and like to identify with the winner, so they admire us."

We finished our snack; it was getting dark. I didn't know what he was talking about. It sounded too simplistic to me even back then, but maybe he didn't think I would understand anything complicated.

Dad told me he had a meeting in half an hour and asked me if I'd like to spend some time at the gym. I said OK, wondering why it was already getting dark when it wasn't even four thirty. This was a strange place; it didn't get light until after eight, and it got dark so early. I asked my father why the time worked so differently here—though I wasn't sure I really wanted to know, because I was afraid he'd tell me something really weird about the place that would just make it seem even more unfamiliar.

"We're much closer to the North Pole," he said. I was grateful he didn't go into any detail. Usually if you asked my dad the time, he told you how the watch worked. Anyway, after geography class, I knew my classmates understood, and I would eventually.

The gymnasium was a ten-minute walk from my father's office. The basketball court occupied the entire ground floor of the sand-colored building. A group of college-age men were in an intense game, using up the full court. There was an area for weight lifting and rope climbing on a balcony on the second floor. A man wearing boxing gloves pounded the heavy bag, which had Everlast written on it in large, orange letters. The large bag hung on a hook next to the smaller speed bag. Another young man, about twenty years old with a brown crew cut, lifted weights as I walked up the narrow staircase.

Before I could say a word, the second man came over to me and introduced himself.

"You must be Colonel Harrison's son. I'm Dan Connolly. I work for your dad."

"How did you know who I was?" I asked, pointing to myself.

"There aren't a lot of kids here your age. Would you like to play in the next basketball game?"

I agreed despite my doubts that my skills were any match for the players on the court. I asked Dan what he did for my father. I noted his eyes were really blue, and almost electric with intensity.

"I'm one of his assistants," Dan said as he put down the barbell and looked at me. "Your dad is a gentleman."

Everyone had only good things to say about my father. This was true of relatives, business associates, my friends' parents, people at the religious school, and now of military comrades. It was as though I had the perfect father. I couldn't complain to Dan about how Dad dominated me without coming across as a whining teenager. Nor did I want to tell Dan about the two drinks my father required to settle down after work, because practicing law riled him up so much. Instead I asked Dan if he was a student.

"Boston College Law School just accepted me," he said. He slammed the dumbbells to the floor and climbed the rope to the ceiling hand over hand.

The basketball game ended, and Dan and I joined three members of the losing team to play the winners. Again I was out of breath within minutes. But I wasn't too exhausted to notice the feud between the two centers. From the outset, they shoved each other. Both were about six feet five and weighed around 230 pounds. I could see the roughness was personal, not just a result of the competition of the game. Finally a hard shove sent one of the Goliaths to the floor, tearing his skin above the elbow. He jumped to his feet, and the two squared off to settle things.

The anger of the two men caused waves of fear to shoot through me. I knew I couldn't be helpful in breaking up a fight between these two monsters. I braced myself for blood…and possibly broken bones or even ambulances. But before the fighting began, Dan came between the two men, even though he was half their size. Dan moved so rapidly that it was impossible to figure out what he did, but it was something, because the two giants desisted immediately. As they backed away, the gymnasium became silent. The game resumed and was over in five minutes.

Three hours later, my father and I were having dinner in the officer's club.

"It was good that Dan stopped the fight," he said. "Those guys could've been court-martialed."

"I know it was good, but I don't know how Dan pulled it off," I said.

"What do you mean?" My dad looked impatiently at me.

I didn't know why he wasn't getting it. Explaining things had always been my strength, even when complicated matters were involved…and this wasn't a complex story. "It looked like the easiest thing in the world. He came between them, and they backed away," I said.

"You know, Dan's the safety for the Patriots, and he missed the football season because he was activated," Dad said as he folded his hands.

"Dan isn't big enough to be a professional football player, and he doesn't act or talk like one," I said, as I scratched my head. Dan Connolly was nothing like the football players I knew. He was smart and friendly, and seemed really interested in other people. He wasn't big enough to be an athlete.

"You don't believe me, but those two guys on the basketball court would," my dad said, as he resumed eating.

I struggled to cut a piece of my steak, but it was too tough. I could quit school and work in the officer's club as a chef and do better than the Air Force chef who cooked this meat. But I couldn't suggest that. My father would tell me "I told you so"—after all, hadn't he said before that with my grades, I would end up working in a luncheonette?

My father stared at me with an exasperated look and asked me what was wrong now.

"I'm just wondering how long it takes before it gets light again," I said.

SETTLING IN

I'd only been at the French school a week and a half when Christmas recess arrived. I spent my free time playing basketball and lifting weights at the gym. My classmates were loaded with homework assignments over the holidays, but I knew I couldn't turn them in.

Dad told me not to worry about it. "You're still getting a lot out of the school," he said. Looking back on it later, I would see that homework was the least important part of my education there. But back then, I dreaded returning to class unprepared.

I tried not to think of my friends playing basketball at the YMCA or going to movies. There would be something going on every day over Christmas vacation back at home. It was important to have groups of friends; it was healthy. People shouldn't have to think so much or retreat into their own minds, as I was doing. Every day I would announce at least five innings of a baseball game or the second half of a basketball game to myself. Military people who saw me walking to and from the gym probably wondered why I was talking to myself. Maybe they thought I was crazy, but I was the lieutenant colonel's son, so what could they do about it?

My father and I went for rides, exploring the Alsatian countryside in our new Peugeot. The scenery was picturesque, but I felt bored just being with my father all the time. He seemed more relaxed and only had an occasional drink at dinner in the officer's club. It seemed much easier for him to transition from work to play than it had been at home.

Two days after Christmas, I went to the gym and saw Dan Connolly lifting weights. We chatted for ten minutes about the Boston Celtics, and then I changed the subject.

"How'd you break up that fight at the gym a few weeks ago?" I asked.

"What are you talking about?" Dan said, as he put down a barbell that held 120 pounds.

That's what I would have loved—not so much to break up a fight, but for it to be such a small deal that I wouldn't even remember. "Those big guys who almost got into a fight in the basketball game…you just came between them. H-how'd you do it?" I stuttered. I was getting nervous, but I had to know. Dan's action had been so far beyond anything I could have done.

Dan smiled. "You mean Upton and Lake. I asked them to stop. They weren't going to fight anyway; they're always ragging on each other."

"It sure looked like they were going to fight. If I'd asked them to stop, they wouldn't have listened to me," I said.

"They would've if they knew your dad was the colonel," Dan said.

"My tendency is to step back," I said. I didn't know why I wanted to tell him these things. There was something different about Dan. He didn't have to prove anything. Even though I was just shy of my sixteenth birthday and didn't have a lot of experience as a judge of character, I saw it in his face and haven't met anyone since where it was so clearly written.

"Fights are good to avoid," Dan said, as he picked up the barbell and began another set of curls. He blew air out forcefully. "Stepping back is a good tendency."

"That's easy for you to say; you aren't afraid," I said.

After he finished his set of ten curls, Dan placed the barbell on the floor. He sat down on a chair and wiped the sweat off his face. "How many fights have you been in?" he asked me.

"Maybe two, if you call the second a fight," I said. I looked down at the floor, but somehow I knew that this was a rare opportunity.

Dan told me he'd been in at least a hundred. He was the son of a longshoreman and had been brought up in East Boston. Fighting was what kids did in his neighborhood. When he was fourteen, he stopped.

"What happened when you were fourteen?" I asked as I sat on a bench that was used for bench-pressing. I took in everything he said, as if he were my teacher. And he was, in a way. Talking with him, I finally felt as if I were in the right place at the right time.

Dan paused for a long time. "I guess I got sick of it," he said. He told me I couldn't get into fights now. "People are big at your age, and you'll get hurt," he said. He also said I'd get into trouble and be kicked out of school. "The last thing a college wants is a guy who gets into fights," Dan said. He used a cloth to wipe the perspiration off his forehead.

"You aren't going to tell my dad we had this conversation, are you?" I asked. I felt that Dan was beginning to wonder whether I was being threatened by someone or something like that.

"Don't worry. I wouldn't know what to say," he said.

"Could you teach me how to box?" I asked him. "We have a heavy bag and a speed bag right here." I walked over and stood next to the two bags and put my hand on the speed bag.

"What makes you think I'm a boxing expert?" Dan said as he stood against the wall.

"I just know you would be," I said, staring at him.

"Forget it. You're going to a French school. Very few Americans could hold their own in a French school. You don't need to break up fights or be a tough guy to get respect. People who act like tough guys don't get respect…they get fights." He bent over, touching his hands to his toes. "You get respect by giving respect," he said.

I couldn't appreciate that advice at the time. The tough guys I gave respect to at home thought I did it because I was afraid of them. And what made Dan think I was even attempting to hold my own in the *lycée* anyway? I couldn't understand half of the things the teachers said.

"The time is past for using boxing to feel better about yourself. There are other ways," he said.

"What happens if I get into a situation where I have to defend myself?" I asked.

"You mean, if your back is against the wall?" Dan asked.

"Yeah," I said, as I got up from the bench and started to pace.

I would look back later and be amazed by his patience. Maybe Dan felt he had to be nice because of my father's position. But as I got to know him, I knew Dan realized I needed something from him, and boxing was a good place to start.

"We can work on the bags. It's a good workout if nothing else. But if you get into a fight, I'll clobber you," Dan said.

I ran down the stairs and out of the gym, almost tripping on the staircase. I don't even remember if I said thank you.

The new year rolled in, as did February. I spent most of my free time after school on weekdays at the gym, learning from Dan about boxing and other sports stuff, and on weekends I learned about European history from my father. I was surprised to find out that I was actually interested in what he said, and that I wanted him to add more details. He responded to my curiosity and was happy to tell me more. It even occurred to me that my father would have made a great teacher. In some ways, I think, that would have been an easier life for him than the one he had as an attorney.

Dad picked me up at school every day at 3:30 PM unless he had a meeting. I know he had other responsibilities, but I never had to wait for him. I spent the rest of the afternoon in the gymnasium, lifting weights, playing basketball, and working out on the heavy and speed bags. Dan coached me when he was there, but a lot of the time he was busy, so he got Nicky, who was a boxer, to help me.

"Your left jab is quick," Nicky said, "but the right cross needs work. You can get more power with the proper timing." Nicky had me hitting those bags for thirty minutes a day. After a while, both Dan and Nicky told me I was improving. But I always enjoyed working with Dan more, even though Nicky knew more about boxing. My interest in boxing was never really about fighting anyway.

Between gourmet lunches at school, afternoon pastries, and baguettes, I gained ten pounds and grew two inches in two months. The damp Alsatian air cleared up the annoying acne I had brought with me to France. Unfortunately there were no girls for me to impress.

My American classmate, Cheryl, was always in a hurry. I ran into her and her father on the base, but she didn't introduce us. Unfortunately it wasn't possible to put her out of my mind, since we saw each other every day. I loved her high cheekbones and the dimples on her cheeks whenever she smiled. I would sneak glances in class when I thought she wasn't looking. When she wore her dark-framed eyeglasses, she looked intelligent and classy, like my mom. But when she took them off, she had a different look, which scared me, because I knew I was looking at the girl she really was. She wore slacks, but once a week, she'd have a skirt on. After staring at her legs and those freckles on the back of her left calf muscle, there were times I had to find someplace out of the way to sit down. I sought out the corner of the courtyard and stared at the wall as though I'd been banished for bad behavior.

We sat at different tables in the dining room, but I always knew where she was. If she was absent from school, I wondered what she was doing as the teacher rattled off words I couldn't understand.

There was no school on Thursdays, so I spent that day at the base library, reading novels, before going to the gym at my usual time. During that time I decided, way back then, to take off Thursdays as an adult, regardless of my profession. It made for a feeling of independence in the middle of the week, when freedom was so scarce.

There was no point in struggling with homework assignments, except in English class. My father found a mathematics tutor through the *lycée*. A retired professor from the University of Strasbourg taught me on Tuesday mornings for a couple of hours in a small classroom across from the school while my classmates were in math class. Even though M. Robin instructed in French, I understood everything. He spoke slowly, as though he were adding items to a bag, and stopped to explain the significance of each one before he started on the next item.

My father also arranged for one of the reservists, a high school physics and chemistry teacher, to meet with me every week. This arrangement also worked out, although I didn't learn much from the man, who had an attention span of thirty seconds. But I figured if he could teach high school physics and chemistry, I could let go of my terror of these subjects, which originated when I first heard the word "isotope" in the eighth grade.

I ventured into the village and tried out my French on the merchants on days my father told me he'd be late. When they saw me, they didn't notice right away that I was American, because I wore a beret and scarf now and had the right shoes. Everybody looked down at your shoes in France. I hadn't ever shined my shoes before I lived there. The merchants understood enough of what I said to communicate with me pretty well, and some of them even said that my accent wasn't bad. But I still couldn't come close to understanding my teachers. They spoke quickly and used strange words.

I often went to the base post exchange (usually referred to as the PX) before going to the gym. I read movie magazines and stared at pictures of Tuesday Weld and other actresses I'd seen on television. It bothered Dad to see me standing in the aisles, engrossed in pictures of her.

"This isn't the place to be reading this stuff," he said. He took the magazine out of my hands and put it back on the rack. "Do you want me to buy one for you?" he asked.

"No, I don't want to buy the magazine," I replied. I looked down, embarrassed. "I was just looking." I had this composite picture in my mind of the perfect woman who would make my life ideal. It was hard to believe I'd be better off with a real, flesh-and-blood person. I waited until I could move again, then went to the gym.

Two days before Valentine's Day, Cheryl sent me a message from across the room in biology class. She felt awful, she said; her throat hurt a lot, and when she swallowed, there were daggers in her throat. But why was she sending me a note? Maybe it was because I was the only other American in the class—or school, for that matter. But what did she expect me to do?

I asked the biology teacher if I could take Cheryl to the infirmary. The woman with the perpetual sneer threw up her hands with a sweeping gesture, as if she were clearing dust off the floor. Her pitch black, straight hair combined with her unfriendly facial expression to remind me of the witch in *Snow White and the Seven Dwarfs*, a movie my mother had taken me to at least five times. She blurted a cryptic comment about "*façons américaines*" and let us leave.

The elderly, red-faced nurse gave Cheryl a pill to swallow and motioned for her to lie on the cot. Cheryl began to shiver, and her teeth chattered. She stared at me with a pleading look, which made her seem tamer than usual. I decided this wasn't an ordinary sore throat. I called my father and reached Suzie, his secretary.

She told me my father was preparing for a meeting with the general and an important visitor to the base—the mayor of West Berlin. He couldn't be disturbed and had already refused two long-distance calls from the United States.

"I have an emergency; you need to interrupt him," I pleaded. She left the line, and I pressed the phone so hard against my ear, I heard my blood pulsate. I paced in a circle for five minutes until my father came on.

"Cheryl Dexter has a terrible sore throat," I told him.

He paused, and I heard silence for about ten seconds. I wondered if we had lost our connection.

"I'll ask my secretary to contact her father. If her father isn't available, we'll take her to the clinic after school," my father finally said.

"This isn't a typical sore throat," I said. Even though I wasn't a doctor, I knew I was right. Unfortunately I also knew how my father would react, and my thoughts were prophetic regarding his next comment.

"From what medical school did you graduate?" my father asked.

"This time you really need to listen to me," I said.

"When my secretary says I can't be interrupted, that's what she means," he said.

The next thing I heard was the dial tone. I sat across from Cheryl and placed my chin in my hands. I would make him eat that comment someday, but for the moment, I was clueless how to get Cheryl through this predicament.

I was shocked and vindicated to see Dan Connolly walk through the door within ten minutes. "Holy cow. It looks like we've got to get her to the clinic," Dan said.

The clinic had only three examining rooms, a tiny laboratory, and an X-ray machine. No surgery could be performed on the base, and all emergencies were medevaced to larger bases in Germany.

An American nurse sat behind a small desk, reading the *Stars and Stripes*. She put out her cigarette in the ashtray, which was full of lipstick-stained butts. A half-empty bottle of Orangina, a popular soft drink, advertised and sold everywhere in France, sat on the desk beside an unopened package of potato chips. Frank Sinatra was singing "Love and Marriage" on the overseas radio network. If I had been much older when I walked in and saw her desk looking like that at three in the afternoon, I would have concluded that she was bored.

As we waited for the doctor to come from the canteen, Dan asked me why I had bothered with the infirmary.

Before I could respond, Dr. Ksarjian arrived. My father must have checked into Captain Dexter's schedule, because the nurse told Dan that Cheryl's dad was on maneuvers over Czechoslovakia and wouldn't be back for two hours.

"What about her mother?" Dr. Ksarjian asked.

"She didn't come to France," I answered.

The doctor fastened a white band around his head with a bright light attached to the front. If I'd seen him on the street looking like that, I'd have thought he was a miner. He tugged on Cheryl's tongue with the white gauze pad in his left hand and gripped a hand mirror in his right hand, angling it toward her throat. He positioned the light on his head so the mirror lit up her throat like the Callahan Tunnel.

He asked her to make a loud noise, but she couldn't muster the slightest sound. I went over and took her hand, something I would never have dared to do if she had all her faculties.

She pressed hard, and I knew that the feeling of that squeeze would be what I needed to get me back to sleep when I woke up frightened and alone at two in the morning. I looked at Dr. Ksarjian. His face revealed confidence and concern. It was the second face I'd seen since coming to France that I wanted to make my own. Dan Connolly had been there both times.

"You were smart to bring her so quickly," the doctor said to Dan. He shone the light from his forehead down Cheryl's throat again.

Dan said, "It was Roy's decision. I was just obeying orders."

The doctor then turned and noticed me for the first time. "How did you know this wasn't an ordinary sore throat?" he asked.

I told him I just knew.

He said I had good reflexes, which was important for a physician. "Some doctors never develop them, despite years of practicing," he said. His praise reminded me of my Babe Ruth League coach, who used to say I had quick reflexes and seemed quicker on the field than I actually was. I never knew whether it was a compliment or criticism.

"You have epiglotitis, a serious infection of the lower part of your throat near the voice box…the same illness that George Washington had," the doctor told Cheryl. He said our first president was treated with bloodletting, but we'd made progress since those days, and she would get antibiotics. It was good Cheryl didn't question him about our first president's fate, because his epiglotitis had ended up doing him in. Then again, even if the question occurred to her, she couldn't speak.

He asked Cheryl if she was allergic to penicillin. She shook her head, and he pulled the white curtain in front of her and stepped behind it to give her a shot. He must have injected her in her rear end, but unfortunately I couldn't see.

After the doctor came out, and pulled open the curtain Cheryl put her hand on my shoulder to pull herself up. Dan and I positioned her in the back of his blue Buick, which his fiancée had talked him into shipping to Europe. I placed a thick, pink blanket that I had stolen from the clinic over Cheryl.

Dan stopped in front of Cheryl's cottage, in the same housing development as ours. The posters on the walls and pillows on the furniture presented a completely different atmosphere than our identical house. It was like being in a home, instead of in a cheap hotel room.

Once Cheryl was in bed, Dan left, but before he closed the front door, he told me to take the shuttle to the base and meet my father at his office at six o'clock. Dad would take me to the officer's club to meet the general and the guest.

I spent the next two hours at Cheryl's. I made tea, but she was asleep when I brought it into her bedroom, so I left it by her bedside. I sat on their living room couch and pulled *War and Peace* out of my green duffel bag. After fifteen minutes, I fell asleep and didn't awake until it was dark. I checked my watch and sprung off the couch. Cheryl was still asleep. I left the light on in her room, so she wouldn't be alone in the dark when she woke up. I caught the shuttle five minutes later.

The secretary told me my dad had already left for the officer's club to have cocktails with the visitor and the general, even though I was on time. He could have waited for me, but he must have thought those guys were more important. I placed my bag on a chair in my father's office.

"They're expecting you for dinner," she said with a smile. I turned away without asking who the big shot was; it had to be some politician from Washington. Since I'd arrived in France, I'd met several members of the Kennedy cabinet, but couldn't remember their names—nor could I separate them in my mind. They all hurt me with their bone-crushing handshakes and bored me with the incomprehensible lingo they spoke. They never asked about me, except my age and how I liked it in France. They expected those questions to be answered in five words. I knew I would daydream at the dinner table for two or more hours, but I was used to it.

My father sat at a table in the center of the lushly carpeted, dimly lit room. People spoke softly at the widely spaced tables, but occasionally loud laughter broke the tranquility. White tablecloths with fancy place settings and expensive wine glasses adorned the tables. Men in uniform smoked cigars throughout the room. The general and a man in civilian clothes sat with my father. The guest at our table appeared to be the same age as my dad. He was a large man, but I couldn't tell how tall he was, because he was already seated. His receding hairline revealed a slightly furrowed forehead. Usually I felt nervous when I had to interact with these politicians, but something about him comforted me. I could tell he was somehow different; he had forgiving eyes. From the way he spoke English, he was obviously British. My father introduced me to him and he stood up to shake my hand. He was a little taller than my dad. I didn't remember his name.

A waiter dressed in a red jacket and black tie with white gloves asked me if I'd like a Coke. He slid a place setting in front of me as I sat down and returned in under a minute with my drink.

The British man asked me how old I was, just as the others had done.

"I just turned sixteen, sir," I answered, as I put down my cola.

He mentioned that he had three sons—one was fourteen, and another twelve, and the youngest was just born.

"Do you have any hobbies?" he asked me. I told him I liked basketball and was a cross-country runner.

He made a joke that he had once won a cross-country race, because he was the only contestant. Everyone at the table laughed. It was as though he was mainly interested in me. I became uncomfortable and felt I was stealing him from the general and my father, so I excused myself to go to the bathroom, even though I didn't need to go. I took my time in the restroom and felt happy for the first time in a long time without knowing why.

When I returned to the table, the guest was telling them about how he was forced to leave his homeland and spend twelve years in Scandinavia—first in Norway, then in Sweden. There was a warrant out for his arrest. The Nazis wanted to put him in one of the original concentration camps for socialists and communists.

"Why were they focused on you?" the general asked.

"Ever since I was a teenager, I belonged to a left-wing group in Lubeck, my hometown. We were constantly battling it out with the Nazis," he said. He told us he spent half his time in street fights. "They knew I had a high profile in a socialist organization and were anxious to get rid of me," he said.

So he wasn't British after all—he was German! I would never have guessed English wasn't his native language. I, who was having such struggle learning French, couldn't believe he spoke my language so well. He even used some English words I had to look up later.

The general changed the subject and asked him, "Willy, do you know what Chancellor Adenauer did during the war?"

I remembered Konrad Adenauer's name from when my father was driving me to school, and we were listening to the announcer E. B. Rideout on the radio. The reporter always talked about Adenauer, de Gaulle, and John Foster Dulles. Mr. Dulles was always traveling to a place called "indoor China." One morning I asked my father why Mr. Dulles never went outside when he went to China. He didn't laugh, but I detected one of his rare looks of amusement he didn't want me to see. He said he'd tell that one to the guys at the office. But he never answered my question. It wasn't until two years after that, when I was in college and the Vietnam War started, that I learned Indochina was what they used to call Southeast Asia.

"Adenauer was mayor of Cologne at the time. The Nazis fired him in 1933 for removing their swastikas from the Rhine River bridges. They put him in prison twice," the man answered.

The "British-German" man talked about himself a bit more, then told us about the time he returned to Germany in 1936 for four months on a mission for the Norwegian underground. He had used a false passport. "They would have killed me if they found me," he said.

The waiter brought steaks. Our guest took a bite of his meat as the general asked him how well he knew the chancellor. He told us he'd just finished a brutal campaign against him for chancellorship of West Germany and his party had lost. One of the main tactics Adenauer used against him was to say he'd been a traitor and renounced his German citizenship.

"My citizenship was revoked," he said, as he put down his fork and didn't pick it up for at least a minute.

Of course I didn't realize at the time that I was dining with Willy Brandt, then the mayor of West Berlin, and future Nobel Prize winner. I couldn't believe this man had almost been chancellor of Germany. He was unlike the American politicians—more like a regular person. But maybe he was meaner than he came across. I thought of the German song about not having a wooden heart and I knew Germans were more complicated than that simple song indicated. What was behind the German man's generous brown eyes?

He told us his opponent criticized him for changing his name to protect himself. "My original name was Herbert Ernst Karl Frahm," he said. He told us that out of respect to his Norwegian friends, he kept his new name, Willy Brandt, after the war.

I stopped listening to them, because they began talking about complicated politics. My mind wandered to beautiful women whom I perceived to be unattainable either because of age, distance, or their lack of interest in me. But I was hopeful that now Cheryl would pay attention to me, since I'd helped her, even though that wasn't the way things usually worked with pretty girls. If you were nice to them, some would become your friend, and others would take you for granted, but none would be your girlfriend. It was the guys who weren't nice to them who became their boyfriends. But if I tried to act like those guys, the girls would say I was a creep. There were different rules for cool guys than there were for people like me.

Mayor Brandt snapped me back to reality every fifteen minutes by talking to me. "I try not to expose my sons to these kinds of conversations," he said, as he winked.

After two hours, the dinner ended. I slept more soundly that night than on any previous night since arriving in Europe.

AN ADVENTURE WITH CHERYL

On her first day back, Cheryl approached me in the courtyard during recess. She looked like her old self. The dimples, which made me crazy, were back. I wanted to grab her around the shoulders and kiss her neck.

She grabbed her scarf and twirled it as she asked if I'd like to go ice-skating in Strasbourg that Sunday. She ran her fingers through her hair and fluffed it, as I tried not to look too excited. I told her I'd let her know tomorrow after speaking to my father, even though I knew he'd let me go. About the only thing I'd learned about pretty girls is you had to act cool.

I daydreamed through class and thought of nothing but her. I filtered out new, important words in history class, like *Ancien Régime* and *Royaume de Naples* and *Guerres Napoléoniennes* while my classmates took copious notes in their blue notebooks, which they called *feuillets*.

Cheryl and I took the train to Strasbourg on Sunday around noon. Her dad dropped us at the Sarrebourg train station and said he'd meet us back there at 9:00 PM. We sat on the train, snuggling against opposite walls of our compartment, talking about school and our lives back home. Her face relaxed more than at school and her eyes sparkled more than in the courtyard.

She flagged down a taxi at the Strasbourg train station before I even saw it and directed him to go to the ice skating rink as if she were a general. It made me uncomfortable, because I knew she could order me around like that once she got to know me better. She sat closer to me in the cab than on the train and talked the whole time. She was tiring me a little with the nonstop chatter, but she looked great. She leaned forward in the seat when we arrived and screamed, "*Nous sommes arrivés*," startling the driver, who drove up to the old rink.

Out on the ice, she did twirls and jumps. There was no way I could keep up with her, so I skated around the crowded rink by myself at my own speed and enjoyed the exclusively American rock music that blared out of the loudspeakers. I looked at the pictures of country scenes on the walls. Toward the end of the session, Cheryl flew by and grabbed my hand, and we sped around for the next ten minutes. It would have been relaxing, except she skated so fast, I couldn't have stopped myself if she released me. Maybe if my father, who played on a championship high school hockey team, had taken me skating more than once, I would have been more on her level. But I'd been forced to develop my unimpressive skills by playing hockey a few times a year with my friends.

After two hours of skating, we walked thirty minutes to the town center. Even though it wasn't even four o'clock, the sun was setting as we reached the narrow, winding streets at the heart of Strasbourg. We went to a Winstube, an Alsatian wine bar, a typical local restaurant with pictures of Alpine skiing scenes hung on the dark walls. Large families were at every table, and their laughter filled the restaurant.

Cheryl said we should order *choucroute garnie*, the specialty of Alsace. It was hot sauerkraut with a dozen different meats. Some looked like regular hot dogs, but others resembled the boiled meat I had to eat as a little kid when I visited my grandmother. If I didn't eat it, she'd threaten to withhold the extravagant presents she gave me, presents that put my parents' modest gifts to shame.

The waiter brought strongly scented cheeses. At first I didn't want them, because they smelled funny, but after Cheryl ate them, I ended up eating more than she. I just didn't like to try new things. She didn't hesitate to order a bottle of red wine, probably because she saw kids younger than us at other tables, drinking it with their parents. At least that's what I thought at the time.

As we spoke, she put her hand on my arm every five minutes; the electricity of her touch numbed my fingers. She knew she had an effect on me, because each time she kept it there longer. I paid attention to what was happening every second. I wasn't thinking about baseball games, basketball games, or unavailable women.

"Things are really different in France," she said, as she took a drink of the red wine. "They didn't ask us for IDs or anything."

"Yeah, but everything here is fifty years behind what it would be in Boston," I said, as I took a sip. I hoped she wouldn't think I was arrogant or too cynical—I worried too much about what she would think. I just really missed seeing familiar, urban neighborhoods and large cities, like Boston. Everything here was on a smaller scale, and that made it seem old-fashioned somehow.

Cheryl told me that back home, it was a hassle being asked for identification every time she went on dates. "In New York, the drinking age is eighteen. We're not a bunch of puritans, like in Massachusetts." I didn't care for the comment but tried to forget what she said. I had to like her; there was no one else here. She was so sexy. She took away the emptiness. Maybe it wasn't important to like members of the opposite sex anyway.

Maybe she was thirsty from the skating, because she poured another glass. Then she surprised me by saying, "I'm concerned about Robert LePerrier."

"What do you mean?" I said, as I sat up from my relaxed position.

"Charlotte told me that he's always saying horrible things about you and how he's going to hurt you."

"Charlotte is trying to get me scared, and she knows you'll tell me," I said. I really wasn't too worried, because Robert never said anything to me. The bullies at home were more direct. But I never could look directly at Robert for some reason.

"He looks at me like he's undressing me, except he wouldn't know how," she said. She moved across the table and sat next to me. I thought she was going to sit on my lap.

We shared German chocolate cake; Cheryl took a piece and fed it to me first with a fork, but then switched to putting it into my mouth with her hand. She pushed it in and didn't hurry removing her fingers.

We spent three hours in the restaurant, but it was like ten minutes. It was the best time I'd had in my life. This must be how the athletes and the cool guys felt, I thought. Afterward we walked down Rue de 22 Novembre, across the Ill River, and down Rue de Maire to the station. It was a quarter to eight, and the streets were deserted. I was grateful for my thick gloves and warm scarf, because it was about fifteen degrees colder than when we'd entered the restaurant.

We'd almost reached the station when a large, barking, black dog rushed toward us. Cheryl was scared, and I wanted to protect her. He was only twenty yards away when a guttural German voice pierced the silence, and the dog stopped and then started barking again. I looked around for a rock to throw, as I had one time when a dog charged me back home; I'd hit it on the head, and it ran away. Now I found a branch nearby and picked it up in readiness, but fortunately, a man materialized out of the dark and grabbed the growling creature by the collar. He said nothing to us and just carted the snarling animal off.

We reached the station to catch our train to Sarrebourg. At five minutes to eight, six youths appeared across the tracks. They were waiting for a train to Munich.

They were teenagers, a few years older than us. They blasted out what sounded like military songs as they marched around the station. They wore motorcycle jackets and had short-cropped hair, and three of them had swastikas and iron crosses sewn on their coats. I knew the swastika was outlawed in Germany, but maybe they could wear them in France. They must be Germans.

The citizens of Strasbourg either were home or elsewhere; maybe they knew that this was a place to avoid at night. The youths made contact with us by yelling first in German, then in English, making comments about Jews and foreigners.

How did these thugs know we were foreigners? It wasn't the way we were dressed. Hadn't anti-Semitism been eliminated with the defeat of Hitler? My parents had told me about tennis and golf clubs where Jews weren't allowed, but that had been it. Now here was bona fide anti-Semitism, and it felt dangerous.

We couldn't exit without crossing to their side. One boy took an empty bottle and smashed it against a wall. He held the piece of jagged glass in his hand and waved it in the air, spitting something in German. Cheryl snuggled against my back, which she was using as a shield. Her hand, which had felt so warm in the restaurant, became an ice cube lodged against my spine.

I had to protect her. Never having been in a similar situation, I had no experience to draw upon. Fortunately she couldn't see my terror. I had nightmarish visions of being cut up, and her being raped. The boxing skills I was developing wouldn't be near adequate to deal with that mob. It was a shame Dan Connolly wasn't with us—he would know what to do. Hopefully they would stay on their side of the track until either our or their train arrived.

It would take a leap of eight feet for them to make it across to our side, or they could come around. I almost checked my watch, but that would telegraph my fear, which would have been as encouraging to them as blood to sharks. Anyway there was a conspicuous clock on the wall, which read 7:59.

Suddenly our train roared into the station. It was as if it had been in the wings all along, just waiting for the situation to become serious enough. There was no faraway light that came ever closer, no increasing sound; it was just there at eight, like a huge, iron shield. A conductor, an older man with a white mustache, stepped down onto the platform and punched our tickets. I pressed my ticket firmly into the man's palm and squeezed his hand. He gave me a puzzled, irritated look.

Cheryl sat close to me on the train. Her knee touched mine and caused me to look at the other passengers, but they weren't watching. A mother held her child's hand as they walked through the car. She smiled as she put him into his seat and slid in after him. She helped him take off his coat and hung it on a hook. I felt a sense of sadness come out of nowhere, but it evaporated immediately when Cheryl said, "You're my hero."

I turned to speak to her, but her beautiful mouth was there. There had been spin-the-bottle games when I was eleven, but after that, nothing; I wasn't used to kissing girls. I heard my friends bragging about making out with girls in their basements while the parents were upstairs, but it never happened to me. Now this great-looking girl wanted to kiss me. I looked around for any GIs who might know me, but there were no Americans except us. She kept her hand on my neck.

"I thought they were going to kill us, and you were so brave," she whispered, keeping her mouth against my ear. I could smell the wine on her breath, but it didn't occur to me how much it was influencing her behavior.

She had no idea how frightened I was. "I was worried too," I said, not comfortable with maintaining a John Wayne facade.

"You didn't show it. I felt safe because of you," she said.

I was about to answer, but she started kissing me again, then let out a sigh. No one on the train said anything, and I was both embarrassed and thrilled.

We arrived in Sarrebourg at nine and waited ten minutes. Captain Dexter didn't show up. "That's weird," said Cheryl, but she just shrugged.

We climbed the fifteen-minute walk to the small enclave of cottages where we lived. She pulled her coat around herself and linked her arm in mine. I finally got up the courage to put my arm around her. It was like going to the baseball game and sneaking into the good seats after everyone else left. I was afraid some athlete would come along and flick my arm off her shoulder, claiming she belonged to him. Even though she'd been giving me positive signals, I was terrified she'd say good night and send me to that empty cottage with my father. I knew she had to get up and go to school tomorrow, just as I did.

But she unlocked her door and walked in, expecting me to follow. She turned on the blue clock radio in the kitchen. Even though we had the same radio, neither my father nor I had ever turned it on. Johnny Hallyday sang, "Retiens la Nuit," a catchy tune patterned on American popular music. He was the singer most talked about by our classmates.

"Charlotte says he's the French Elvis Presley," Cheryl said.

"How did you become such good friends with Charlotte?" I asked. I knew Charlotte was best friends with Robert LePerrier's older sister and wondered what other things she might say about me.

"She's the only one at school who speaks good enough English to talk to me. Her dad's an English professor at Strasbourg U."

She sat down next to me on the couch, and her breast pushed against my chest. It was better with just the two of us, but a little scarier, since I wasn't prepared for what Cheryl had in mind. I didn't want to come across as a guy on his first date.

When the next song came on, Cheryl asked if I wanted to dance. I knew something unusual or upsetting was going to happen—I would say something stupid and reveal who I really was, and she would say she had to get up early, look at her watch, or yawn…and then, three minutes later, ask me to leave.

She leaned against me as we swayed back and forth. Her hand was on the back of my neck. She buried her head in my chest. Maybe I would be OK. We'd been through an ordeal already; how many bad things could happen in one night? I had to pretend to know what to do. The idea came to me to fake it. When the song was over, she went into her bedroom, but didn't close the door all the way.

I waited as she changed clothes. Maybe she wanted me to come into her room, since she left the door open. Possibly she wanted to find out if I could take a hint. But she might kick me out if I walked in there. I didn't trust her, but really it was myself I didn't have confidence in. My dilemma was resolved when she came out wearing slacks and a blouse she often wore at school.

We started dancing again. She rubbed my neck, and this time she stuck her tongue deep inside my mouth and pushed it against mine. I copied whatever she did; I felt myself rubbing against her, and her pushing back against me. I felt warmth going through my body and wanted to stay with her forever, even though I didn't trust either of us.

"How about more wine?" Cheryl asked.

Before I could answer, she pulled out one of about fifty bottles from a cabinet and opened it with a corkscrew, as if she were a bartender. I was concerned about her drinking but told myself to forget it.

She saw me staring at the cabinet.

"My dad uses it to drown his sorrows," she said.

"What do you mean?" I asked.

"My parents are getting divorced." She took a drink of the red wine. I looked at her eyes, and instead of her frequent wild look, I saw sadness.

"When did you find this out?" I asked, leaving my glass untouched.

She told me her dad begged her mother to come here, but no one in the family besides Cheryl was willing to come to France. "He's lonely, and it's hard for me to watch," she said. She told me her dad got drunk every night, and that she didn't think she'd ever get married.

"And he's flying planes during the day?" I put my hand over my mouth. I knew pilots were supposed to be alert.

"It's nothing new," she said. She told me how frustrated she was being four thousand miles from home. Other than meeting me, France had been a disappointment. She took another deep gulp of her wine, and within five minutes she had almost finished the brimming glass—to add to the two she'd had at the restaurant. Maybe she had a drinking problem too, but I had to forget it. Disappointment in her wasn't something I could afford.

"I cross the days off the calendar every day," I said.

She told me she had had visions of going to museums and fancy restaurants, then ended up in this farm country. "Did your father tell you the truth beforehand?" she asked, as she poured her fourth glass of wine.

"I knew what I was in for," I said and stood up and stretched. I was wondering if it was my place to say something about all the alcohol she was consuming, but I didn't want to fight with her, then have to struggle to get back in her good graces. It didn't occur to me that she might be asking for help.

"When I walked into the school and saw those outhouses, I decided I would use the WCs (water closets)," she said. She stood up and turned off the radio and put Mozart on their phonograph. She told me about the time she had to go to the bathroom suddenly and went into one of those WCs, even though she knew they were only for the faculty. There was no toilet paper, but she had to go badly. Afterward, when she looked over again, there was just enough toilet paper for one person.

The story unsettled me, but I filtered it out. Girls weren't supposed to talk about their bowel movements, especially in front of guys.

Her father stumbled into the cottage; it was around ten thirty. He tripped and fell onto the floor, fortunately not injuring his face.

He called from the floor, "Cheryl, I'm home."

"I can see, Dad," she said. She made no effort to help him. She crossed her legs in the chair and held onto her wine. "I'll see you in the morning," she added.

"I need to talk about your mother," he pleaded. I buttoned my coat. It was time to leave. I had no business hearing this conversation.

"Don't go. This goes on all the time," Cheryl said, as she tried to unbutton my coat. But I'd had enough. It had been one of the strangest days in my life, and my father would have kicked any guest out if he felt like Captain Dexter must be feeling.

"My dad must be back from his weekend trip, and he'll wonder where I am," I said, as I took hold of the doorknob.

I exited into the bitter cold, but it was only a minute until I arrived at my own cottage.

"Where the hell have you been?" my father hollered as I opened the door. "I've been back since seven, and you can't imagine the thoughts I've had."

I told him I'd been with Cheryl and didn't get back from Strasbourg until late. Dad's explosions had scared me ever since the time he slapped my face, when I was nine. It was the week after my mom was admitted to the hospital for her mastectomy. My cheek burned every time I saw him for the next three months. I didn't even remember why he did it. It was always so hard to feel comfortable and trusting around him.

"You were supposed to return to the base for the night yesterday," he yelled.

"And I did, didn't I? Look, it's late to be getting into an argument. I just want to go to bed," I said.

"Well, I hope you had a nice time, anyway." The angry tone in his voice evaporated. It always amazed me how quickly his temper subsided—but it was what might happen in those seconds before he calmed down that terrified me.

I sat at the kitchen table across from him and told him how I almost got mugged by Nazis at the Strasbourg train station. I spent half an hour relating the incident while he chewed on his fingernails. I told him Cheryl's dad drank a lot at night and flew planes the next day.

He wasn't surprised. "People don't understand or want to know about the armed forces. They want to know they're protected, but they don't want the details of what military people actually do. Out of sight, out of mind," he said. He took a drink of bourbon from a glass on the kitchen table.

"This is the first time I've seen you drinking other than at dinner over here," I said.

"The only reason I'm having one now is because of you," he said. We looked at each other and broke into laughter for about thirty seconds. After that anything one of us said made the other laugh.

All the same, I woke up twice that night from nightmares. After the second time, at 5:00 AM, I turned on my light and read *War and Peace* until it was time to get up.

CONFLICTS AND COMPLICATIONS

February became March, but the ides hadn't come and gone. It was now light in the mornings, like back home. I spent most Thursdays with Cheryl. It wasn't as if we were in bed all day having sex—far from it. Our relationship evolved to an almost platonic friendship, except for rare occasions. Cheryl would get romantic when she was on a train. I thought about buying her a merry-go-round to keep her in continuous motion, but I wouldn't have known where to find one.

The first Thursday in March, I walked to Cheryl's around ten. I tried to kiss her, but she brushed me off. "I'm not in the mood," she said. I went into her bathroom and checked my skin and was relieved not to see any pimples. I was reassured her negative response wasn't on the basis of broken-out skin. I always thought any rejections would be on the basis of the state of my complexion; it was what I was most sensitive about.

"I had to put my father to bed last night. He passed out on the living room floor," she said. Her eyes were red, and her face swollen. She had eye makeup smeared down her cheek. I wanted to walk out and go to the gym. I'd thought having a girlfriend would make my life perfect. My relationship with Cheryl was my first lesson about not wanting something too badly, because I might get it. But it was nice to know that not every negative reaction from girls was due to my complexion.

"Do you think it's safe for him to be flying a plane?" I asked.

She told me it didn't bother him and never had.

I had read that drinking dulls one's reflexes and told her so.

"I'm trying to get a job this summer working as an interpreter at the United Nations," she said. She paced around the cottage and didn't look at me. It was as though she were talking to a third person in the room. I wondered who that might be.

I suggested she ask M. Guérin, the principal, to write her a letter of recommendation. I swallowed and looked at the floor, imagining how lonely this place would be if Cheryl left. I felt as though she didn't want me here, since she wasn't really talking to me. She was probably wishing I were someone else. I almost asked her who she would really have liked to be with right then. I got up to leave. She saw me start to put on my coat, and a scowl spread across her face. "All you want is to pretend life is fun all the time. Are you my friend or not?" Cheryl snapped.

I was relieved, in a way, that she didn't really want me to leave. Even though I wanted to go to the gym, I wasn't about to turn down a pretty girl who wanted me to stay at her house. Dad had told me girls got moody at certain times of the month. I put my hands in my pockets and looked at Cheryl. A tight line going down the middle of her forehead replaced the dimples—or at least it distracted my attention.

"How about if we walk into Sarrebourg after we listen to music?" she suggested. I said fine.

We listened to Johnny Hallyday sing about five songs. Three of them were American songs that had been translated into French. At about a quarter to twelve, we walked down the hill into Sarrebourg to have lunch at one of the *brasseries*. Several men shot glances at Cheryl in the restaurant, but she didn't seem to notice. Afterward we went for a walk in the countryside. Just outside of town was a vast stretch of country. She had bought a stretched canvas and some paints in one of the stores, so we sat under a tree while she painted the landscape. I tried to read from my nine hundred pages of *War and Peace*, but it was cold and windy and hard to concentrate...although Cheryl seemed to be fine drawing, even with cold hands. I was impressed by her talent; she'd never said anything about art.

I thought Cheryl was beautiful, and I guess I was flattered to be with her, but really trusting her was another matter altogether. I never felt I could tell Cheryl what I was feeling any more than I could with my father. I sensed her toughness and saw how she treated her own father when he was in need. She'd think I was a wimp. I needed some tenderness from a girl, the kind I had gotten from my mother, but I only got it from Cheryl when she was in the mood, and it was always on her terms. The key was not to appear too deprived—not easy for someone who was terrified of being abandoned.

It was strange being friends with a girl. I needed this relationship, but at the same time wished I were in the gym, playing ball with the guys. At times, walking the streets on a Saturday night with my friends back home appealed to me more than I could have imagined it ever would. I halfway wished that Charlotte would come along and take up Cheryl's time and attention instead of me, but if Charlotte actually came to my rescue, I would have felt alone and excluded.

Another Thursday we took the train into Strasbourg to visit a couple of art museums. Cheryl put her hand on my shoulder and pointed out how each artist used light in their picture. She was in such a good mood and laughed at all of my jokes. If my father had shanghaied me there, I would've been bored, but with Cheryl, the museum was fun. It would have been nice if spending time with Cheryl was like this all the time, but I had no way of predicting her moods, unless a train was involved. On the ride back, she leaned against me and put her hand on my leg. When we got to her cottage, we kissed on the living room couch for about twenty minutes.

The next Thursday, we were on the base after going on a long walk. I was looking at pictures of movie actresses while Cheryl was looking in another part of the PX for some sunglasses.

"I was wondering where you were on Thursdays," said Dan Connolly, who tapped me on the shoulder. He had just come back from the gym.

Before I could respond to Dan, Cheryl came over, wearing her new glasses. Without breaking stride, she yanked the magazine out of my hand, causing a paper cut on my index finger. She placed it in the rack as though that was where it belonged, and it shouldn't be disturbed. She smiled at Dan and thanked him for coming to her rescue the day of her sore throat. "I was worried Roy wasn't going to get through to his dad," she said, as she fluffed her hair and took my arm, and we walked out.

I waved good-bye to Dan, but none of it sat very well with me. She acted as though she owned me; she had devalued me in front of my friend, even though I was the one who had come to her rescue. I couldn't imagine a woman doing that to Dan. I knew I could never trust her, but I needed her…or at least that was what I thought.

My father and I got to travel to Rome the next weekend, because he arranged temporary duty (TDY) there. All of the guys on the base talked about TDY. They were free tours of the world paid for by the U.S. government. The higher the officer's rank, the more TDY was available.

"We have to order the world famous fettuccine Alfredo," my father told me in the cab between the Hotel Michelangelo and Alfredo's restaurant. Alfredo himself spent five minutes at our table, serving us the egg noodles and cream. Even though we couldn't speak the same language as the waitstaff, we laughed most of the time. There were four American movie actors in the restaurant, but none received more attention than we did.

The next day, my father saw me studying frescoes on the ceiling of the Sistine Chapel. It was probably surprising to him to think of me as somebody who took an interest in art. Maybe he didn't realize how much I had changed while we were in Europe. He took off his glasses and cleaned them. "You look like you know what you're looking at," he said.

I told him about the museums I'd been to with Cheryl, and how she explained the paintings. I asked him if he knew who painted the frescoes in the Sistine Chapel.

He must have realized how little I really knew him as a person, instead of just as a father. Maybe he was even afraid that I thought he was uncultured and ignorant in some ways. "Of course I know," he said and turned away, his face red.

*   *   *   *

Just before our one-week spring vacation in mid-March, M. Richard, the physical education teacher, approached me after our daily soccer game and suggested we play basketball at the base. Since the *lycée* had no court, we couldn't play at the school.

I asked my father, and he arranged a morning trip for my class. He suggested my classmates remain on the base for the entire day. We could have lunch at the canteen, and go to the PX and each get a pint of ice cream. The students could see the planes. My father went out of his way to personally invite the *censeur*, but she declined.

A van arrived in front of the *lycée* at nine thirty and carried the two *seconde moderne* classes to the base. The small stands were half full of American soldiers. Although my father couldn't be there, he would meet us at the airstrip later. Dan Connolly sat in the first row.

Unlike soccer, basketball was a game I played frequently. Because the French students rarely played, this was my chance to shine. Also I could show off in front of the men at the base, many of whom thought of me as just the lieutenant colonel's son.

M. Richard divided us into two teams. I took control of the game and scored twenty-two points in the first half, so the other team put two defenders on me in the second half, and I only scored four points. The game ended in a tie, but was marked by a nasty incident.

As I went to drive to the basket with the score tied in the last minute, Robert LePerrier tripped me. He denied it even years later, when we had our conversation in the Tuillerie gardens, but I knew it was deliberate. I was barely able to block my fall with my hands. I could have broken half my teeth and my nose.

Later, some of the officers who had been watching told me the crash was like a piece of the ceiling plunging to the hardwood floor. It jarred everyone in the gym. Dan Connolly yelled to the referee, but he was on the other side of the court and hadn't seen what happened. There were loud rumblings in the stands. Two of my teammates, Bertrand and Abdelak, screamed at Robert. Robert stood in the middle of the court and yelled "*Qu'est-ce que tu veux que je fasse?*" as he shrugged holding his palms up.

Bertrand raised his fist and shouted at Robert, "*Ta gueule!*"

Although I got up slowly and he outweighed me by thirty pounds, I walked over to Robert and threw a punch at him. I don't know if the courage came from anger, the safety of all those American soldiers surrounding me, the boxing lessons, or somewhere else.

"What've you got against me?" I screamed in French. My punch missed by a mile. I'm sure Robert knew this was not the place to finish me off, so he took one step back, as though he were the sensible one. The coach, Dan Connolly, and five soldiers placed themselves in between me, Abdelak, Bertrand, and Robert. The game ended in a tie.

Dan Connolly asked me if Robert was the same guy who spilled soup on my hand in the school dining room. I told him I didn't know for sure if it was him. Jules Falkstein was standing next to me that day, and he knew it was Robert, but he didn't say anything then.

The next day, Cheryl came up to me in the courtyard after geography.

"I heard there was a fight at the basketball game yesterday," she said.

I told her Robert LePerrier tripped me, and I could have broken all my teeth.

"And they're such nice teeth," she said, as she touched my arm. It was unusual for her to touch me at school; she acted most of the time as if she didn't know me that well. She shocked me when she said Abdelak and Robert had a fight in the park behind the school, which was broken up by one of the surveillants.

"How did you find out?" I asked.

"Charlotte knows everything," she said. "She heard about it from LePerrier's sister."

I knew I had a friend in Abdelak Bonnini—or at least we shared an enemy—and wondered what I could do to help him. Maybe I could tell the *censeur* that Abdelak was sticking up for me in that fight, but I knew how little my opinion mattered. They wanted to get rid of me as much as him.

"Is it worse being an Algerian or an American in France?" I asked Cheryl.

"Algerians get treated badly all over France. They're second-class citizens," Cheryl said.

"Did Charlotte tell you that too?" I asked.

"She did, but it's in all the newspapers. Algeria has set off terrorist attacks in France, because their country wants independence, Fortunately, they finally will get it since they signed a peace agreement with France yesterday at *Evian-les-Bains* in the Alps," she said. Her eyes lit up as she explained the situation. She rarely had that kind of expression on her face. Maybe she would be happier working for the United Nations.

I told her politics was as confusing to me as history. I was just trying to get through the year.

About a week later, Dan Connolly told me about an unexpected meeting with Jules Falkstein. Jules approached him in the town square outside the *patisserie* and said he was my classmate.

After Jules introduced himself, he complimented Dan about his insightfulness in surmising that LePerrier was also behind the incident in the dining room where my hand was scalded.

"I knew it," Dan told Jules. "Roy kept telling me it was an accident." He looked at Jules and shook his thin hand gently.

"Roy isn't used to the school and doesn't see that some people are trying to hurt him," Jules said as he fingered his navy blue beret.

Dan asked for more information about Robert LePerrier, smiling so my classmate wouldn't run away.

"LePerrier tried to ruin four of my paintings two years ago," Jules said, as he turned around to look at the school gate.

Dan asked him what had motivated Robert to do that.

"My father went to their house and talked to Robert's father, who said he and his son thought we were Jewish, because we have a Jewish-sounding last name."

Dan asked if Robert stopped the behavior. Jules told him that Robert did stop, but only after his father had told him Jules wasn't Jewish.

"My dad thought he was an ex-Nazi," Jules said, but then turned away. He said he had to get back to the *lycée* but gave Dan his parents' phone number, where he could be reached on Sundays.

"I don't require much prodding when it comes to confronting 'ex-Nasis,'" my dad said later, as he stood up from his desk and looked over the map of Germany on his wall. Dan told me that my father then explained that his idol, Winston Churchill, called them 'Nasis.' "He wouldn't give them the dignity of pronouncing their party's name correctly," my father said.

My father, who never had a conversation with any of my teachers back home, let alone a principal, drove to the *lycée* at noon wearing his dark blue Air Force uniform. He told me about his meeting with the *proviseur* and the *censeur* that evening. The same secretary who was in the lobby in December escorted him upstairs. As with his previous visit, there was little greeting from the principal and *censeur*.

"If the school is too strong, we would understand if his father would like to withdraw him," the *censeur* said as she suppressed a smirk.

My father told her that it wasn't me who was complaining, but others who were in a position to observe.

The school officials didn't want to hear what he had to say.

"Many of the students at the school are envious of Robert LePerrier. He's a natural leader, athlete, and student," the *proviseur* said. Although the woman spoke the words, the *proviseur* looked directly at my father as the *censeur* translated.

She continued, "It may be that this school presents too much of an adjustment for your son. Many of the teachers say the classes are too powerful. Maybe he'd be better off at an American military school, where they instruct in English. It would take a superior foreign student to survive in this school, and your son is not that."

The principal's nose looked redder than usual. My father stood up to leave, but suddenly turned and spoke to the principal, expecting him to understand without translation.

"What about Robert LePerrier's father's activities in the Nazi party during World War II?" he asked.

"Who told you that?" the *proviseur* asked in English, as he fiddled with his right cuff link.

"I don't know if it's true, but it would explain his boy's behavior, since my son has done nothing to him," my father said.

The *proviseur* continued in English. His speech was almost as fluent as that of the *censeur*, although more strongly accented. He said that M. LePerrier was head of research at a pharmaceutical company and one of the leading scientists in France. When he said that, his entire face reddened, not just his nose. My father said nothing, but stood up with his hands folded in front of his chest.

"Lieutenant Colonel, to make such charges without evidence *n'est pas en bonne forme*," the principal said after a moment's hesitation. My father didn't speak French, but he knew what the expression meant. Soon after, he left the school.

It wasn't like Dad to say something so accusatory based on so little. He always thought things out, especially in matters that could be viewed as scandalous. He always told me to think before I acted. He must have known what he was doing—or maybe he just felt helpless and had to shake them up any way he could.

It had to have crossed his mind to withdraw me from the *lycée*. The school officials didn't want me there and had never been welcoming. But he must have reasoned I was no longer complaining about the place and was learning French. To have me sit idly at the base would be boring and unrewarding for me.

For once he was reading me correctly. Maybe my father was growing from this trip too. But he didn't give me any suggestions about protecting myself. Maybe I expected too much from him in those days. I didn't realize at the time that the whole ordeal might have been beyond one person's capability.

THE BERLIN WALL

I sat in the canteen on the base, engrossed in the sports section of the *Stars and Stripes* while taking frequent bites of my oversized hamburger, made with lettuce and tomato and doused in mustard and ketchup. I gulped Coke from the large, red plastic cup with Coca-Cola inscribed on the outside. I was becoming well indoctrinated in the pleasures of junk food at this canteen. I never cooked hamburgers at home, because Dad didn't like them, and we rarely ate in restaurants.

I couldn't read the newspaper while I ate, because the hamburger required two hands. Reluctantly putting it down, I dipped my french fries into the ketchup. They weren't quite as crisp as the *lycée*'s, but I wasn't complaining. "Moon River," the most popular song in the canteen, was playing. I loved the phrase "there's such a lot of world to see," even though coming to Europe had been the last thing I'd wanted. I felt busy, happy, and grateful for all these things: the food, Coke, music, and opportunity to travel. I would cook hamburgers at home if we ever got back.

I must have been pretty immersed in the sports page, because Dan Connolly's arrival at my table escaped my awareness. When I looked up, there was Dan with a hamburger. I read to him that Wilt Chamberlain scored a hundred points in a basketball game three nights ago against the New York Knickerbockers in Hershey, Pennsylvania.

"Yeah, and the next night, they played at Madison Square Garden, and the fans gave the Knicks' center a standing ovation for holding him to fifty-seven," Dan said. He added that those games were played three and a half weeks ago, and I must have been reading an old paper.

"His team will never beat the Celtics. It's one star player against a great team," I said.

"I want to talk to you about that guy in your class...Robert LePerrier." Dan smiled, but his eyes looked serious. He always got to the point.

I rolled my eyes. More and more people kept bringing up this jerk's name. What did they expect me to do?

"Is it about the incident in the gym?" I asked.

"I heard from one of your classmates that he's done some other things," Dan said.

"Like what?" I asked

He told me what Jules Falkstein had had to say about the hot-soup incident.

I started to read my newspaper again. It was more fun than this conversation. I knew I was being rude, but I didn't want to hear about threats to my safety. Why was Dan getting so concerned anyway? He wasn't an alarmist.

Suddenly a song took over the speakers. It was a slow ballad called "Once in a While." I'd heard it over the past few years on the radio but couldn't recall where or when. While it may sound corny, in this removed environment, this American enclave called the canteen, goose bumps overcame my body, especially on my back and neck. A chill ran up my spine. This stopped me from eating, drinking, and reading, and extinguished every conversation in the room for me as suddenly as if someone had pulled the jukebox plug out of the wall. The clatter of the kitchen dishes ceased equally abruptly.

The music was like a sonar-equipped probe that plunged to the depths of my mind, dislodged an anchor, and guided my most deeply protected feelings to the surface. Was it the soft tenor voice of the lead singer, who was drawing the words out like a fine thread, or the harmony of the group? It was probably the words and the music together. "Once in a while, will you try to give one little thought to me, though someone else may be nearer your heart?"

My mother had said those words to me as she lay in her bed the one time I visited her in the hospital. Mom hadn't made a lot of sense during the first hour and a half I sat with her. But all of a sudden, her blue eyes became clear, and she looked at me, and we connected. She told me to think of her once in a while, using the exact same words pouring out of the speakers. The music transported me to that hospital room. I could barely see or hear Dan Connolly. I wanted to plead to the sky that nobody was closer to my heart than she, and never would be.

I had felt her loss every day but never thought about the specific things we'd done together, and how much I'd enjoyed that time and longed for it to be that way again. Now I was five again, and we were on our daily walk to the park, waving to the engineer of the train and going to the record shop to buy a new record. I wanted to stay with her but couldn't. The memory had surfaced too quickly. I couldn't focus; I was like a diver coming up too fast and getting the bends.

I had no idea how much time I'd lost. I knew I could never cry in front of Dan Connolly. Running to the bathroom might be an option, but I'd have to open my eyes to find the way.

Dan sat there, looking at me but not staring. "This song really hits home for you, doesn't it?" he said. How could someone who tackled giants with thighs like tree trunks be so sensitive to other people's pain?

I cleared my throat and said, "I really love the Skyliners," hoping he'd think I just liked the group. I got the words out, but my eyes remained fixed at the floor. I couldn't let him see how soft and vulnerable I was; he was such a strong man.

"It's not the Skyliners." Dan put his hand on my shoulder.

"I'm positive this is the Skyliners," I said. I tried to be tough to overshadow my weakness. I forced myself to look up for the first time. My eyes were moist; I hoped he didn't notice, but he didn't miss much.

Dan shook his head back and forth. "The Skyliners have a woman singer in the group," he said. "Try the Chimes."

* * * *

Three days later my math teacher, M. Edouard Bernet, an older man with thick eyebrows that came together in the middle, walked around the classroom with his usual cigarette dangling out of his mouth, the ashes threatening to burn his hand. I moved my fingers back and forth as though they held a pair of tweezers. The urge to trim this teacher's eyebrows at the point where they met in the middle obsessed me. His ashes floated to the floor as always.

Earlier that morning, this teacher had called me to the blackboard to solve a solid geometry problem that one of my classmates had partially solved. After I got it, he announced to the class my math skills were now on par with everyone else's. I would tell M. Robin next Tuesday if I couldn't find him before then.

Suddenly a knock on the door interrupted us. The teacher ambled over to find the *censeur* waiting outside. She beckoned to me with her hand, and I could see my father behind her in the corridor.

It must be important for them to be interrupting the class. I racked my brain for anything I might have done. Could Cheryl have said something about me? Were they kicking me out of the school? My father put an end to my wondering.

"We're going to Berlin for the weekend," he said, as though he were giving me an expensive birthday present. I asked why he hadn't told me before.

"I just found out an hour ago. I have an emergency meeting there," he said. He had my suitcase and ordered me to get in the car. He said it with the same smile the dentist had when he was about to drill my teeth. I didn't want to go since I'd been looking forward to going to Strasbourg with Cheryl on Sunday; it was one of those rare weekends when she wasn't going away with her father.

"You never let me get used to anything," I snapped.

"This is the opportunity of a lifetime," he said.

When had I heard that message before? I threw my math notebook on the floor. "You can't do that in public," he said, as he looked around to see if anyone had noticed my display of temper. Fortunately the *censeur* had returned to her office.

I bit my upper lip and left a note for Cheryl with the secretary, then climbed into my dad's Peugeot 404. We were off to Frankfurt to catch the overnight train to Berlin.

We crossed the gray Alsatian countryside and, within fifty minutes, left Strasbourg behind. Minutes later we crossed the Rhine River, which separated France and West Germany. Every time we traversed that river and entered Germany (or Deutschland, as the Germans called it) and the signs changed from green to blue, my stomach tightened. I felt that Germans were boogeymen who would harm me because of my religion and could read my ethnicity on my face with their scientific minds.

This time, instead of army bases or the Heidelberg Castle, we were headed to Berlin, the scene of the big problem my father was always talking about. My father had explained that, after World War II, the city had been divided into four sectors: U.S., British, French, and Soviet. He told me that the Russians, whom I thought of as a bunch of scary-looking, bald people who liked to eat borscht, were keeping a million people behind a big, ugly wall—a little bit like the one outside my school, but enormous and very dangerous. The Berlin wall divided the city into East and West Berlin. Some of the Berliners were separated from their families and had no means of getting home. I knew something was going to happen there, although I wasn't sure whether I would be attacked, kidnapped, or just mocked.

My father, ever the military man, calmly gripped the wheel of the Peugeot 404 and guided the car along the autobahn at a rate exceeding seventy miles per hour. Nonetheless almost every automobile on the road passed us. As we neared Frankfurt, I asked my father why, if it was so important to arrive in Berlin immediately, we weren't traveling by plane.

"Because you, as a civilian, aren't allowed to fly on a military plane, and they like us to deal with the Russians, not the East Germans," he said. I didn't understand the second reason and asked him about it. He said that the Soviets were threatening to sign a new peace treaty with East Germany, giving the East Germans the rights to control the border between East and West Berlin and East and West Germany.

"But we won't recognize that treaty and prefer our soldiers and their dependants to travel on the 'duty train' between Frankfurt and Berlin," he said. I didn't ask him about the duty train but he explained it anyway saying it was a military train run by the U.S. government.

"Because the Russians and not the East Germans inspect the duty train as we cross the border, using this train is a way of not acknowledging East Germany as a sovereign nation," he said. He went on to talk about this treaty for a long time as though it was more the reason he'd been activated than even the wall. He said Khrushchev had brandished it over Kennedy at a meeting in Vienna the past summer but Kennedy wouldn't sign it, so Russia made threats to sign another one with East Germany. I didn't understand what he was talking about since I thought treaties were for peace not for intimidation. It wasn't until years later that I learned that this "treaty" was a device Khrushchev cooked up to nullify the Potsdam agreement and get the Americans out of Berlin.

It was becoming dark, and ice formed on our windows as we reached the outskirts of Frankfurt. For the first time since I'd arrived in Europe, I was in a city with skyscrapers, just like home. People were bundled up in overcoats, walking the packed streets. They had been here all my life, and I had never known the place even existed.

We reached the train station two hours before our scheduled departure for Berlin. The street signs were written in a fancy, cursive script in a language I couldn't understand, despite my three months of studying it. I'd seen writing like that on the few bar mitzvah invitations I'd received, and the Detroit Tigers had those kinds of letters on their uniforms.

The guttural German language filled the air in the large, brightly lit train station. Multicolored, electrical advertisements decorated the walls in the same type of script as the street signs. Yet when Dad asked people for directions, they answered in perfect English as though it were their native language, and all of this other stuff was decoration, just a facade.

My father bought me bratwurst with mustard and sauerkraut on a huge hot-dog roll, and it was the best I'd ever had. When I told him that, he said, "This is the city that frankfurters were named after, so a sausage sandwich made here had better be good."

There were ten parallel sets of train tracks in front of us. People stood at circular, chairless tables, gulping beer out of huge glass mugs, which they held by the handles. The suds on the top looked like bath bubbles.

My father had to go to the bathroom. While he was gone, I walked over to a large, colored map on one of the walls. "Berlin" was written in large letters and appeared on the other side of a red dividing line from Frankfurt. My father came over to me at the map.

"Why isn't Berlin just part of East Germany?" I asked him.

My father wiped his mouth with his sleeve as he drank the beer from the glass, which was broader than any I'd ever seen. If he had on a ten-gallon hat, he'd have looked like a cowboy in a Western. "I'm glad you asked me," he said and explained the Potsdam Conference and the division of Germany by the Allies at the end of World War II. I remembered his mentioning that in his lecture at my high school.

"Even though Berlin is 115 miles inside the eastern half of Germany, it was too important to give to any one country, so they divided it into east and west, just like they did with Germany," he said. He traced the lines of division with his finger. "So you have to go through East Germany to get to West Berlin. The city of Berlin is completely surrounded by the Soviet sector."

I felt better when he explained it. It was the first time I had any grasp of how this strange country worked. I didn't understand their language or their writing, but they all seemed to understand mine. I asked him why the Soviets had to put up the wall, and he told me that they had to keep people from escaping to the west. The East Berliners would do almost anything to get away from the horrible lives they were forced to live under Communism. Crossing the wall was an extremely dangerous thing to do, because soldiers were posted there with orders to shoot anyone climbing over the barrier. I finally was beginning to understand what it meant to be going to Berlin right now.

"As bad as things can get in our own country," he said, "at least we've never had to build a wall to keep our people in. In fact, sometimes we've had to adjust immigration laws to keep too many others from coming into the country. That's a result of the advantages of democracy."

We boarded the train for Berlin at seven, while my friends in America would be finishing their lunch. While they would be returning to afternoon classes, I was headed to what was in my mind undoubtedly the most dangerous place on earth. After having dinner in the dining car, I went to bed in one of the sleepers and passed out with my clothes on, not stirring the entire night. Neither the pounding of the rain on the roof of the train nor the late-night interruption of Russians boarding at Helmstadt to inspect travel visas woke me.

A white carpet of snow covered the ground to greet us in Berlin at eight in the morning. Cold, clear air blew in our faces as we stepped off at the train station, which was also a zoo. Before I could look around to see any animals, hotel personnel met us and escorted us to a limousine, and we headed to a military hotel in West Berlin near Templehof airport. I looked around to see any dangerous people, but didn't spot any.

We arrived at our hotel after a drive of only ten minutes. The boulevards in West Berlin were wide, colorful, and already populated with people strolling and chatting in their heavy overcoats, even though it was still shy of nine o'clock. Our lodgings were for senior officers in the United States military and were located in an old, three-story, ivy-covered brick building with extensive grounds. The employees helped us bring our luggage through the elegant lobby and up to our suite. I had expected to be in a dark, gray apartment building; our hotel was a pleasant surprise. As I looked out the windows of our spacious rooms, there were no police outside, and people walked down the street as though they were free. I wondered what all the fuss was about.

"How well these people speak English!" I said, as we settled into our luxury suite.

"Don't be overly impressed. This skill stems more from financial incentive than pursuit of scholarship," my father said.

"I don't think you're giving them proper credit," I said.

"Well, that may be. I'm not big on giving credit to Germans," my father said, as he removed his hat and placed it on a large, mahogany dresser.

Our suite was filled with Old World furniture and a large, upholstered, turquoise couch. Both beds had tall wooden posts from the frame at the foot of the bed. The long casement windows looked out on a residential street with large, wooden, two-story homes, extensive lawns, and trees that were bare of leaves.

My father combed his hair and put his hat back on. He told me he had to rush off but would be back around three. Even though I knew he had a meeting, his leaving scared me. But I figured I'd be safe in the room.

I sat on my bed and read my book. After about ten minutes, I went to the window. The sky appeared overcast; some rain or even more snow might be in the offing. Maybe I could go out for a while. It wasn't as if anyone were being mugged or molested outside. I fastened my scarf around my neck, pulled my gloves tight on my hands, and buttoned my green military coat, including the upper buttons around my throat. I took the elevator to the lobby and asked the concierge if he knew someplace interesting and safe to walk.

He motioned with his hand, and a driver in a blue uniform appeared. The driver told me he was taking me to Charlottenburg, an historic palace with widespread grounds behind it. There were multiple paths for walking and a large field to play soccer.

"There are millions of people there all the time with children. It's as safe as can be," the driver, whose name was Max, reassured me in his accent, which reminded me of how my grandparents spoke.

"I'll come fetch you if you just call this number," Max said, as he handed me his card. He also gave me some change and suggested I use the coins, which were called marks, at phone booths.

Still I had fears of being captured and held hostage in a dark basement, where my father would never find me. But Charlottenburg was a calm, manicured park where people of all ages, sizes, and shapes crisscrossed the paths behind the castle. Seeing the large number of children comforted me. No one would try anything with them around.

The Germans didn't look any different from the people back home. They didn't all have blond hair, blue eyes, and light skin, and none of them stared at my nose. Two birds fluttered above and landed in the tops of two adjoining trees, chirping at one another.

After walking for about forty-five minutes, I stopped for hot chocolate in a small snack bar. The woman knew I was American and barked out "two marks" as though she were a lemonade vendor on the Boston Common. I sat at the end of a long, green wooden table and removed my black leather gloves, relying on the paper cup to take over warming my hands.

Three teenaged girls down the table were laughing. Out of nowhere, a question sprang out: "Are you a member of the U.S. military?" I turned around and found nobody there. I pointed to myself, and the girl nodded; she meant me. The ringing clarity of her speech, with only a trace of an accent, jolted me.

Her ability to speak my language when I had no knowledge of hers provided her and her friends with an advantage over me. It was as though they had a large window through which they could see in, but I could only discern vague shapes looking out. It was feelings of helplessness like these that inspired me to become fluent in German in later years.

"How did you know I was American?" I asked.

"Because of your U.S. Air Force coat," one of the girls replied.

I told them I was a student and not old enough to be in the military.

"What are you doing here then?" the first girl asked.

I told her I was accompanying my father. I didn't want to give out too much information.

One of the girls suggested I see the wall. "Hopefully it will not be here very long, although my father told me that it would never come down," she said.

"Does it affect you?" I asked.

She had upset me. This was the first time anyone told me it would never come down. According to my father and the guys on the base, it would be a matter of weeks or months. I worried about missing my senior year as well, which was more than I'd bargained for. But at the worst, I'd go home for college in a year and a half.

"It affects us all." Her voice strengthened, as though she'd turned on a microphone. "We can't go across, even though we've all got relatives there."

One of the other girls said she used to go to the museums, since all the good ones were on the east, but now she couldn't.

"But they'll allow foreigners across. You can get a day pass or take a tour. They just won't let Germans go," she said.

"Why did they put it up, anyway?" I asked. I thought I knew but wanted to hear their point of view.

"Because people were escaping from the east at a rate of over ten thousand per month. The Communists can make life very dreary and oppressive," the first girl said.

The girls excused themselves, as they had to catch a bus. How did they know words like "oppressive" in English? I would never have used that word in conversation.

I'd enjoyed the exchange, even though I wasn't supposed to like Germans. These friendly young ladies had parents who had killed six million Jews less than twenty years ago, humiliating and torturing them in the most brutal ways. Although these girls were just being born back then, they were still Germans and had inherited the genes of those who committed the monstrosities. Could I have been too open and friendly?

I felt nervous and needed to call Max to pick me up. It weighed on me that I might not be leaving France at the end of the school year. Now I had something else to worry about in addition to my complexion, my relationship with Cheryl, and all the uncertainties of my current life. Max picked me up within ten minutes and took me on a mini tour of West Berlin, even though I told him I wanted to go back to the hotel. He said it would be interesting. My father had warned me Germans were willful.

We ventured down the main street, called the Kurfurstendamm, which teemed with people who toted packages out of Kaufhaus des Westens and Wertheim's, the two largest department stores in Europe, according to Max. But I wasn't paying attention to the shoppers or department stores. I was looking at the nearby memorial church, which had been bombed in World War II and was only partially reconstructed. Seeing this living monument of World War II, with its broken-down walls, caused flutters in my chest. I'd never seen any evidence of the damage bombs could do and felt vulnerable in this strange German city. With all the gossip on the base about whether the reservists would be going home soon, I realized how serious things could get if bombs started flying. How sheltered we all were back home, where my friends were at the Saturday-afternoon movies.

"Max, please take me back to the hotel," I pleaded.

Fortunately this time he listened, and we arrived back at the hotel in ten minutes. I nestled into a large, stuffed chair as American officers lounged around the spacious lobby, enjoying beer and hot cider. My chest felt calmer, and my breathing slowed, as I basked in the milieu of English conversation and U.S. military uniforms. I was privileged to be like a little puppy who had come in from the cold and was allowed a low profile by the fire.

But my tranquility was short-lived; my father, who always stirred up my calm, glided in the front door. He was wearing his Air Force hat with the lightning emblazoned on the visor and his blue Air Force coat. He moved to the bar as though he were powered by the same electricity that was displayed on his eyeshade. He brought a beer and Coca-Cola and sat down on the couch next to me. He handed me the Coke and said he wanted to talk about school.

That was the last thing I expected from him. He'd already told me that all he cared about was that I show up. I told him the classes were too hard and poured the Coca-Cola into a big glass with a handle, which was supposed to be for beer.

"I don't care about that. I'm concerned about this Robert LePerrier kid. Dan is convinced he's trying to hurt you," he said and looked worried. A warm feeling, which started in my stomach and rose up my spine, caused my face to flush.

I told him Robert didn't bother me, and he was just a weird guy.

"I can't allow you to get hurt. You're all I have," my father said. He took a gulp of the beer and turned away.

I reassured him I'd be fine, but since my conversation with Dan, I had this subject linked with memories of my mother, and my mind darted to the time I woke up from my hernia operation in the seventh grade, and she was sitting by my bedside with ten presents. Even though I had heavy bandages on half of my stomach, I knew I'd be OK, because she was there. If she were with us now, this place wouldn't seem nearly as scary, even though I knew my father was strong.

My father finished his beer and looked at me, but I couldn't tell him I was thinking about Mom. He seemed excited to be in this creepy place and looking forward to the evening. He was planning on going to dinner with General Holmes and the mayor at a restaurant called Copenhagen.

"I can sit with you in the dining room if you don't mind eating early," he said.

I was thrilled to hear that, because the last thing I wanted was to go out in the freezing night and listen to boring politics.

After my dinner of a hamburger, french fries, and a Coke in the dining room, I came up to my room with my father and plopped onto my bed. My father put on his jacket, scarf, and heavy gloves. He reminded me he'd arranged a tour of East Berlin for us in the morning. Dad was surrounded by other military people at the base who were all talking about Berlin, and he was intensely involved in the current situation, so he was excited about actually seeing East Berlin.

On the other hand, I felt terrified at the idea, something like the way I had felt back home when he started talking about moving to France and putting me into a French school.

"What if they don't let us come back?" I asked.

"It's very important to see East Berlin," he said and walked out the door. I was amazed that he was more worried about Robert LePerrier harming me than getting detained behind the wall.

I lay in bed reading and fell asleep before nine, but before I did, I wondered when he was going to quit subjecting me to all his strategies for my growth and development and just leave me alone. I would've been fine going back to Charlottenburg the next day and renting some skates with my marks. Maybe those girls would be there again. But he had plans for me, and they always seemed so important to him.

His hand on my shoulder was my alarm clock. We went down to the dining room but I couldn't touch my favorite breakfast of blueberry pancakes and maple syrup.

"Don't worry, nothing will happen," my father said, as he finally saw how scared I was. Usually he chose not to see these fears of mine. I felt a weight roll off my shoulders when he offered those words of reassurance.

It was a cold, clear March day—a duplicate of the previous one. I pulled my mittens onto my hands. My father and I were two smokestacks talking to one another in front of the hotel, as the van rolled around the circular drive. I held onto my passport as though it were a shield.

Our small group boarded the van. We consisted of three U.S. colonels (including my father), the wife of one of the officers, me, and the German tour guide, who drove. As we started out in West Berlin, nothing seemed of interest. I was actually becoming bored—a welcome feeling—until I saw it.

At first I wasn't sure what it was, since it seemed to rise out of nowhere. However, once recognized, there was no mistaking it—an ugly monster spreading itself as far as the eye could see. Like a disease, it implanted itself into the center of one's consciousness, forcing all other considerations to the side. The wall stood about ten feet high and was topped with barbed wire. There were two other walls behind it. The guide told us the smaller walls were to prevent East Berlin border guards from escaping.

We moved into the French sector along a narrow street called Bernauer Strasse, where the wall intersected with the side of a building. The windows were boarded up, so people couldn't escape by jumping to the sidewalk below.

The guide spoke in his accent, which made him sound like a younger version of my grandfather Otto. "Those wreaths on the sidewalk in front of the buildings are memorials to people who jumped to their deaths in search of freedom," he said.

He told us the buildings on the Bernauer Strasse were in East Berlin, but the sidewalk below was in West Berlin. In the days following August 13, the day the wall went up, people jumped into nets, trying to escape, while East German police guards ran up the stairs into their homes, trying to stop them.

"What happened to those who were afraid to jump?" asked the woman in our party.

"Police hauled those people who were paralyzed by fear, and unable to jump, back into their rooms."

"Are people still trying to escape?" she asked.

"People in the east still manage to escape daily by tunneling, escaping in car trunks, and even swimming across the Spree River," the guide pointed out.

In my mind, a cold, unyielding Goliath stood before me, seething with contempt for a piteously small David. I was too young to realize it would require someone with more than a slingshot to bring it down. I had no idea as a sixteen-year-old what real strength meant; to me, athletes who hit home runs in the ninth inning and actors who fought five people at once had real strength, not single mothers or cancer patients. I thought Lincoln was our strongest president because he won the civil war and freed the slaves, and never took into account that he endured four years of uncertainty, frustration, losing his son, death threats, and intense criticism to keep our country together—a country that, if not unified, may not have been able to defeat Hitler eighty years later.

The van left the Bernauer Strasse and moved to the famous Checkpoint Charlie, the critical spot where the Russian and American sectors of Berlin converged. What I saw made me feel as if I were ascending a roller coaster without a seat belt; I would have to hold on. Two booths stood fifty yards apart. Russian and American armored tanks faced each other, and signs in four languages affirmed that we were about to leave the American sector. Soldiers were everywhere, toting rifles and a variety of large weapons I'd never seen before. My mouth felt like cotton; fortunately I wouldn't have to say anything.

The van crossed to the East Berlin side of the checkpoint. Hostile-appearing Russian or East German officers inspected our passports. I figured they were going to board the van and remove only me, because they realized they scared me. But my father seemed unaffected by their glares, and this calmed me. After an endless wait, we entered what appeared to be a gray, uninhabited ghost town when compared to West Berlin. The red on people's shirts, pennants, and flags screamed out above the grayness that East Berlin was in the hands of Communists.

We drove past deserted, boarded-up buildings. The van swerved to avoid debris on the street. It was as though we'd traveled from the luxury of Beacon Hill to the slums of Roxbury in one block. We moved onto Wilhelmstrasse and viewed the outside of the Reich Chancellery, Hitler's old office building. I was terrified and thrilled. Our guide showed us the location of the bunker where Hitler and Eva Braun committed suicide, along with Josef Goebbels, his wife, and his six children.

We then passed Goebbels's office, and the guide mentioned he had been the minister of propaganda during the reign of the Third Reich.

"What was the real name of the position?" asked the colonel's wife.

"What do you mean?" the guide asked, as he pulled the van to the side of the street.

"Well, they didn't call him minister of propaganda, did they? I mean, that's like calling someone minister of exaggeration and distortion," she said.

"They did call him minister of propaganda, and that was his official title. It was only after Goebbels that the word took on the connotation of deceitfulness. Before Goebbels, propaganda meant public relations," he said.

I thought about John Pelters, one of the substitute linemen on the high school football team, whom the guys called Goebbels in the locker room because of his strange accent. He was a stocky guy who always looked uncomfortable and was forever muttering to himself. I wondered if they would have called him that if he were a starter.

I was relieved to see Checkpoint Charlie emerge once again from the grayness. After what was probably a short wait that prompted me to again imagine never being allowed to come back, we returned to the west. It was as though a thousand lights had been suddenly illuminated, and a hundred musical instruments began playing in synchrony. The coloration changed from a brooding gray to the penumbra of the rainbow. Democracy was Technicolor, and Communism was red and gray—a simple lesson for a freezing Sunday in March 1962.

The hotel lobby was a welcome sight as I staggered into the welcoming arms of the same overstuffed chair that received me the previous afternoon. I fell asleep immediately—or maybe "passed out" is more accurate. I don't know how long I was out until my father gently shook me by the shoulders for the second time that day.

"We have to leave for the mayor's house," he said. I fell back asleep, but ten minutes later, he awakened me again and guided me out of the chair. There was no time to discuss East Berlin. I think I nodded off again in the car on the way to the mayor's. I couldn't process everything I'd seen.

The chauffeur dropped the two of us off in a section of West Berlin known as Zehlendorf. The house was a medium-sized duplex, on a quiet middle class neighborhood on a pleasant cobblestone side street off the Am Schlachtensee, the main thoroughfare, which had the same name as the lake behind the mayor's residence. Their address was Marinesteig 14.

Willy Brandt himself answered the door wearing slacks and an open-collar, blue shirt. His wife and sons were there, the youngest in a crib. Mayor Brandt's wife was a tall, blond woman who greeted us with a smile. The mayor's oldest son and I went outside to take a walk partway around the lake. When we returned, the two men were in the middle of a conversation.

"I was in Nuremberg campaigning for the chancellorship, August 12th, the night before the wall went up," the mayor said.

"What did you do first?" my father asked.

"Well, they didn't reach me until about five in the morning, when they woke me up on the campaign train. We had just reached Hanover, so I took a flight to Berlin, and the police chief met me at Templehof airport," he said.

"What did you do then?" my father asked. He was leaning forward in his chair, so excited to be talking to this man in his own home.

"We drove to the Brandenburg gate and saw East German soldiers, roadblocks, and barbed wire everywhere," he said.

My father asked him if he tried to call President Kennedy. Mayor Brandt answered that he did, but JFK was out on his yacht. "I heard he got the news quickly, but he didn't want to do anything too fast, as long as it was just East Berlin that was involved," the mayor said as he sat forward in his chair.

I couldn't put the wreaths I'd seen that morning on the ground out of my mind. I asked him, "Have you really seen people jumping from windows?"

The mayor paused and said with an expression of great sorrow on his face, "Yes, I have, Roy. Unfortunately, it was a common occurrence in the days immediately after the wall went up."

There was a long silence at this point. I shifted in my chair and looked out at the lake. The sun was setting over the freezing water. The mayor asked my father how he felt about being in Europe, away from his law practice, helping Germans. My father's answer surprised me, because he never would have said it to me—in fact he had acted just the opposite.

"I'm pretty comfortable in France, but the trips to Germany, particularly Berlin, make me pretty uneasy," he said.

The mayor turned in his chair. A few creases formed in his forehead. He spoke with great seriousness and intensity as he said, "We need the American presence desperately. I am concerned that, although the United States government is committed to defending West Berlin, it may not be prepared for the tactics the Soviets would use to extend their influence."

"Like what?" my father asked.

"In the past, some examples would be the brutal suppressions of rebellions in East Berlin in 1953 and in Hungary in 1956…and now the wall," he said.

"Do you feel we've done enough to protest the wall?" I asked. I would never have asked that question if I hadn't seen the wall that very day and felt its effect so acutely.

He turned and looked at me. "I feel that the Allies could do more," he said.

My father brought up something about an economic boycott, but I couldn't remember what the mayor said in response. I was just too tired and overwhelmed by then. My father asked Mayor Brandt a long string of questions. At one point, I remember my father asking him, "Did the younger generation question their elders about the Holocaust?"

The mayor said, "No, Steve."

I guess no one mentioned it then. In later years, of course, it would become a bone of contention.

The visit to East Berlin combined with the visit to the mayor's house was really too much for one day, and we didn't end up staying very long. The mayor tried several times to ask my dad some personal questions of a more lighthearted nature, but my father's exuberance prevented any kind of buoyant atmosphere. I had the feeling Mr Brandt really didn't like to get into these heavy conversations at his home on the weekend, but didn't want to chip away at my dad's enthusiasm. The conversation went on for another half hour and we left. We were picked up by the same chauffeur and driven back to the hotel.

On the train back to France the next day, I asked my father a million questions abut the British-German man.

"I thought you weren't interested in political stuffed shirts," he said, as he looked over at me with a rare twinkle in his eyes.

NEAR-DEATH EXPERIENCE

The magic date of June 27, the end of the French school term, was no longer a mirage, but a visible finish line. I had survived Berlin and viewed going home to be a downhill path; I would make it. But one certainly couldn't judge the passage of time by the weather; even though it was already March 29, the temperature was only in the low thirties, with a typical Alsatian chill. As usual, our gym classes paraded in sweatshirts and shorts to the stadium.

We were about to enter the stadium when we came upon a dead animal in the middle of the road. A gray football with a tail and a set of evil, sharp teeth, it lay still in the middle of the street. It was too big to be a rat or squirrel. I was glad I hadn't encountered it while it was alive. We surrounded it, but no one wanted to try to move it. Our circle remained intact as we stared at it. Finally M. Richard grabbed the rigid tail and dumped it on the side of the road.

On this morning, instead of making us play soccer, our teacher decided for some reason known only to him that the game would be rugby. In my three and a half months at the *lycée*, with the exception of the basketball game at the base, the menu had been soccer. It was like going to a forty-flavors ice cream shop and ordering vanilla every time, but no one had complained.

Despite the bruising nature of this new game, my classmates dressed in the same clothing as for soccer. The objective was to run with the ball across the opposing team's goal without being tackled. Unfortunately no one explained to me to drop the ball once I was tackled. Communication problems were the most irritating, because they were preventable, and the result of insensitivity and laziness rather than human error, which was much easier to pardon.

After ten minutes of running up and down the field, the ball rolled into my hands. I knew I had to pick it up and run. I surprised myself by dodging two would-be tacklers, but Bertrand Lutz, a usually gentle six-foot-three guy with a large mop of brown hair in a *C*-shaped curl over his forehead, grabbed me around the ankles and brought me down like a sack of potatoes.

Despite the hard fall, I wasn't injured, and I held the ball like a trophy to my chest. The football players back home always smirked about fumbles being the ultimate weakness. But I held on, and they would have been impressed. But suddenly Robert LePerrier began kicking me in the chest to try to dislodge the ball.

Before I knew it, he'd kicked me twice, which caused M. Richard to blow the whistle and scream to stop the game. I held onto the ball despite the punishment. The coach scooted across the field, as I clutched it to my chest. My eyes were locked on his to detect a flicker of approval for my act of manliness.

M. Richard arrived, waving his arms like a referee at a football game. "*Monsieur Harrison, vous devez laisser tomber le ballon, autrement vous vous ferez beaucoup mal,*" he screamed. I couldn't get used to the way the French pronounced my name. Not only would they drop the *H*, but also they would always put the accent on the last syllable.

Now that M. Richard was there, Robert inched backward, and I began to feel the pain of his blows. I knew that second kick had jolted me far more than the first. If I were the left-field wall at Fenway Park, and a line drive had hit me with the same force as Robert LePerrier's second kick, the rebound would have been retrieved by the shortstop rather than the left fielder.

The students milled around, but no one spoke. The coach put his finger in Robert's face, but Robert pushed it away and said, "Let's get back to the game." Jules Falkstein walked into the stands. Two other students joined him, and the three sat there.

I stood up for the first time, and Richard finally asked if I was all right. I told him I was fine.

"You need to understand the rules," he screamed, as though I were supposed to be born knowing them.

My pain diminished, but my breastbone was tender when I pressed it, so I left it alone. I walked over to Robert and said, "You've been waiting to do something like this, haven't you?" I said it in French, the language I always spoke in now in school.

But he didn't get to answer, because Didier Colon, a classmate who rarely spoke, said that Robert hadn't been waiting. "He's been doing these things all along," he said.

Robert waved his hand dismissively. "It was legal what I did. You aren't supposed to hold on to the ball when you're tackled."

This was my introduction to people defending unethical behavior on legal grounds because of a lack of any other justification. There would be times after that when I would wonder if the law was designed for crooks to manipulate rather than for the courts to provide justice, but I could never tell my father that. He was a lawyer, after all, and had great respect for the law.

"From now on, we'll play soccer," the coach announced. Despite Robert's protests, we didn't resume the rugby game.

As we marched back to school, two classmates came over and dropped the ball at my feet. "*Tu dois laisser tomber*," they said. Why couldn't someone have told me before? It was hard to believe that out of all the people in my class, not one would have thought to explain important rules to me. They knew I'd never played before, but they weren't thinking about me. People were concerned with what affected them personally. It was no different back home; the thoughtful person was the exception.

I tried to forget the incident and enjoyed my lunch of beefsteak and *pommes frites* with cider and French bread. But that afternoon at the gym, it hurt my chest to shoot the basketball, so I went to the library instead. I said nothing to my father.

In soccer the next day, I was able to run up and down the field just fine. But in French literature class that morning around eleven, I suddenly felt as if I couldn't get enough air. I tried to breathe, but my lungs were stuck, and I didn't know how to free them. Breathing was something I'd just taken for granted; I never thought for a minute about the lungs in my chest. I became nervous. The room spun, and I couldn't see the teacher, who was only fifteen feet away. I moved my hands for someone to see, but the class and world went on, despite my inability to breathe.

I needed help; I was going to faint. I looked for Cheryl but couldn't see far enough. Pierre Aboghast was within my reach, and I grabbed him like a raft. I remember his blue eyes staring at me, as wide open as an empty hockey net, as he looked at me. He interrupted the teacher by screaming out, "*Quelquechose ne va pas avec l'Américain. Il est malade.*"

I was going to die, and the people back home would finally think about me and realize I was gone. But how would Dad get along? He'd already lost my mother and hadn't come close to recovering. All the thought he'd put into my future would go out the window. He really did care about me. Although it hadn't registered until now, I was finally enjoying my life.

Those were my last conscious thoughts. Almost everything I know about what happened after that point I learned from my father, Dr. Ksarjian, and Jules Falkstein.

Three classmates carried me to the infirmary and called my father.

He sped down the hill from the base, cursing himself for not having removed me from the school. He made it to the *lycée* in six minutes. The *censeur* waited for him at the front door and showed him into her office. I was flat on my back on the couch with four students surrounding me. My neck and head were swollen, as though they had been inflated with air.

Without waiting for explanations, my father picked me up as though I were a little boy and placed me in the back of his automobile. I do have some recollection of how gently he handled me. The students asked if they could come, but he said there wasn't room.

"But I saw everything that happened," pleaded Jules, so my father relented and made an exception.

During the drive up the hill, my father rifled the clutch through second, third, and into fourth gear within five seconds. A big truck carrying hay blocked his way. He kept the clutch in fourth and sped around the truck. Another car was coming in the other direction on the narrow, two-lane N4. My father wedged in between the two vehicles. Jules told me later he thought he was going to die then too.

My father carried me into the clinic, and only after he'd placed me on an examining table did he ask Jules what happened.

Dr. Ksarjian arrived, and Jules told them what had occurred during the rugby match the previous day. The doctor asked me if my chest hurt, but I didn't answer. They sat me up, and my breathing seemed a little better, and that meant something to the doctor.

"We need a chest X-ray immediately," Dr. Ksarjian said. He did the procedure himself. It took both the nurse and my father to support me while they took the film.

Five minutes later, Dr. Ksarjian stood in front of the view box, staring at the films. He told my father my heart was very enlarged. He took my blood pressure and said I had a large amount of blood in my pericardial sac from trauma to the chest, and that the blood would have to be removed immediately.

"Can you do it?" my father whispered.

"I've never done a pericardiocentesis, and it has to be done under fluoroscopy," the doctor muttered. He wiped the perspiration off his brow and sat down, cradling his head in his hands with his elbows on the desk. "We need to medevac him to Wiesbaden," he said. The moisture from his hands made smudge marks on the desk. Jules told me he didn't think doctors were supposed to sweat.

The doctor and my father drove to the landing strip in my father's Peugeot. My father told Jules he couldn't take him in a military plane but had the presence of mind to thank him for all his help. My father could be considerate, even under the most stressful situations, when people outside the family were involved. His secretary, Suzie, drove Jules back to the *lycée*.

One of the seventy pilots on the base was waiting for us as we arrived at the airstrip. They placed me in a seat at the front of the aircraft and took off immediately. The doctor took my pulse every five minutes. My father kneeled beside me.

As the flight progressed, my breathing became more labored, and my neck veins appeared ready to burst. My father gripped my hand. "My God, Roy! Your hand is as cold as the ocean at Bar Harbor!"

He looked very worried, and he kept holding my hand in his as he said, "This is truly the worst hour of my life, Son. I can't go on without you. Losing your mother, whom I adored, devastated me, but to suffer the loss of my boy would be more than I could bear." He said that the dark cottage with the two nondescript pictures on the wall would be purgatory if he had to live there alone.

He smiled for a moment as he touched on a memory of his. "Sixteen years ago, at another air base, in Ohio, the dark hair on the back of your head preceded the rest of your body into this world," he said.

But then he again looked stricken and shook his head back and forth, moaning, almost to himself: "I can hardly believe it. Now here I am, asking myself if it is all going to end on another Air Force base, halfway around the world. Already one of the trio who shared the magical moment of your birth is gone. My only real successes in life have been my relationships with you and your mom."

Moisture clouded his glasses, and he was unable to read his watch, which he checked every three minutes. The doctor kept listening to my heart and measuring my blood pressure; his shirt was soaked with perspiration. "Come on, Roy, hang in there, we're almost there," the doctor pleaded repeatedly. Rain splattered the windshield of the plane. A few times, the aircraft lurched, causing the doctor to fall forward into the aisle between the rows of seats. By the time the plane landed, the doctor could barely get any blood pressure reading on me.

An ambulance sat on the airstrip, awaiting our arrival. The ambulance driver and his coworker jumped out and loaded me onto a gurney, placing it into the back of the ambulance. They sped the three minutes to the emergency entrance to the hospital and raced me into the radiology department and fluoroscopy suite. My father and Dr. Ksarjian, who were also in the ambulance, ran behind them.

They watched through a window outside the X-ray room as I was placed on a table in front of two enormous metal machines. My father and Dr. Ksarjian watched as a man named Dr. Cook, dressed up in a green robe with a large, black apron covering it, injected carbon dioxide into my arm. Another man dressed in white came out and explained the accumulation of fluid in the sac that held my heart.

A long, silver needle became suddenly visible on the screen as it entered my heart sac. It drained dark, bloody fluid from my chest. The man standing next to my father and Dr. Ksarjian told them that if I had been brought in a half hour later, it would have been too late to save me. My father staggered to a chair and sat down. He lowered his eyes to the floor and didn't move for five minutes.

That was when I woke up on a big, flat table and saw a person with a green mask and two very big, brown eyes peering down at me. I thought I was in the middle of a dream on a spaceship, and he was a Martian. He asked me something, but I couldn't focus, because I was too busy trying to figure out whether I was alive and dreaming, or dead. But it was easy to speak and breathe.

It took me about half an hour to realize I hadn't died. My father told me what had happened since I passed out at the *lycée*, but it wasn't until after we had returned to the United States that he told me about all the thoughts that went through his head during that shaky period. I was so excited to be able to speak, I tried to tell the German X-ray technician my life story, but he just smiled and told me to rest.

They held me in the radiology department for about an hour. Finally they wheeled me upstairs to a brightly lit room with two beds and a view of the green countryside, with cows and horses grazing in the distance.

A nurse came in and measured my blood pressure. "Just press the button if you need anything," she told my father.

My father kissed my cheek; I couldn't recollect his ever having done that before.

A little later on, I talked with Dr. Ksarjian. I said, "I guess my dad was pretty worried for a while there, wasn't he?"

Dr. Ksarjian told me, "That's an understatement, Roy. Your father was beside himself. Why, he must have kissed you twenty times while you were in the airplane!"

"Really? Wow! You know, my dad and I didn't always get along all that well. He could be sort of military and rigid sometimes, and I didn't always meet up with his expectations. So we didn't communicate much, especially after my mom died, and we didn't have a go-between and peacemaker."

"Roy, I think that may be different for the two of you in the future. I'll tell you something: In the plane, your dad swore that if you survived, he would never criticize you again." The doctor went on to tell me all the other things my dad had said in his moments of agony.

Over the next few days, my father let me watch unlimited television on the U.S. overseas network in the hospital room, even though he had called it the "idiot box" and said if I watched it, my buddies would get way ahead of me. He made frequent trips to the PX to bring me every type of snack. I devoured the sports page of the *Stars and Stripes*.

When he wasn't running errands, my father remained in my room. During the third day, he rolled me in a wheelchair to one of the outdoor patios. I didn't need a wheelchair, but it was a hospital rule that if I left the floor, I needed to be transported that way. The birds chirped, and the sun felt warm on our faces. We both wore windbreakers supplied by the hospital.

For half an hour, both of us sat silently on the patio. Even though in the past it was hardly unusual for us to be together without talking, this time I was getting uncomfortable, because I wanted to communicate with him, but I didn't know what to say. Probably if we had been at home, my father would have gone into another room instead of just sitting there.

I finally got up my courage and asked him, "Dad, you never told me how you and Mom met. It's something I've always wanted to know, but I've been afraid to ask you in case it made you feel too sad remembering her."

"I never told you that?" he shook his head in disbelief. "Well, I had a job at that time doing stock inventories at a supermarket chain while I attended law school in the evenings. I lived with my parents, brother, and sister, and money was short. My wages paid Mom and Dad's rent."

"I didn't realize you worked your way through law school, Dad." Knowing that about him helped me understand why he was so careful and frugal sometimes.

"Well, I did. It wasn't always easy, but the supermarket job had its bright side. On weekends, you see, your mom also worked at one of the stores, since her uncle owned the chain."

"At first, your mom thought I was too serious, but after she broke up with her boyfriend, she noticed me," he said. "She had even called me a 'drip.'" He smiled, remembering that silly little word from a long time ago.

I laughed hard; none of my friends would use that expression. It was something a man who parted his hair in the middle would say.

I asked him, "Would you ever like to get married again?" I never thought I could ask him that.

"How would you feel if I did?" he asked. He looked at me as though it would matter what I said.

I told him, "I can't know for sure, but I think I'd be happy for you. But no other woman could take the place of my mother."

His next statement jolted me, and I've never forgotten it: "She really doted on you. At times I might have been a bit jealous." He stood up, went to the window, and looked at the green hillside.

"You, jealous of me?" I repeated in disbelief.

"She spent much more time with you than she ever did with me. I couldn't have admitted it at the time, but there were times when I resented it," he said.

Neither of us spoke for a minute. My father stared straight ahead, as though my mother's face were in front of him. I'd seen that wistful look many times but never knew what it meant until then.

He said my mother knew how to have fun, and he was always the boring one, worrying about my grades.

"Mom always gave me encouragement," I said.

He told me he thought compliments would jinx people; my father was superstitious, which was no surprise.

"How come you never got out of the National Guard reserves?" I asked him. I knew my mom had nagged him about that for years.

"Everyone asks me that at home," he said. "I joined to make extra money, but I've always liked the guys, and they kept promoting me. It's different from my law work, and it's fun being a lieutenant colonel."

* * * *

We returned to the room, and I turned the television back on while Dad took a nap. Dr. Cook breezed in as the afternoon wore on, wearing his long, white coat, which covered his green surgical scrub suit. His thick, brown mustache and large, brown-rimmed glasses gave him more the appearance of an absentminded professor than a doctor as he settled into the leather chair, which was in need of reupholstering. He sat ensconced in the chair, as though he had arrived at his final destination for the day.

My father sprung from the bed and turned off the television.

"I'll never be able to repay you," my father said. "We're lucky you were here." He turned around and went into the bathroom, but was back out in ten seconds, putting his glasses back on. I realized that when people had skills my father didn't, they earned his respect. By becoming a doctor, I might earn the esteem he gave Dr. Cook.

Dr. Cook laughed. "You won't find me anywhere else unless I'm on vacation."

The doctor was forty-eight and had spent the last ten years in the military after practicing medicine for five years in Lexington, Kentucky. The business aspects of medicine had drained his enthusiasm for being in private practice as a cardiologist, and he'd opted for life in the armed forces. He had married a German woman five years ago and had two young children.

He told me that most of the time, his patients were people much older than I. Dr. Cook wanted to know more about me and asked me several questions about my life. I could sense that he was interested in me as a person, not just as a medical case. We talked some, and he warned me about taking care of myself in the future.

"Maybe you should leave rugby to the Europeans," he said. "It's a crazy game anyway." He wanted to repeat a chest X-ray in the morning, and if that came out OK, I could be discharged.

After he left, I told my father that Dr. Cook was a doctor who made you feel like a person instead of a patient with a number tag on. He was so different from Dr. Dunbar, my mother's surgeon. "Remember, Dad, how Dunbar would come into the hospital room wearing his three-piece suit, look at the chart, tell Mom a few jokes, and leave?"

The funny thing was, although I don't think he ever asked me a single question about myself or even learned my first name, Dr. Dunbar gave me the first inkling that I might want to become a doctor. Anyone who could do something as miraculous as surgery and open up the human body would obviously never get sick himself or have any personal problems.

About twenty minutes later, Dan Connolly strode in the door. He said he was surprised at how good I looked and was sorry he hadn't come sooner, but every time he tried to leave, his commanding officer had given him something to do.

He turned to my father and told him that my father's secretary, Suzie, had spoken with the mayor of Berlin yesterday, telling him what happened to me. The mayor said he was going to call here.

Dan and my father talked about work, and I returned to *77 Sunset Strip* on television. After ten minutes, two girls accompanied by a military policeman knocked on the door. The officer asked if these civilians could visit me.

My father asked if they were classmates of mine.

"No…but I've seen you before, *n'est-ce pas?*" I asked the younger girl. I knew her from the courtyard, but she wasn't a classmate. She unbuttoned her blue coat, which revealed thick corduroy pants with a brown vest.

She spoke in French. "I'm in *quatrième*. My name is Jeanne LePerrier; I'm Robert's younger sister. Because he's unable to come, I'm visiting with my cousin."

I translated for my father and Dan and added that her class of quatrieme would be equivalent to the ninth grade in our high school system.

The other girl was older, either a college student or young working woman. She stood straight as a flagpole, while the younger one tapped her feet on the linoleum, which her eyes studied.

"How did you girls get here all the way from France?" my father asked.

"We took the train from Strasbourg and a cab from the station," the older girl answered before clearing her throat. Her name was Isabelle, and she was Jeanne's cousin, the daughter of Jeanne's father's sister. She was a psychology major at the University of Strasbourg; her mother lived in Paris, and her father in Lyons. She was twenty.

My father offered them chairs. At first the older girl sat quietly, but she became increasingly involved in the conversation because of her proficient English.

"Jeanne's brother didn't mean to harm Roy," she said, but even I, naive to begin with and very attracted to her, could tell she didn't mean it. Although she was beautiful and dressed seductively, she wasn't a good liar.

I couldn't take my eyes off her. Her tight pants drew attention to her long, slender legs, and her shoulder-length, dark hair shone as though it had been freshly washed. She had full lips with a minimum of makeup. She spoke English easily, with a different accent than the one I heard my classmates use in English class.

The girls sat in the room for about fifteen minutes. They didn't say much after introducing themselves and asking me how I was feeling. They must have felt they had to stay awhile out of politeness or guilt.

"I'm sorry you were hurt." The younger girl broke the silence. She looked again at the ground and wiped one of her eyes. The older girl looked outside at the view.

"Everyone wants to know when you'll be back at school," Jeanne said and Isabelle translated.

"We're not sure," my father said. He had a bad habit of answering questions for me. But I was so happy to be alive, I couldn't let small things bother me.

My father looked at Jeanne and said, "I appreciate your going so far out of your way to visit Roy, but I am curious why you came instead of Robert or your parents." He looked over at Jeanne for an answer.

Jeanne said nothing and looked to Isabelle. They conversed rapidly and briefly in French.

"Her father is out of the country, and Robert is sick," Isabelle answered.

"What about your mother?" the lieutenant colonel inquired.

"She wanted to come, but the *lycée* wouldn't let her off," Isabelle answered.

Jeanne spoke again, but Isabelle didn't translate this time. I couldn't understand what she said.

After another five minutes, Jeanne got up from her chair and put on her coat. She announced, "*on doit partir*" and asked me if it was possible to buy food at the hospital if one wasn't in the American military.

My father told them he'd take them to the cafeteria, and they could leave their pocketbooks in the room. "It's my treat," he said.

The three of them got up to leave. Dan Connolly remained in the room with me.

"I don't remember what happened after I passed out in my classroom. I could have died, couldn't I?" I asked Dan the question I didn't want to ask my father.

Dan took off his coat and loosened his tie. "Ksarjian is a great decision maker," he said.

I told Dan I'd changed my choice of careers and wanted to be a doctor.

He told me that was pretty good, since he was six years older than I and had decided on law school only in the past six months.

"What did you want to be before?" Dan asked.

I told him I had wanted to be a sports announcer.

Dan looked surprised, since I'd never announced any games for him. Our relationship was pretty formal; I was always afraid of doing something stupid that would make him think less of me. It was a fear I didn't have with my parents' friends or my relatives. In retrospect my fears were unjustified, because Dan was the least judgmental of people.

"Any particular sport?" Dan asked, as his eyes locked on mine.

I told him I had wanted to be like Mel Allen, whom I viewed as having the perfect life.

Dan nearly fell out of his chair. "What makes you think that?" he asked.

"He's the Yankees announcer, and he's always broadcasting the World Series and the Rose Bowl," I said. I really saw no other possible point of view on the matter.

Dan was having a hard time suppressing his laughter. "I love going around the country too, but I'm not going to be a bachelor when I'm his age. I want to come home every night to my family, and so will you."

It was the last thing I expected Dan to say.

"How do you know what I'm going to want when I'm older?" I asked. I didn't think he understood me that well. He surprised me by asking next why I'd want a job where someone could fire me for any trumped-up reason.

This dose of reality was more than I was prepared for. "They could never fire Mel Allen. If they did, people would be lined up to give him another job," I said.

Dan shook his head. "They could fire anyone. But it won't happen to me, because I'll have my own law practice, and it won't happen to you either."

My father and the girls came back. I was shocked to see Mayor Brandt with them. He had a meeting nearby in Frankfurt and had decided to pay me a visit. Suzie must have told him I was pretty sick.

"How're you feeling, Roy?" asked the mayor. He handed me a book—an English edition of *The Tin Drum*. "It's been very popular here; I think you'll like it…if you ever finish *War and Peace*," he said.

After I got over the shock of seeing the mayor, I introduced him to Dan Connolly before my father could. These two famous people might have been my father's friends, but today they came specially to see me. I must have been a worthwhile person for people of such caliber to go out of their way to see how I was doing. I would tell myself that in the future anytime things didn't go as I'd hoped.

My father asked Dan if he'd drive the girls back to France. Dan said he'd be happy to, but he had to leave in the next ten minutes. My father accompanied them to the car while Mayor Brandt remained in the room with me.

He removed his coat and scarf and folded them on my father's bed. He sat down on the chair next to my bed where the doctor and Dan had sat.

"It must be hard not having your mother anymore," he said. "You are such a brave boy." He looked around the room and walked over to the bureau to grab a checkerboard, which was folded on top of the bureau, and placed it on my bed.

The mayor told me about his own childhood. It was as though time were frozen, with just the two of us in the room, and spending time with me was the most important thing he could be doing. Maybe that was the way many politicians made people feel—but not the ones I'd met on the base. He told me he'd been close to his own mother but had never even met his real father. His mother and grandfather, whom he called Papa, brought him up.

"Today is March 31, 1962. This is the exact day in 1933, twenty-nine years ago, when I boarded a boat at midnight and left Germany for twelve years. I was afraid the Nazis would come after me and drown me," he said.

I jumped one of the mayor's checkers and kept listening as I held onto a black checker. I didn't want to put it down.

"It was a cold, dark night, and there was a powerful wind blowing in off the North Sea. I remember pulling the two woolen blankets I had been given by the boat's captain securely around myself to ward off the penetrating cold," he said.

"Why were they after you? I asked, as I put down the checker and started biting my fingernails.

"Despite my age, the Nazis considered me a dangerous opponent of the government. They would have put me into prison at the minimum...and most likely have me killed."

Then the mayor jumped me and got his first king. It wasn't fair; there was no way I could concentrate. Despite my ignorance of history and politics, I knew somehow that the mayor was telling me things he wouldn't tell most people. I didn't understand why, since he was my father's friend, not mine. I had asked my father in Berlin why the mayor was so interested in him, and he said it had to do with some articles he'd written. I never knew my father wrote articles; he seemed to read most of the time, although on weekends I would find him writing on the desk in the living room with a million books open.

But I really did wonder why Mayor Brandt had told me such personal things about himself. Maybe it was easier to talk to a foreigner. Or it might have been that he thought my near-death experience had made me more understanding. I thought that it had, in fact. I guess he also could have identified with me because I had only one parent. Maybe he shared so much because it was the anniversary of his escape that day. I didn't know. I would never have the answer to those questions.

I asked him if he left because of Hitler. I'd heard my dad talk about Hitler and all the bad things that happened in World War II, but I'd never spoken to a German about him. But I could ask the British-German man, because he wasn't really German, at least not to me.

He looked at me, and that warm look left his eyes. He said, "Where freedom is given no timely defense, it can be won back, only at the cost of great and terrible sacrifice." He told me this was the lesson thus far of the century.

He was giving me a private speech. I read *The Tin Drum* eventually, but his comment that day was his real gift. I couldn't have imagined how many people would try to take away my freedom in the future, but I would discover many different ways it could happen.

My father returned to the room, and he and the mayor talked for another fifteen minutes. I listened and didn't turn the television back on. The checker game went unfinished.

CONFRONTATION

They discharged me from the hospital the next day. I told Dr. Cook I would keep in touch with him; I sent him a note every March 29 for ten years.

We drove the Peugeot that one of Dad's assistants had driven to Germany through the black forest, and I noticed the scenery for the first time. The blue sky and canopy of trees, whose leaves were just beginning to appear, were a broad, protective awning. Until my near-death experience, I had viewed each day crossed off my calendar as one less to be endured, one closer to returning home. I would stop doing that, because I would never have those days back. Every minute had value, even if nothing exciting was happening. Feelings of mediocrity were indulgences; something would always prove them to be illusions. It was just a matter of being able to persevere and tolerate temporary, unpleasant feelings.

My father broke the silence as we crossed the Rhine, and the signs changed back from blue to green. He told me he didn't want me to return to the *lycée*.

"I had spoken to the principal about the LePerrier kid before this episode," he said.

I turned to my father, who was full of annoying surprises. "Why'd you do that? You could've have told me," I said.

"To try to prevent a disaster like the one that landed you in the hospital," he said.

I wanted to go back to the *lycée*. I told him they could put me in a different gym class from Robert, since everything seemed to happen in physical education class, but my father was firm as usual. He said it would be one thing if the school would cooperate in my protection, but they didn't want American students.

"How about the military school in Verdun for the last two months?" he said, as though that would be an acceptable compromise.

I slammed my hand against the dashboard. Despite the last episode with Robert, I felt more secure in school than I ever had. I wasn't going to Verdun.

We drove over a stone bridge that looked as if it had been there at the time of the French Revolution. My father pointed out that I had never liked it there anyway, but I told him I was learning French and enjoyed my classmates—and even had a girlfriend, something I thought I'd never have.

He told me, "We need to have a conversation about Cheryl. I want to tell you something I found out recently. Captain Block smelled alcohol on her breath the other day in the canteen."

"Hmm, what was the captain doing so close that he smelled her?"

"Look, it's not just that. She asked when you were coming back, but she didn't visit you or even call while you were in the hospital, did she?" he said. He had that "I told you so" look on his face that made me want to explode.

"Cheryl is having a rough time, because her parents are getting divorced, and her dad drinks every night," I replied in her defense. But I knew he was right about her.

All the same, my feelings for her could only survive if I told myself that Dad was wrong.

"Just keep coming up to the plate. One of these days, you'll hit it out of the park," he said. He was worried about my getting hurt by girls like Cheryl, either now or later, but he didn't know how to say so except through some tired, old cliché that I found tedious. But I knew what he meant—and in a way, I was feeling the same thing.

After I was absent a few more days, the *censeur* called the base.

"Roy will not be returning to the *lycée*," Suzie announced. "*Le colonel viendra bientôt chercher ses trucs quand il aura un moment de libre.*"

The *censeur* must have loved hearing that, but couldn't show it. Cheryl, Abdelak the Arab, and I were such burdens to her, she must have put her hand over her mouth to conceal her joy.

When the school officials announced I wouldn't be returning, half the class descended upon the *censeur*. "It's his family's choice," she said with her arms folded in front of her as she sat behind her oversized desk.

But my classmates claimed Robert was the problem. Between classes, instead of the courtyard, the *classe de seconde*'s destination was her office.

"Maybe we can talk his father into bringing him back," she told them after three days. She probably assumed my father would be as resolute as usual in his decisions. She had every reason to believe that, based on the way he wore that uniform at the school as though he were commander in chief of the U.S. Air Force. The *censeur* called the base and told Suzie a few of my classmates wanted to meet with my father and me.

Dad walked to the library during lunch and found me alone in the book-filled room with a pint of strawberry ice cream in one hand and *The Tin Drum* in the other. In my five days since returning from Germany, I spent all my time in that room. My father hadn't forced me to attend the military school; he decided I could finish the year on the base. It wouldn't be fun, but it was safe. There was no point in arguing anymore; I knew he'd never change his mind.

My father told me to be in his office at sixteen hundred hours, when two or three of my classmates would be coming to say good-bye. I kept checking my watch to make sure I wouldn't be late. I expected Jules, Abdelak, and maybe Bertrand. We'd sit around for an hour not knowing what to say. But it was nice they wanted to say farewell.

Imagine my surprise when I saw almost my whole class sitting in the room outside my father's office, where the men who worked for my dad usually sat. My dad had given everyone except Suzie the rest of the afternoon off. I swallowed hard when I saw my English and physical education teachers too. I'd only recently learned the two of them were a couple—an unlikely one, I'd thought.

Classmates with whom I hadn't shared a word all year were there, but when I walked into the room, their faces turned to me as though I were their leader. It was spontaneous and couldn't have been feigned.

"Roy is making a unique contribution to all of our educations. If you will allow him to return, we will make sure nothing further happens to him," Mlle Keller, my English teacher, said in her British accent.

My father asked if Robert LePerrier was with them.

Abdelak and two of his friends stepped forward. "You don't have to worry about him," Abdelak said with his omnipotent smile.

My dad removed his glasses to wipe them with his handkerchief. The sun broke out from behind the clouds. The rays of light made the room feel twice as bright. I could tell my father hadn't expected this turnout any more than I had, and for once was nonplussed about what to do. He told the group he'd give the matter more thought, then sent Suzie to the PX for two large chocolate cakes and twenty pints of ice cream, along with a few cartons of Coca-Cola. She needed four employees from the PX to carry everything back.

My friends stayed two hours. The military police came twice because of all the noise. It was like a birthday party, with everyone holding paper plates and eating chocolate cake with ice cream. Laughter filled the room. Mlle Keller and M. Richard loved the American ice cream in the pint cartons as much as we did.

After everyone left, my father told me, "Maybe I can send you back. But I'm going to have to make demands on them, and I don't know how happy they're going to be."

A few days later, he told me at dinner that he received a message that a local clockmaker was waiting at the sentry's office at the front of the base to speak with him that afternoon. This man's son was a classmate of mine.

He had them bring the man to his office. M. Falkstein related his experiences with the LePerriers and emphasized the boy's father had been a Nazi. He apologized that he hadn't come sooner.

"My son told me Robert LePerrier has been targeting your son," he said. "A few years ago, he did the same to us."

Robert LePerrier had damaged several of his son's paintings. Apparently the LePerriers thought the Falksteins were one of the rare Jewish families who remained in Alsace after the war, since they had a Jewish-sounding name.

M. Falkstein had forced himself to go to the LePerriers' house to speak with the father, a wealthy research scientist and scientific director of a large pharmaceutical company in Strasbourg. Two months after this visit, a German from Kiel came into M. Falkstein's store to buy an antique clock. He told M. Falkstein he'd worked at that same pharmaceutical company but had been fired. When M. Falkstein mentioned M. LePerrier's name, the German had said M. LePerrier was an ex-Nazi; the German was sure of it.

"What did you say when you heard that?" my father asked him.

"Nothing, but I believed it, having met M. LePerrier," the merchant said.

My father asked him if he remembered the man from Kiel's name, but he didn't, although he had records and would be able to come up with it, he told my father.

"Why do you think it had to do with being Jewish?" my father asked him.

"When I told him we weren't Jewish, the son's behavior stopped," the clockmaker said.

My dad asked why very few Jewish families lived in Alsace. "The Jews of Alsace were either killed or left the area during the war, and few have returned," Jules's father said.

My father walked M. Falkstein out to his car and asked him where his place of business was located. "Maybe I'll buy an antique, European clock," he said, smiling for the first time.

"I can get you a great price," M. Falkstein said.

* * * *

So I went back to the *lycée* and was greeted like a long-lost hero by everyone except the biology teacher and Robert. At that time, I still didn't know the biology teacher was Robert's mother. During physical education, instead of participating in soccer, I practiced high-jumping. I was the worst high jumper in my class back home, but one of my classmates showed me a new way to go over the bar called the western roll. I perfected it while my classmates scampered up and down the field, playing monotonous soccer.

One morning Abdelak Bonnini's brother, one of the surveillants, approached me while I was in the midst of conquering my fear of heights by climbing the rope near the high-jump pit. He had never before spoken to me. I had reached the top of the rope when he distracted me by telling me about his brother's fight with Robert LePerrier several weeks ago after the incident in the basketball game. It was hard to concentrate, because I was twenty feet above the ground and a tad dizzy. But I remember him saying he didn't tell the censeur because he was afraid his brother would be suspended.

The next day, the *proviseur* shook my hand for the first time in the courtyard and pronounced it good to have me back. I didn't care whether it was from guilt, fear of recriminations, or genuine affection, because for the first time, I felt valuable to other people—the only real importance a person could have.

I was booked up with invitations to my male classmates' homes every weekend through the middle of June. My schedule was so packed, dad complained he needed an appointment to see me. Sometimes I'd visit sprawling farmhouses and end up milking cows at five o'clock on a Sunday morning. Other weekends I'd be a guest at an apartment in one of the small towns in Alsace or Lorraine.

* * * *

Since the incident at the stadium, my classmates avoided Robert. The mathematics and English teachers turned away when they encountered him in the corridors or courtyard. While I wasn't witness to these occasions, people reported it to me as though I were their supervisor. I had never felt so important.

I also heard about Robert's home life from Cheryl, who got regular updates from Charlotte, Robert's older sister's best friend. Cheryl said he stopped doing his homework and would wake up in the middle of the night and pace in his room for hours. In geography he broke out in a sweat and couldn't catch his breath. It happened in French class too, and soon he had these unexplained attacks several times a day. While I could see he wasn't himself, I only learned the full extent of his suffering directly from him, thirty-seven years later.

Over the next three weeks, he must have lost ten pounds. He used to be the star of the soccer game, demanding the ball every minute. Now he was a hazy shadow in the background that could barely run. During one game, he got a leg cramp and sat out, but Bertrand thought he was faking it. He took a few days off school, and from what I understood, he pretty much stayed in bed.

Robert had bags under his eyes, and his face showed the weight loss. Everyone would go out of his or her way to tell me how badly he was doing. Even though people acted as though I had ousted him, and the respect I now felt had been previously his, I never felt a sense of victory. I loved the attention and interest, which I'd been craving all my life, but when I thought of Robert, what I felt was more pity than satisfaction. It was my first lesson that loving other people was more satisfying than defeating them.

Robert's sister cried to Charlotte that he remained in his room rather than joining his family for dinner. They really weren't a family anyway, just related individuals living together, she complained. While he'd always received respect from his classmates in the past, Robert would never invite friends to his house. His parents, Jean-Claude and Marie, never asked anyone over either. It would have been unheard of for them to go to a restaurant or a movie as a family.

Marie LePerrier sent her daughter upstairs with Robert's dinner every night, but it came back untouched. His parents could hear him tramping in his room as they tried to read their newspapers in the living room. Robert's mother tried to discuss the matter with her husband, but he said he had to go to the lab. He left and didn't come home until the next evening. She decided to walk up to her son's room. Her voice was unsteady, and her hands trembled. She told her daughter she felt the onset of a pounding headache.

Robert was lying on his back, fully clothed, staring at the ceiling with the television on. His clothes and belongings were strewn randomly throughout his room.

I only learned about this and other conversations decades later, from Robert himself. He had tears in his eyes when he started telling me, but he quickly regained his veneer of toughness. He recalled every detail of that conversation with his mother from 37 years ago. My own eyes must have almost bulged out of their sockets because he asked me if I had a thyroid condition. I told him I'd had a check up two weeks ago and was fine.

"Robert, I think it is now time that I tell you why your father hates Americans," his mother said after she entered his room and stood beside his bed.

"I had given up asking that question, because you never gave me an answer," Robert said, as he shifted his gaze to the television.

"Don't you want to know why?" she asked, leaning forward as though she were tempting him with a bag of candy.

"I'm sure if you knew, you would have told me." He turned on his side to face her, but didn't meet her eyes.

She sat down in the chair near his bed and said, "He hates them because of some things that happened during and after the war."

Robert sat up on the edge of the bed. "You mean before I was born?" he asked, as he gazed at this mother for the first time since she entered his room.

"Your father helped Klaus Barbie kill people in France," she said.

There was silence in the room for what seemed like a long time. Robert finally said, "Wasn't Barbie a high-level Nazi who was well-known for his war crimes? He killed Jews, didn't he?"

"Klaus Barbie killed Jews and a lot of French people," she admitted.

Robert pushed himself off the bed and paced around the room. He didn't want to hear this information, but he'd suspected the truth all along.

"Did my father kill children?" he finally asked her. He glared at his mother. He'd always liked little children, which had helped him feel that he was different from his father.

"He never killed children himself, but he loaded French-Jewish children onto a train that was headed to a concentration camp. That was what Germans did back then."

"So what you're telling me is that my father is a murderer." Robert raised his hands for emphasis.

She said nothing but attempted unsuccessfully to light a cigarette, her hands trembling. Robert made no effort to help her.

He finally commented, "I always knew there was something wrong with him, but I thought it was because he was a scientist."

After lighting the cigarette on the fourth try, Mme LePerrier dropped it on the floor, then put it back in her mouth. She turned her back to Robert and dabbed her eyes.

She looked at his wall, with its numerous pictures of teams Robert had played on over the years. "I thought your father was going to become a very important man in Germany," she whispered. "You see, we thought Germany would win the war. Then war crimes wouldn't have mattered. The Americans would have been forced to respect and obey people like your father."

Robert's head throbbed. He never got headaches, and the hammerlike pounding on his skull caused him to squash both his hands over his temples.

His mother admitted her husband and Barbie raided schools, removed Jewish students, and killed members of the French underground.

Robert thought about his own behavior toward the boys at school that he thought were Jewish.

Mme LePerrier got up from her chair and placed her hand softly on his shoulder. He pushed it away as if it were a wasp landing.

"I still don't know why he hates Americans," Robert said as he got up, walked across the room, and slammed his hand against the wooden desk so hard his palm turned purple.

"I'm telling you, so you won't feel guilty. It has to do with things that happened before you were born. I've always been proud of you. You're not like my father or brother," she said. "Those cowards wouldn't have had the guts to put this American idiot and that sissy Falkstein in their places."

Robert dragged himself through classes, but his sleeping didn't improve. He kept to himself and stayed out of the courtyard. During lunch, rather than eating at school, which was his custom and which his father paid for, he went home and lay on his bed, returning thirty minutes late for afternoon class. One of the surveillants smelled alcohol on his breath and warned Robert he'd report him. Robert told him to mind his own business.

The math teacher called on him, but he was unable to solve a simple homework problem at the blackboard. The back of Robert's neck turned red as a raspberry as M. Bernet asked him the same question four times, and he couldn't get it.

"*Eh bien alors. Qu'est-ce qu'il y a?* You never have trouble with problems like this," the teacher pleaded. He finally called on Bertrand, who immediately solved the problem, although no genius himself.

The next day, in the chemistry lab, I was working on an experiment with Jules Falkstein, who was my lab partner. We wore plastic glasses and blue smocks to protect our clothing. The professor began to bellow, and I shoved in the earplugs I'd bought at the base for these daily outbursts in physics.

But this time, the sound came from more than the stone-deaf teacher's personal public address system. Big Georgette Kramer screeched, and I couldn't miss the flames coming from the back of her blue smock. I hadn't communicated with Georgette much before this incident—in fact the only thoughts I'd had about her were fantasies of shooting basketballs through her enormous, round earrings. I had visualized attaching a backboard to her head. Her lab partner, Astrid Duprée, pulled the smock off her, but Georgette had a violet burn on her right arm.

Orange flames leaped around the laboratory. The teacher flew across the room and doused the fire with a large blanket. The lab became clouded in black, thick smoke, which irritated everyone's throats and lungs. Between the teacher's hollering, Georgette's screaming, the coughing, and the shrill alarm, the noise was deafening. My classmates bolted out the door, but Jean-Paul Gully edged me out the casement window, and we leaped five feet into the courtyard.

Within minutes a fire truck drove through the gate and into the courtyard. The firefighters hurried into the main building and stayed inside half an hour. It was the only time during my six months at the *lycée* that the black steel gate would be fully open. Georgette's parents arrived and escorted her out. Her arm looked like a lobster as her parents guided her through the yard. She continued to sob. My classmates said her parents were going to take her to the hospital.

The *censeur*, *proviseur*, and all the teachers were out in the courtyard together for the first time since I'd been at the school. Nobody forced us to stand in lines; we were free to mill about the yard for an hour. When we went to English class, Robert and Georgette weren't with us anymore. Bertrand said Robert had knocked the Bunsen burner onto her smock. He was out of school for a few days after that incident, but I don't think he was officially suspended.

*   *   *   *

Despite my lack of fervor for revenge for my own injuries at the hands of Robert LePerrier, my father was of another mind. His energies were moving in the direction of a lawsuit after his meeting with M. Falkstein. He called the *censeur* and asked questions about M. LePerrier, but she kept him at bay by telling him they dealt exclusively with his wife, who was a biology teacher at the school. Looking back, if it had been my child and not me, I would have felt the same as my father. But I was too happy to be angry—maybe unrealistically so.

Suzie called Jean-Claude LePerrier at work. He was in Lille but would return the next day. When she didn't hear back, she called again. This time M. LePerrier was doing an experiment. Suzie conveyed my father's message that if he didn't hear from M. LePerrier by five, he'd contact an attorney.

"*Pourquoi ça?*" asked M. LePerrier's secretary.

"He'll know," Suzie responded.

At three before five, my father received a return call from M. LePerrier. My dad usually didn't talk with me about his confrontations, but he went over the whole telephone conversation in the officer's club that evening with me.

My father told M. LePerrier he wanted to speak in person about what was going on between Robert and me.

"I'm busy with an experiment and can't make this a priority," the scientist told my dad.

"I suggest you get over here tomorrow morning," my father said. He didn't hesitate to mention M. Falkstein's story about the man's past from World War II as though it were connected to what was going on between Robert and me. While I understood the association, I couldn't imagine my father would ever get M. LePerrier to admit there was one. But I wasn't a lawyer and have never thought like one.

"I don't know what you mean," M. LePerrier said. There was silence on the phone for thirty seconds. Then he said, "I live near your base. I can be there eight thirty in the morning."

"I'll leave a message at the front gate for you," my father said.

My father was in his office when M. LePerrier arrived at eight thirty, escorted by a member of the military police. I learned most about what happened in this office encounter from Suzie, who was present the whole time, but I also got a few details from my father. Maybe it was because Dad didn't want me to become a lawyer that he never told me about his skills in confrontation.

M. LePerrier strode into my father's office dressed in a dark, pin-striped suit with a red silk tie and planted himself in the chair opposite my father's desk. He removed his fedora and tossed it on the desk as if it were a hat rack. No sooner had it landed than my father picked it up and handed it back to him.

"There's a hook on the back of the office door," he said.

"Who's the woman?" the visitor asked.

"She's my secretary," my father replied.

"Are you going to have her record this meeting?" he asked, a flush coming to his cheeks.

"I thought you might need a translator," the colonel said.

According to Suzie, M. LePerrier became condescending at this point. He reminded my father about their conversation the previous day.

"It's you Americans who need the translators," he said, as he settled back in the chair. I must admit he was right about that.

Suzie didn't leave. She told me that at this point, my father turned around as he heard the harsh sounds of two black crows cawing on the ledge outside his window. As if their noises weren't piercing enough, one of them banged his wings against the windowpane. My father swiveled around and hit the screen with his palm, and the two of them flew off, continuing to make the harsh sounds. Suzie told me she thought they weren't much different from my father and his guest.

The colonel asked, "M. LePerrier, why was Robert making such efforts to harm my son?"

M. LePerrier didn't answer and just stared at my father. Apparently it was quite a glare. Later on my father told me he had felt the force of it in his stomach, but he refused to take any chalk tablets, because that would have telegraphed to his guest how much the glare was affecting him.

M. LePerrier finally shrugged and said, "I have no idea what you are talking about."

"It's one thing to fight, but another to try to kill someone," my father said in a soft voice, as he folded his hands on the desktop. He was probably using the gentle voice to get M. LePerrier to underestimate him. My dad told me later about similar tricks he'd used with judges and attorneys in court. Unfortunately he had never wanted me to be with him in the courtroom in action, so I never saw that part of his personality.

"I'm sorry your son was injured, but he shouldn't be playing rugby if he doesn't understand the rules. It's the fault of the instructor for assuming he knew the system," M. LePerrier said. "It can be a violent game," he added, as his eyes burned into my father like laser beams, according to Suzie.

Even my father admitted to being more uncomfortable with this man than anyone he could remember, even in court.

Dad took a drink from his cup of coffee, and M. LePerrier fidgeted. "Do you think I put him up to it?" he asked, as he leaned forward and placed his elbow on the desktop. Suzie said he had a hard time keeping himself or his property off my father's desk.

My father asked him to explain why a sixteen-year-old who had never been to the United States should dislike Americans.

"Where's he getting his information?" my father asked.

"What my son did was within the rules of the game," M. LePerrier repeated, as he now appeared to be relaxed in the chair. He pulled a cigar out of his suit pocket.

My father asked him about the tripping at the basketball game. "Twenty American GIs in the grandstands agreed Robert could have knocked my son's teeth out," he said, adding that not all of those people could be mistaken.

"These things all sound like accidents." M. LePerrier waved his hand in the air as though he were swatting a fly. "And you Americans all stick together," he added. My father told me that after he made that comment, he wanted to nail this guy, whatever the cost.

He told M. LePerrier that every episode was witnessed, and no one said they were accidental.

M. LePerrier leaned forward. His fingers drummed the desk. He started to light his cigar. There was no way my father was going to allow him to smoke in his office.

"But you have three ashtrays on your desk. Aren't they for people who smoke?" M. LePerrier protested.

"They're not for you."

M. LePerrier sprung to his feet. His smooth features morphed into a hard frown, while his laser eyes focused on my father's glasses. He croaked, "If you want to sue me so badly, go ahead. You ought to talk to an attorney before you start throwing around threats."

M. LePerrier reholstered the cigar in his pocket and prepared to leave.

At this point, my father said, almost casually, "M. LePerrier. I'm curious. What exactly did you do during the war?"

"Why would that be any of your business?" he snapped as he settled back into the chair.

"Because I've heard that you were a Nazi, and that would explain your son's behavior, since my boy has done nothing to provoke him."

"My wife says your son is a nuisance," M. LePerrier said. He squirmed in his chair and couldn't seem to find a comfortable position. "Your boy bothered many people at the *lycée*."

"So it's your wife who's behind this. Maybe she's the one I should have called," the colonel said and told Suzie to call the *censeur*.

"You don't need to do that," he said. His face lost color and his voice was now soft and even. My father must have been experienced at these types of encounters. He used the patience he never revealed to me to hold out until the person he was questioning showed some vulnerability—perhaps a statement or gesture. He told me later that he'd trained himself to wait hours if necessary, like a hawk patrolling the sky. It was trial and error, but he seemed to have found M. LePerrier's weakness. Usually it took him longer to discover these things.

Finally M. LePerrier spoke again. "I was conscripted into the German army when they took over Alsace-Lorraine in 1940, just like every other Alsatian male."

"So you fought for the side of Germany?" My father gripped his coffee cup by the handle and sipped it slowly with his eyes riveted on M. LePerrier.

"Of course I fought on the German side. I was conscripted. You know what that word means, don't you?" He turned the light on the lamp on my father's desk with a quick flick of his wrists.

"Why would anyone have thought you were a Nazi?" the colonel asked, as he scrutinized the man's facial features.

M. LePerrier looked away quickly and said, "I don't think this conversation is going to work out very well."

"Work out well for whom?" my father asked. "Do you think maybe things would go better with your wife?" She would be my father's ticket to getting cooperation from this man.

"She has nothing to say to you," M. LePerrier said.

"We can bring charges against her as easily as you. She is your son's parent too," he said, as he gained momentum.

"You do what you have to do, Lieutenant Colonel," M. LePerrier said, as he stood up and took his hat off the hook on the door.

My father looked at Suzie. "My secretary will call the sentry, and he'll escort you to the front gate," he said.

THE LAWSUIT

My father spent a week getting the name of René Creteuil, a French attorney. He made an appointment on a Thursday afternoon, because he thought the attorney might have questions only I could answer. It wasn't how I wanted to spend my free day in the middle of the week.

As we sped across the farmland on the forty-five minute drive to Strasbourg, my father asked Suzie endless questions about M. Creteuil. "You need to concentrate on the road, or else you'll get us killed," she answered.

We took the Wacken Boulevard exit off of highway N4 and within five minutes were pulling up to the French attorney's office, which was located in a four-story, wooden building on Avenue Herrenschmidt, opposite a park full of women pushing baby carriages or walking dogs. I could smell fresh paint the minute we entered the building. My father banged his knee on the blue and white bicycle locked to the brass banister at the bottom of the stairwell. He hobbled up the first two flights, then resumed his normal step for the final two.

"How did you get this guy's name anyway, Suzie?" He grimaced as he paused on the second landing.

Suzie answered between gasps that three people in the liaison's office said he was the best. While climbing these stairs, she was paying the price for never being without a cigarette in her mouth.

M. Creteuil's secretary, who looked like an overly dressed-up model, was typing when we entered. The freshly varnished wood on the walls coordinated with the beige carpeting to give the office a light, airy feel. The recently renovated suite occupied the entire top floor of the building. I felt challenged to find even a single object out of place. The great Cathedral of Strasbourg, with its gothic steeples, dominated the view from each room.

René Creteuil appeared to be in his midforties. He moved with a spring to his step and was tall enough to be an NBA player. But his milky complexion, ultrathin physique, and delicate features didn't give the appearance of an athlete. He actually reminded me more of the left field foul pole at Fenway Park.

After escorting us into his office, M. Creteuil motioned for my father and me to sit on the couch and held out a chair for Suzie, but my dad preferred the beige leather armchair nearer our host's desk.

A picture of Charles de Gaulle covered the wall behind his desk. The full-size photograph of the president revealed that he and M. Creteuil were the same height. I would see this picture everywhere in this country. It seemed as if being a soldier was the clearest route to being head of a country. As I sat on the white couch, I thought of at least five examples in my own country.

There were pictures of two other men on the sidewalls, one of whom had a flowing, white beard.

"Is that man with the white beard Victor Hugo?" my father asked.

"*Exactement*," said M. Creteuil, who could not conceal his pleasure.

Suzie told us the third portrait was of André Malraux, a member of de Gaulle's cabinet.

My father told M. Creteuil about his ordeal getting into the building, and the attorney apologized. "I should keep that bike farther back," he said.

I knew Dad would ask how the lawyer kept his weight down. It was one of the things he admired most about the French; he repeatedly commented on how few French people were overweight. Sometimes my father, who was so smart in his work, couldn't see that anyone who climbed four stories several times a day and drove a bicycle to work would be unlikely to be overweight. Also, the more we ate in French restaurants, the more familiar we became with the small portions characteristic of continental cuisine.

M. Creteuil wore wire-rimmed glasses, like my father. He listened carefully and made notes on his yellow legal pad, just as Dad would have done. The pad was the only object on his broad mahogany desktop, other than a black blotter. Attorneys did the same thing all over the world.

After fifteen minutes, M. Creteuil advised my father he had three legal options.

The first would be to file a complaint with the police. "This would be the easiest and costs you no money," he said.

"How long would it take?" my dad asked, sitting back in his chair as he glanced out at the cathedral.

"It depends on the town where you're filing...on how busy the investigating officer is, and how much interest he would have in the case," the attorney answered and continued to write. He called his secretary, and she brought in coffee for the four of us on a tray with very fine cups and saucers. Suzie later said it would cost her three months' salary to buy a set of those for her dining room.

M. Creteuil held the cup and saucer as though he knew how much they cost and was giving an etiquette class. He asked, "Does your base have any influence with the local police?"

"I would have to ask the general," my father said and asked what his other alternatives were.

He told us our second option was to file a *plainte avec constitution de partie civile*. This way the investigating judge would make all the inquiries and would decide whether he had enough evidence to bring a case to trial against M. LePerrier. "Since you have many responsibilities, and your time in Europe is short, this would relieve you of the burden," he said, as he folded his hands in front of him on the desktop.

"I would like to get publicity for this trial," my father emphasized.

"Then this would not be the best way, because the interviews take place in private," M. Creteuil said, as he set the teacup on his desk and brushed away some invisible dust.

My father shifted in his chair and looked out again at the cathedral. He shot a glance at his watch. Suzie coughed. She told me later she thought my dad was going to get up and leave.

M. Creteuil put down his coffee cup and said the third way would be a *citation directe*—like a regular court trial in our country. He said it was the most expensive route, but if we were planning to return to the states soon, it would be the quickest route, and we'd have more exposure.

"Let's go with the *citation directe*." My father sprung from his chair and extended his hand to shake that of M. Creteuil. His sudden movement startled me and I ripped the napkin in my hands.

"Not so fast," the Frenchman put up his hand. He told my father that if he chose that path, he'd only be allowed to try the adult, not the underage son.

My father said that was fine with him. "I believe if you discipline someone's boss, it's the best way of punishing him or her," he said still standing.

But the lawyer said that even if the son's actions were premeditated, no one would ever convict M. LePerrier of attempted murder.

My dad sat back down and explained what he'd heard about M. LePerrier's past during World War II. Then he asked, "Can we bring up that the father was a Nazi?"

"Just because someone was a Nazi doesn't mean he was a criminal. There were millions of Nazis, and most of them didn't break the law," M. Creteuil said. "The judges would say the whole line of inquiry is irrelevant."

My father sat back in his chair and clutched his hands together. He said nothing for the next minute. Then he looked straight at M. Creteuil and told him the direct citation was the best route for us to take. He didn't care about the money, and if we lost, so be it.

"I think it's going to be difficult," repeated the attorney, who dropped his head and fingered his desk, directing his attention to some imperfection in the woodwork he appeared to have just discovered. "But, just for my interest…you have only mentioned Robert LePerrier's father. So I am wondering what role the mother might have in all this. Sometimes it's the mother who is influencing the kid. She also is his parent and an adult."

"I don't think that's the issue," my father said. "But there is something about the father I don't like. Would you be willing to take on this case?"

The Frenchman maintained his congenial smile. He said he realized we were upset about what happened to me, but thank goodness I was all right. "The times of the Nazis are over. You can't punish every bad man on earth," he said. "Besides, the public is focused on the Algerian situation right now."

"Yes, I'm aware of that. But new wrongs don't eliminate the need to investigate old crimes. Even if you don't agree with me, would you represent me?" my dad asked, as he leaned forward in his chair.

M. Creteuil picked up his pad and placed it on the side of the desk. He folded his hands together. He said that as much as he wished to help, he didn't feel this trial would be in the best interest of me or my father. "You also could be at risk for a countersuit for malicious prosecution. Furthermore, court costs are prohibitively expensive in France," he said.

"Is that your last word?" my father asked. He placed his palms on his knees, with his face directed toward the floor. M. Creteuil stood up and offered a handshake to my father and me, and smiled at Suzie.

"If you get any more information, let me know," the Frenchman said.

We were silent on the ride back to the base, but I was relieved we were dropping the case. I wanted to move on with my new life. A lawsuit would mean continuing to think about all the things I wanted to put behind me now.

But from my dad's point of view, it was a shame we didn't know about Dan Connolly's adventure in Strasbourg that day.

Dan's car must have passed ours, going the opposite direction. Despite the lack of traffic and the brightness of the day, we must have been like two trains passing in the night. There couldn't be many blue Buicks in that part of the world, but we never saw Dan speeding past our car toward Strasbourg, possibly because of how fast we were driving ourselves or how much we had on our minds. I wonder how many other obvious things skipped past my attention back then.

Dan was headed to Strasbourg for a birthday present for his fiancée. He arrived there at 1500 hours, as the guys said, and found an underground garage near Place Kleber. After visiting three jewelry stores, he hadn't seen anything he liked. He exited the last store, which bordered on the cathedral. Even though it wasn't tourist season, there were sightseers around, possibly because Easter was approaching.

Dan bought a ticket to tour the world famous church and endured the fifteen-minute wait. As he stood in the queue, his eye took in the grandeur of this building, built in the thirteenth century.

Suddenly someone touched him on the right shoulder. He turned, expecting to see one of the men from the base, but instead found himself face-to-face with Isabelle, Robert LePerrier's cousin, whom he'd met at the army hospital in Germany.

She was wearing a sea blue dress, and her hair was pulled back into a ponytail. She greeted him as though she'd found a long-lost friend. Then she immediately reached back and removed the elastic band from her hair, which fell down to shoulder length.

"I was hoping I'd run into you again," she said, as she smiled at Dan, who was surprised, because she'd made no effort to communicate with him during the three-hour ride from the army hospital in Germany.

She asked if he'd like to have some coffee.

"Why not?" he replied.

"I had the feeling you didn't want to be at that hospital," Dan said, as they entered a bakery and sat down at one of the tables. "It seemed like you were dragged there against your will." He told my father the next day that he had hoped to get her talking about her uncle. Dan recounted much of the conversation with Isabelle; my imagination could fill in the rest.

"You were right." She smiled. "I just went because my cousin, Jeanne, was driving me crazy."

"Why was Jeanne the one who went to visit Roy?" Dan asked. It was the question he and my father had hoped to get answered on that drive. He asked why her brother hadn't gone to the hospital, since he was the one who actually injured me.

"Are you kidding me!" Isabelle laughed. "You don't know their family very well," she said.

"How would I know them?" Dan shrugged as he sipped the coffee. He decided he didn't like French coffee; it was too strong and bitter.

"No one in that family takes responsibility for anything. The father is a horrible man; the mother is as cold as ice, and her son, Robert, is a machine. The older sister is also distant. No one has any emotions except Jeanne, so she feels everything for the whole family."

"You sound like a psychologist," Dan said.

"That's what I'm studying. Jeanne and I have these conversations all the time," she said, as she fidgeted more than he remembered her doing during their encounter at the hospital. She fluffed her hair every three minutes and asked to be excused, returning with fresh lipstick and rouge on her face.

"What did you mean when you said that the father is a horrible man?" Dan asked.

"He tells Jeanne I'm a whore, because I like to dress like a modern Frenchwoman instead of an Alsatian farm girl. He says I look as though I come from the interior of France."

"The interior of France?" Dan repeated.

"Yes, that's how Alsatians refer to people who come from other parts of the country—they say those people are from the interior of France. They view themselves as Alsatian, not French."

"It's almost like they feel they have their own country," he concluded.

"Exactly. They even tried to become independent before World War I, but neither France nor Germany would let that happen," she said.

"Well, maybe Jeanne's father is just trying to protect his daughter," Dan said, trying to get her to say as much as possible about her relatives.

"That's not the reason. He doesn't like me because he and my mother can't stand each other."

Dan didn't say anything but forced himself to drink the coffee. It wasn't so easy to nurse it along.

She went on as though she were talking about a mundane soccer game or fashion show. "He tormented my mom when they were little. Mom spent her whole childhood trying to get away from her older brother, Jean-Claude. The two of them haven't spoken since the war. My mother feels as though he was a traitor to France."

Dan took another sip of the coffee. From now on, he would order tea.

"Why does she think he was a traitor?" he asked.

"During the war, Jean-Claude was in Lyon, and he worked with Klaus Barbie. Have you ever heard of him?" Dan figured Isabelle was taking advantage of an opportunity to vent her mother's anger. He hoped she would continue.

"No, I haven't," Dan said.

"Well, he tortured and killed many people in the French resistance, including Jean Moulin."

"Who was Jean Moulin?" Dan asked.

"Jean Moulin is the symbol of the French resistance. They are talking about moving his ashes to the Panthéon in Paris. Jeanne's dad was involved in killing him." She banged her two fists against the table, which reverberated with such force that people at the two neighboring tables looked over at them.

"Why has he never been tried for that?" Dan asked.

"There was no proof. Another man was tried twice and released, and Barbie ran away somewhere, probably to South America."

"Well, if you know this, why don't you tell the police or someone?" Dan asked. I can picture him scratching his head at this point, flexing a huge muscle in his right arm.

"They wouldn't care. There are no witnesses; at least that's what my mother says," she said.

"Well, if your mother knows, why doesn't she come forward?" Dan asked.

For the first time, Isabelle asked if he and my father were planning to do anything about what happened to me. She put her coffee cup on the table and looked at Dan, her eyes wide open.

Dan was honest with her; he told her he didn't know what the lieutenant colonel's plans were, but the more information he had, the more it would help him to decide. "If it's true your uncle is a very bad man, that might influence him," he said.

She replied, "The only reason my mother knows anything about the things he did is Jean-Claude told her in a moment of weakness at my grandfather's funeral."

"Was he feeling guilty?" Dan asked.

"If he was, it must have been momentary. I don't think he knows what that word means. But he did tell her that of all the things he did with Barbie, what bothered him was the killing of Jean Moulin."

Dan sat there, not saying anything, then asked Isabelle for a pencil. She rummaged through her large, shiny, black purse and pulled out a ballpoint pen and a pad of paper. He wrote down the names Jean Moulin and Klaus Barbie.

Isabelle sat back in her chair for the first time. "Anyway, would you like to go for a walk on the campus? It's a beautiful afternoon."

"I would normally love to, but I'm here today to find a present for my fiancée," Dan said.

"I sensed you might have a fiancée," she said, her face lightening. "I could tell you weren't interested in me the way most men are when I first meet them."

She sat still for about ten seconds, then took out her pad of paper and pen again and wrote down her name and phone number. "If you would like to talk more about my cousins, please call. I hate my uncle. He tells Jeanne horrible things about my mother and me. I'm not allowed in their house. He once told Jeanne that he would kill me if he thought I was trying to influence her. He scares me."

Dan walked the woman back to her school and strolled through the lively park adjoining the parking garage. He took a deep breath of the balmy Alsatian air and drove his Buick back to the base. The next day, he informed my father of everything Isabelle told him.

My father told Dan he had consulted an attorney who said there were millions of Nazis, but most of them weren't criminals.

"But according to Isabelle," Dan replied, "this man wasn't just a Nazi, but a criminal. He killed an important French resistance leader named Jean Moulin."

My father wrote down the name.

Dan told him M. LePerrier helped this criminal, Klaus Barbie, torture Moulin in prison, and Moulin died.

My father wanted to know how Isabelle knew these things, and Dan told him her mother was M. LePerrier's sister. My father asked Dan if her mother would speak to them, but Dan could only say she lived in Paris.

Dan contacted a family friend, an officer in the Boston police department. The police officer got in touch with Interpol and reported back there were no records on anyone named LePerrier. However, he found information on Klaus Barbie and Jean Moulin.

Dan learned Barbie left Europe in the early 1950s and was presumed to be in South America. He'd been sought by the French government to testify in a case but couldn't be located. The Israelis were also interested in him, because he tortured Jews and deported them to Auschwitz. By all accounts, Barbie was an exceptionally brutal man.

My father was able, through his position in the Air Force, to contact the Mossad, the Israeli secret service. They had an abundant file on Barbie and a minor one on Jean Moulin. The Israelis viewed Moulin as a friend who had favored an Israeli state. There was actually more information on Moulin's father, Antonin, than on Moulin himself. Antonin, a former professor at the University of Montpelier, had been very supportive of the Jewish Captain Alfred Dreyfuss in the 1894 case that created a permanent separation between church and state in France. Dreyfuss had been convicted of espionage in 1894. But after a few years it became evident he had been framed and was innocent. The French military wouldn't admit they made a mistake and, the elder Moulin, a Freemason, had been outspoken in his criticism of them in their ignoring the facts of the case. However, it was the writer Emile Zola who was most effective in freeing Dreyfuss with his letter "*J'accuse*" which appeared in the newspaper *L'Aurore*. The other French newspapers wouldn't print the letter.

Barbie's file revealed that there was a research scientist who worked closely with him named Guillaume Sendef. Both these men disappeared after the war.

"I wonder if LePerrier was Guillaume Sendef," my father mused to Dan.

"Isabelle left me her phone number; I can ask if he changed his name," Dan said. He called her and came back twenty minutes later to say, "They are one and the same person."

After hearing the above, M. Creteuil still couldn't muster much fervor for pursuing this case.

"I tried to tell him there's no interest in France for tracking war criminals," he told Suzie, who called to deliver the new information.

"My boss is a persistent man," Suzie said.

"He's also a smart man. He knows the main issue in this country right now is Algeria's recently hard won battle for independence…"

She interrupted him. "Once he makes up his mind, nothing will get in his way…"

M. Creteuil then returned the favor, cutting her off, something he might not have done to my father. "He knows about the Algerian situation and about the terrorist attacks all over France. He even said he was aghast there were troops on top of the Arc de Triomphe," he said.

"You said if he was a Nazi, it was not that big a deal. But we found out he might have been a Nazi war criminal…that might be *quelquechose d'autre*," Suzie said.

M. Creteuil said if the lieutenant colonel made similar inquiries in his own country, he would encounter the same apathy toward Ex Nazis. He would find

Americans were concerned with the Russians. "They are the reason he's in France. His anger has blinded him to reality," M. Creteuil said.

"LePerrier's son almost killed Roy!" Suzie yelled through the phone.

"I feel for the colonel that he lost his wife at such a young age," he said. "You see, I remember the details you mentioned when you first called me about this case."

Suzie told him her boss was determined to pursue this case with or without his help. M. Creteuil must have reasoned if someone else took over, they might not be able to protect my father from M. LePerrier's retaliation. He called Suzie back three days later and said he had changed his mind.

He filed a *citation directe* and received a court date on June 20. It was ten days before we were scheduled to depart.

JEAN MOULIN

My classmates lived all over Alsace-Lorraine. Some lived as far as Colmar and Mulhouse; others lived in nearby small towns, like Wassalonne.

Their families would turn my weekend visits into occasions. When we went to dinner on Sunday afternoon, we'd spend four hours in a restaurant. "Why do they serve the salad and cheese at the end?" I asked Jules.

"This is the way we do it," my genius classmate answered, as we savored Sunday lunch in a four-star restaurant on N4. Jules's father, mother, three sisters, and two cousins and aunt talked, smoked, giggled, yelled, ate, and drank for five hours during a six-course meal. At times the cigar smoke was so thick I couldn't see the people on the other side of the table.

"Why don't they serve water with the meal?" I asked. "With all the fountains you have, I can't find a water fountain in the entire country."

"Drinking water from fountains is not in the French mentality," Jules said.

Everyone laughed throughout the afternoon. By the third course, they were all singing. They sang in English as well as French and were particularly fond of Frank Sinatra.

"No, I don't know him personally and neither does my dad," I told them.

Time stood still on those Sunday afternoons. A day was like a person—similar to many others, but with a uniqueness. There would never again be a May 3, 1962.

No matter whose home I visited, everyone smoked cigarettes or cigars. At first the smoke made my eyes tear and irritated my nose, but I got used to it. A pig's knuckle wasn't my idea of a good meal, but everyone loved them. They poured me wine and expected me to drink it; I didn't tell my father, because I was afraid he'd put a stop to these visits. It was too bad Cheryl didn't get to come; she would have loved all the alcohol. Despite the smoke and liquor, when I looked back later, I would never remember feeling as relaxed as I had on those irretrievable Sunday afternoons.

"When are you going back to America, Roy?" Bertrand's father asked one Sunday afternoon. Everyone pronounced my name "Rwa." I was used to it by now.

"I don't know and I don't care," I answered. The letters I used to sweat out and answer the same day they arrived were now piling up, and I debated whether to answer them at all.

"You speak French beautifully. Have you learned it all in one year?" he asked.

I could tell people appreciated my learning their language, as if I were doing it for their sake. I tried to be modest and told him my survival was at stake at school, and I wouldn't be able to eat there if I didn't ask for the food in French. But it was nice to get positive feedback from an adult.

The weather had become warm. The meadow behind our cottage, gray all winter, was now a wide, green carpet that extended as far as the eye could see. Cheryl responded to the change in season in her usual unpredictable way. Since one of her boyfriends at home had a motorcycle, and she wanted her own, she decided to rent a small motorcycle from one of the shops in Sarrebourg.

We would drive the *velo* on Thursdays, all the way to Saverne. Cheryl had no inhibitions about speeding downhill, which terrified me, but I couldn't say anything. Even if she were a guy, it would have been hard to admit my fear. On the way back, she let me drive and put her hands tightly around my waist. I know she wanted me to drive fast, but I couldn't. As we climbed up the steep hill of Saverne, I didn't think the bike would have the power to make it to the top, but it did.

After my father and I returned from a weekend in Germany on a Sunday evening in early May, Dad looked up from his writing on the living room table and asked me what I knew about a man called Jean Moulin.

"I have no idea, Dad. Who is he?" I asked, as I lifted my head out of the *Stars and Stripes*. I was reading about Dick Donovan of the Cleveland Indians, who had the best pitching record in the American League at 6-0. I handed the paper to my father, thinking he'd be interested.

"Well, he's not alive anymore," my father said.

I didn't know what he was talking about—I couldn't understand how someone could pitch from the grave.

"I mean Jean Moulin!" my father yelled, as he threw the newspaper down on the floor. My father's outbursts didn't bother me as much now. They happened much less frequently, and it was just who he was. I knew I was starting to grow up when I stopped taking his mood changes so personally. He told me Moulin was an important French politician during World War II and wondered if I'd studied him in one of my classes.

It was a catchy name, Jean Moulin. The Moulin Rouge was one of the few landmarks I knew about before coming to France. But I was more interested in Dick Donovan.

The next afternoon at the gym, Dan walked up to the weight-lifting area, where I was in the midst of climbing the rope. I was excited about using the scissors technique of wrapping my legs around the rope to climb, which I'd learned at school. It was a great exercise for my upper body, but could be rough on my palms. While I descended, Dan asked if I'd learned anything at school about a person named Jean Moulin.

"I don't know anything about him, but my dad asked me the same thing yesterday," I said, as I wrung my hands. The rope always burned no matter how facile I'd become.

"This kid at your school, LePerrier…his father may have been a criminal during World War II, and we think he may have murdered this French leader, Jean Moulin," Dan said.

Jean Moulin was murdered? Now the name stuck—I remembered that *moulin* meant "windmill" in French. I woke up the next morning and told my father that Dan also asked me about Jean Moulin.

"Dan was the one who told me about him," he said.

I told him Robert LePerrier hadn't come near me since I'd returned to school. I was finally happy, no one was bothering me, and now my father was stirring things up again by investigating Robert's father's activities during the last world war. I felt I had won and had experienced the thrill of victory, and didn't need the exhaustion of war. I went into the bathroom and put on the beret I'd bought the past week in Saverne on one of my Thursday jaunts with Cheryl.

"If I had to change my name and live in France, I'd want a name like Jean Moulin," I told my father, who winced, probably because he thought I'd made up another of my nicknames.

I asked my classmates about Jean Moulin. Most of them were familiar with the name but didn't say much. But M. Robin, my math tutor, told me he'd actually met the man as we stood next to one another at the blackboard.

"We lost one of every eight young Frenchmen in World War I. That's why they called us the lost generation. I didn't think we'd ever recover," he said during our Tuesday morning tutorial.

I asked him if Moulin fought during World War I, and he told me Moulin was born in 1899 and was too young at the start of that war. He joined the army in 1918, but didn't see action, because it ended too soon.

I was beginning to get interested in the history of this area, because it had become a picture and not a bunch of abstract concepts, like those I'd been forced to study. I asked him why France did so much better against Germany in World War I than in World War II.

"The Germans were able to overcome us in World War II because we were not mentally prepared for another major battle," he said. He told me I would have liked Jean Moulin, and I asked him why.

"He was strong, yet gentle," M. Robin said. He told me Moulin parachuted into the country in the middle of a freezing winter night in January of 1942 after meeting de Gaulle in England to plan the strategy of the French resistance. He told me to ask my history teacher, Mme Lanier, about him: "She knew Moulin very well. Your father is paying me to teach you math," he said and picked up his chalk.

I kept hearing the phrase "the resistance" whenever I asked about Moulin. Jules, who knew everything, said it was an underground movement during the war against the Nazis. He didn't know any more than that.

Mme Lanier taught both history and geography. She was a tall, blond woman, probably in her forties, with a large wedding ring on her left hand. She dressed fashionably, more like someone from the interior of France. I always thought she had more going on beneath the surface than her pleasant expression conveyed, but didn't know what gave me that impression. Maybe it was because she moved around too quickly, as though she were restless somehow. She always left immediately after class and never joked around—but then again, neither did any of the other teachers.

She'd never shown the slightest interest in me. In fact I wasn't sure she even knew I was in her class. Whenever I'd encountered her in the hallways, I felt invisible. But I was determined to find out about this man, mainly because I liked the sound of his name. Names were important; I guessed that was why movie actors changed theirs. I walked up to her after class the same day I spoke with M. Robin and asked her about Jean Moulin and the French resistance.

In the entire five months I'd been at the *lycée*, it was the first time she'd heard my voice. She probably didn't know I could speak French. She'd never called on me in class, and I'd never volunteered. I'd never even attempted the homework.

"I'm curious how you've become interested in Jean Moulin," she said, as she shifted a coffee mug around her desk. She told me none of my classmates took much interest in that aspect of French history, even though it was crucial to the identity of France. "As I would hope you've noticed, the curriculum over the past months has been the Napoleonic wars," she said.

She said we would be covering World War II next year in *classe de première*, but without anywhere near the detail we had seen in the Napoleon material. She looked disappointed at the idea, as though World War II were maybe a special interest of hers. But I didn't know why that might be, and I wasn't concerned with her personal history at the time, although I would have loved to ask her later, if I could. She took her pencil and tapped it against the desk. After thirty seconds, she said she'd bring me something to read tomorrow.

The next day, she handed me a small book. The title was *Premier Combat*, written by Jean Moulin. It had not yet been published, but was bound and had a cover. "If you can read this, you will know Moulin," Mme Lanier said.

I thanked her as I put it into my duffel bag.

"Do you mind telling me what piqued your interest in him?" She repeated her question from the previous day.

"Nothing specific," I said.

She pointed to my green bag. "I can't allow you to remove the book from my classroom," she said. It was her only copy. She said I could read it during class and would need a dictionary. "I hope the book isn't too strong for you," she said.

The next day, she handed me the hardback before class. There was a picture of a dark-haired young man with benevolent, black eyes on the cover of the book. He wore a dark scarf around his neck and a business top hat, which would have been popular in America in the forties and fifties.

Moulin described his experience in June 1940, when he was the prefect in Chartres, a town in the middle of France that had a world famous cathedral. It took me two days to learn what exactly a prefect did. The best I could ascertain was that a prefect was a national official who was head of a municipality. It seemed Moulin's job was to administer the town's affairs. While there was also a mayor, Moulin's position was higher.

Moulin wrote that he was the youngest prefect in France. He answered only to the secretary of the interior, a man named Georges Mandel. My father told me France was a Catholic country; I wondered if Mandel could have been Jewish.

The hour passed so quickly, I couldn't really get very far into the book. When class ended, I sat and glared at the clock, the way some of my overweight patients later in my life would frown at the scale.

I begged Mme Lanier to let me take the book into the study hall, but she refused. I offered to leave my gold pocket watch, which I inherited from my grandfather, as collateral, but she smiled and put the book into the locked bookshelf behind her desk. I told her I had to read sentences over and over and needed the dictionary to look up every fifth word. It was time-consuming, and the hour of class wasn't sufficient. But she told me that was what researchers did: they located original documents and translated them, using a dictionary.

"Just proceed through the book methodically. All worthwhile things require patience." She suppressed the first smile she'd ever let me see. "I'm going to test you on the content," she said, as her usual serious look took over her face.

After reading five pages, I realized the book was a diary, covering four days in June of 1940, from June 17 to June 20. At that time, people were pouring into Chartres from Paris, and all over northern France, to avoid the Germans, who had annihilated their country in six weeks. Moulin referred to the Germans as *les Boches*. I couldn't find the word in my dictionary, but my classmates told me it was an unflattering name for Germans. Finally my English teacher said the corresponding American term was "the Krauts."

Chartres was a town of about twenty thousand people, but 19,300 of them had fled, including police officers, firefighters, butchers, bakers, and electricians. They were headed to Spain, Italy, Switzerland, or Portugal. There were no basic services available to the people of the community, including running water, electricity, and food. Many of the members of Moulin's office staff had run away as well.

But the city was far from vacant. Refugees from the north filled the streets; the idea of living under German rule was intolerable to them. The only hospital overflowed with sick, elderly people with infections. There were no doctors, medications, or supplies. People broke into buildings to pillage, and many stray dogs and cats became aggressive and had to be shot and buried.

Moulin worked twenty-four hours a day; he didn't mention sleep in his narration. I put my hand over my heart as I struggled to translate the words. The American soldiers in the PX, the gym, and my father's office claimed French people lacked courage and had opted for surrender. They didn't know Jean Moulin.

Some French troops broke into Moulin's house and stole his car, which meant he had to get around on a bicycle. Although the Germans hadn't arrived yet, Moulin described extensive damage from their bombs.

Moulin wrote it was his patriotic duty to stay and attend to the needs of all his people. He was mainly concerned with the lack of food, describing how many people starved in the streets. He was able to locate transients who were bakers, and got them to open one of the bakeries. However, caring for sick, old people without doctors, nurses, or medications overwhelmed them.

I arrived at class ten minutes early and planted myself in the back of the room with the book. The next thing I knew, Mme Lanier would shake my shoulder to tell me my time was up. I never heard the chairs scrape the concrete floor as my classmates got up to leave. I surrendered the book as though she were confiscating my lunch money.

Everyone turned to Moulin in Chartres. Was he a role model or a martyr? While I always grilled my brain for even the most improbable excuse to avoid unpleasant tasks, this man, with every justification to abandon an impossible situation, had persevered. But he didn't reveal much about his feelings; maybe that was why Mme Lanier said he was a murky character. When I asked her if that was the reason, she blushed and offered some vague answer. I wondered about the exact nature of their relationship; when I asked M. Robin, he said to ask her.

Finally the Germans arrived in Chartres. After a few days, they went to the prefecture and were friendly and respectful. They wanted Moulin, as the official in charge of the municipality, to sign a document that certified that a French Senegalese unit of soldiers had murdered a number of women and children in France. They offered it as a formality. Mme Lanier told me Senegal was a country in West Africa about the size of South Dakota which had belonged to France until two years ago.

Moulin wrote in his diary that he knew the Germans had committed those barbarous murders and were seeking to affix the blame elsewhere. There was no way he would implicate his countrymen in such a gruesome crime. Because of his refusal, the Germans became unpleasant. First it was verbal abuse; then they assaulted him.

At this point, I got up and walked into the corridor and paced for five minutes. I walked into the WC and stared at my face in the mirror. I found a pimple on my forehead and started to squeeze it, even though Dr. Clayton told me never to do that. Maybe I wanted to create a sore on my face so that I could get someone like Dr. Clayton to take care of me. I knew I couldn't go back to class and focus on my reading just then.

I went into the park in back of the school. Two people who were with their dog in the other side of the park came running. They wanted to know if I'd been attacked by the wild boar that had been sighted in the area. I told them I was fine, wondering if I'd let go of the scream I'd been feeling. I waited down there until five minutes before the end of class.

Now I talked nonstop to my father and Dan about Jean Moulin. My father said he didn't understand how I had no anger about a guy who almost killed me, yet was outraged about a guy I didn't know who was murdered twenty years ago.

The next day, I resumed reading the diary. The Germans forced Moulin to get into a jeep and drive to a faraway place, where they showed him the mutilated bodies of ten women and children.

"This crime was obviously the work of black soldiers," the Germans claimed.

"They are victims of bombs." Moulin mocked them with his hands.

"Can't you see that black people did this?" the Germans screamed in his face.

"How can one distinguish a crime carried out by black people versus one by whites?" Moulin scorned them.

They brought him back to Chartres and made him stand on his feet for hours. They smashed his face with their bare knuckles and shoved sharp wooden sticks under his fingernails. His eyes began to swell, and he couldn't see clearly. Although he craved rest for his feet, they wouldn't allow him to sit. They ridiculed France as a country of cowards. They used the word *laches* over and over. Up until this point, I had thought Jews were the only ones tormented by the Nazis. My father and his friends had emphasized German anti-Semitism as though we had a monopoly as victims of their barbarity.

Moulin continued to refuse to sign the paperwork. Finally, at about eleven at night, they placed him in a tiny room with a sleeping black soldier and made him sleep a foot apart from the man on the wooden floor. The Germans promised to return early in the morning. Moulin wrote he would no longer be able to hold out; he'd sign the document in the morning.

However, he found a jagged piece of glass on the floor and slit his throat deeply. He would rather die than betray his country, even though the Germans had said he didn't have a country anymore. Moulin wrote that there would always be a France.

The soldiers returned at five, two hours earlier than expected, and at first didn't notice anything unusual. Suddenly they became aware of blood all over Moulin's body and woke up the lieutenant. The officer crashed into the room, cursing his men for waking him at an unthinkable hour. However, when he discovered Moulin and the condition he was in, he and his men rushed the bleeding Frenchman to a medical facility. He was treated there and escaped after being sewn up. The Germans didn't come after him.

It took two weeks for me to finish reading the one hundred-plus pages of this diary. My teacher said my face was flushed, and my eyes blazed as I recounted the reading material.

"*Je vous enstime de plus en plus,*" she said, as she leaned toward me. But she emphasized it was up to me to show people what I could do. "You can't expect them to go searching for your hidden talents," she said. "You have to come out of your shell." She smiled as though I were a turtle.

I told her I would have read the book in two days if I didn't have to look up so many words, or if I could have taken it to the study hall. I knew she could see how proud I was of myself.

Mme Lanier walked over to the red, white, and blue flag in the corner. She came back to the desk and pointed to Moulin's picture on the book cover, explaining how he wore the scarf to cover up the scar from his throat slitting. She said he couldn't speak properly for many months. She said there were many others in the French resistance who risked and even gave their lives to save France—both men and women.

Most of the men on the base snickered about French bravery and emphasized that the French had surrendered to the Germans. But it was clear to me their loss was more due to denial and inadequate preparation than lack of courage. Like their neighbors in England, they had ignored the slow rise of a tyrant. M. Robin said England didn't surrender because they had two advantages France didn't: the English Channel and Winston Churchill.

When I mentioned my newfound respect for French bravery on the base, an avalanche of opposition engulfed me. I brought the comments back to Mme Lanier.

She folded her arms in front of her chest. The pleasant expression, invariably there during our discussions about Moulin, disappeared. "It was General Leclerc who liberated France," she said and told me she'd bring me information about him too.

"General Leclerc, my ass!" my father exploded, as we drove to the base after school. "There were thirty-eight divisions under Eisenhower who could have liberated Paris, and Ike handed out the plum to Leclerc. It was the allied troops, not General Leclerc. The reason French people acted so arrogant was because they didn't want to admit to themselves that they needed help. What other propaganda has your history teacher filled you with?" he asked.

"She told me your hero, Roosevelt, one of our few great presidents, was bigoted against Jews, blacks, and Japanese Americans," I replied viciously.

"On what does she base that amazing statement?" he asked.

I parroted her comments. "Roosevelt didn't try to protect blacks from lynchings, he put Japanese Americans in camps, and wouldn't let Jews into the country during the war."

My father gripped the steering wheel, and his knuckles turned white.

✳ ✳ ✳ ✳

After history the next day, Mme Lanier stood up to pack her books into her black leather satchel. She placed the bag on the desk and sat down. She took off her black eyeglasses and looked around the room. I moved up to one of the brown wooden chairs in the first row of the classroom and waited for her attention.

She looked up and spoke before I could ask my question. "Since you've developed such an interest in Jean Moulin, and your French is so much better, I'd like you to give a presentation to this class about him. While I'm teaching, you can study additional materials about the other periods in his life. If you want to do further studying, you can go to the library in *centre ville*."

I went home every evening and planned my day so I'd be able to get to the town library and look at books about Moulin for an hour. My father gave me the Mossad and Interpol reports. M. Robin told me the names of several veterans of both world wars with whom I could speak.

I loved to ask my teacher provocative questions that would set her off. After my father and I visited Normandy, I told her we visited a cemetery filled with Americans who died in France in both world wars.

She pounded the table. "America didn't get into World War II to help France. The citizens of your country were 90 percent against getting into the war until Pearl Harbor. After you declared war on the Japanese, Germany declared war on you." She turned red and said we got into World War I to make money for weapons companies. "Your former president Eisenhower called it the 'industrial-military complex' in his farewell speech just last year," she said. Her comments surprised me; I thought the only reason our country ever entered a war was to save people from suffering. I still had a lot to learn—from teachers, from my father, and from life.

I spoke to everyone I could about my new hero. I learned about his participation in the Spanish Civil War to prevent the fascists from taking over.

"No, he never got married," said M. Robin during the break in our tutoring session. "I guess he was too committed to the country. I know there were several women."

I found a dark scarf in one of the shops in Saverne and wore it on the cool days, of which there were still several. Mme Lanier chuckled when she saw me with the beret and the scarf.

I developed a reputation on the base of being a French partisan. One day my classmates and I were out for a nature walk in biology about a mile from the school. A group of American GIs came by in a truck and recognized me. They stopped the vehicle and asked if I wanted a ride back. Because they were clearly offering the ride only to me, I declined and thanked them anyway. My classmates talked about how much French I'd learned during the year as the truck drove away.

My father heard me rehearsing my lecture in my room and asked if he could listen. I wasn't sure why he wanted to, since he couldn't understand French, but he said he'd get a good idea about my delivery. I said fine; let him see what it was like to sit through a lecture in a foreign language! Maybe he would realize what he'd subjected me to.

He sat down at the small desk on the side of my room and listened to my presentation without interrupting. He told me I'd have to rehearse it six times.

"Did you practice the speech you gave at my high school six times?" I shot back. The work involved in implementing his suggestion was overwhelming—and another example of his insensitivity.

He told me he ran through it several times, and that was what was necessary to make it appear effortless. "There's no other way," he said and walked out of the room as though he'd shot me with a hypodermic needle full of doubt and needed to move on to the next person.

So every night the week before my speech, I rehearsed my talk to the wall in my bedroom. Finally the day of my lecture arrived. Mme Lanier announced that there would be a special presentation today from Roy Harrison, the American student. She explained that while the class had been studying Napoleon Bonaparte, I had been preparing a presentation on Jean Moulin, head of the French resistance during World War II. I stood in front of the class, and she sat at her desk. Everyone put their books down and looked at me; it was seventeen minutes after one when I began.

I outlined Moulin's life, from his boyhood in Montpelier until his tragic death at the age of forty-three at the hands of Klaus Barbie. I spent ten minutes going over his ordeal in Chartres, where he almost committed suicide. Everyone was leaning forward, probably because I was so interested in the subject myself. The words just poured out of me. It was as though my six rehearsals created a tape, and I put it on play. Although it was in a foreign language, the speech gave itself.

Even I enjoyed listening to it. It reminded me of the time my father gave the lecture at my school. Robert LePerrier sat quietly during most of the talk but began paying rapt attention toward the last ten minutes, although I didn't find out exactly why until much later.

But even then I did realize there was something different about the way Robert looked at me. I didn't feel the pressure of his eyes, as I often had when he stared at me in the courtyard. It was as though he'd been blowing a silent wind at me for months and had just now quietly turned it off. I felt its absence more than its presence, or at least I thought I did. He now seemed very interested in what I had to say.

At the end, Mme Lanier added several comments, one of which was that André Malraux, the minister of culture, was considering moving Moulin's ashes to the Panthéon, where Victor Hugo and the Curies were buried.

The class gave me a standing ovation at the end. Even Robert stood up. Cheryl came up and told me she never could have done that and kissed me on the cheek. I received admiring looks from my classmates, who probably thought I didn't have it in me to give a presentation in French. But maybe it was because I'd presented one of their countrymen in such a positive light. I wasn't sure, but I thought my teacher had a tear or two in her eyes when I mentioned Moulin's parachuting into France in the middle of a freezing cold January night after meeting with de Gaulle in London.

Thirty-seven years later in Paris, a much more mature Robert LePerrier told me that his attention became riveted the minute he heard the name Klaus Barbie. I mentioned Moulin had been tortured in a prison in Lyon and murdered by Barbie in the second part of my talk. Barbie had been the man Robert's father had worked for during the war, according to his mother. She had never mentioned the name of Jean Moulin.

Like the rest of the class, he developed a sense of outrage as he listened to my presentation. His father had always told him about the importance of a pure France and the need to rid the country of Arabs, Jews, and foreigners. Yet M. LePerrier may have supported a foreigner who had killed French patriots. Could his father have given support to a man who would torture and kill the courageous Jean Moulin?

Robert had gone along his whole life believing that cleansing France of impurities was the right thing to do. He'd sought to punish me, whom he'd viewed as weak and spoiled. But then he realized I had been courageous enough to get up in front of the class and paint such a positive picture of France. It was one of the things Robert wanted to tell me when he went out of his way to see me in Paris.

But that day in 1962 at the French *lycée*, the teenaged Robert couldn't say anything to me after the lecture. He did ask Mme Lanier if he could read about the torture of Moulin by Klaus Barbie. She said she didn't have that part of the material, since I'd found it myself. When he asked her to get it from me, she told him he'd have to ask me himself.

The next day, for the first time, he approached me in the courtyard. I knew something was different about how he felt about me even before he said a word. There was an apologetic quality to his eyes and an air of embarrassment conveyed by his posture. I felt it more than recognized it.

Abdelak, Pierre Aboghast (the boy I once reached for when I couldn't breathe), and Bertrand immediately came up to us. They thought Robert was going to start something, but I knew he wouldn't. He just asked if he could borrow my reading materials about Barbie's torture of Moulin. I told him I'd bring it the next day. He said thank you, tried to smile, and walked away, his head a little bent. He returned them a week later and thanked me again, but didn't tell me what he thought or even if he'd read them.

But when we had our meeting in Paris, he said he read everything. He questioned his mother about whether his father was involved with Jean Moulin's murder.

She ripped off her glasses and asked him, "How did you hear about Jean Moulin? Who gave you these materials?" She shouted out the questions, as though she could not receive the answers quickly enough.

He told her about my presentation in class.

"I didn't know that the idiot could speak French," she hissed. "He does nothing in my class. I tried to have him removed, but the *proviseur* wouldn't let me."

Robert quoted her verbatim, despite the decades that had passed, as he quoted everything related to this matter. I added the detail about her hissing based on my remembrance of her.

"You don't know anything about him," he shouted at her as he gathered his materials and walked upstairs. His mother paced around the living room; I felt a warm feeling inside when he told me that.

Later that evening, Robert approached his father, who was staring absentmindedly at the ceiling in their living room. Robert wasted no time in asking him whether he had anything to do with the torture of Jean Moulin.

Already prepared for this line of questioning by a hysterical phone call from his wife earlier in the day, M. LePerrier denied any involvement with those activities and claimed he'd been assigned to serve as a clerical person in Klaus Barbie's office. He advised his son not to believe anything I had told their class in my lecture.

M. LePerrier was most agitated, because he'd received a summons that day that he was being taken to court because of the attacks against me. He paced back and forth as though competing in a speed walking endurance race. "I just can't believe it. This crazy American military officer is going to carry out his threat," he said. He turned then to Robert with a grim look on his face. "Why do you always have to make matters worse?"

Robert was used to being criticized by his father for lack of restraint and ignored the question. Instead he said, "I've been learning some history about the way that Klaus Barbie treated Jean Moulin." He repeated to his father what I had emphasized. Naturally the books I gave Robert supported my account, so he had some details available to him. When he was finished, he turned his back on his dad, muttered that he had homework to do, and walked upstairs.

Jean-Claude LePerrier started talking to his wife about his past. Robert said he must have been incredibly upset, as he never talked about such things. He either must have thought Robert wouldn't overhear or was unaware his son was sitting on the top stair. He told his wife he'd been a spectator when Barbie's gang barged into the big house overlooking the Rhone in Izieu and terrorized the Jewish orphans.

"He still got you that new name and identity," Mme LePerrier said. Robert always smiled when he talked about his mother, but I think it was because he felt he had to apologize for her. I think deep down he knew she was the most anti-American and anti-Semitic member of his whole family but couldn't admit it to himself.

Robert heard his father describe how, on many occasions, he'd been involved in phone conversations in his minuscule office in gestapo headquarters. Barbie would stand in the doorway and interrupt and keep talking at him until he released the phone. M. LePerrier obviously felt Barbie owned him.

Robert climbed down the stairs so he was just out of sight. His mother suggested they go into the backyard, but M. LePerrier ignored her.

"I never really believed in any of the things Barbie did. Most of the time Klaus just wanted me to observe as he interrogated people," he told her.

He was afraid he would lose his job at the pharmaceutical company. His wife blamed it all on their daughter and niece.

"I'm sure it was Isabelle the whore who told them," she said. "Your sister has always filled Isabelle with venomous lies about you."

M. LePerrier continued to walk back and forth. Robert could hear his steps, and could imagine his father pacing with his hands joined behind his back, as he often did.

"I've never had anything against Jews, particularly Jewish children," M. LePerrier said. "If only Robert didn't hurt that boy, the Americans would never have met Isabelle."

All those years later in Paris, after we left the Panthéon, Robert told me that the only memories his father had been unable to erase from his mind concerning the Barbie era involved the treatment of Jean Moulin. Barbie had made him actually enter the cell and watch while he bashed the Frenchman's head repeatedly against the wall. He'd been amazed that Moulin wouldn't give his boss any information. He'd never seen anyone like him. While M. LePerrier held contempt for most of his countrymen who had fled the Germans or become collaborators like himself, Moulin was not a man whom he had been able to dismiss.

Moulin had seen him in the cell. Their eyes had met several times. He would never forget those eyes, dark as night, showing no fear. M. LePerrier wondered at times if he would receive his due someday because of that horrible torture.

He had actually admired Moulin. And it had not been his idea to torture him. He couldn't believe Barbie had the gall to lie to Heinrich Himmler, second in command under Hitler and head of the SS, and say that Moulin had banged his own head against the wall. One evening when he and Barbie were out in a posh restaurant after several drinks, and everyone else had gone home, Barbie confided to him that Himmler should be a clerk in a post office.

All the same, nobody showed such self-confidence and resourcefulness in dealing with the assorted problems caused by the French resistance—problems that arose daily in Lyon. Klaus Barbie was an unparalleled decision maker. There was no problem that he couldn't solve single-handedly, it seemed to M. LePerrier. Or could it perhaps have just been delusions of grandeur that motivated him?

Robert was astounded to hear those admissions. I guessed that was why he remembered it all so distinctly. Also, I supposed my father must have really gotten to M. LePerrier. He probably used a lot of his attorney skills in the meeting they had in his office. In later years, people told me how scary my dad could be in any legal proceedings, meetings, and, of course, in the courtroom, as though they were surprised such a gentleman could be so tough. I would just nod, not wanting to let them know he sometimes ran a court in our home.

THE TRIAL

Two days later, around five in the afternoon, the doorbell rang as I sat at the kitchen table, doing English homework. It was a lesson about a woman who had lived in London her entire life and had never seen the dome of St. Paul's Cathedral. I really didn't know why they thought it was noteworthy enough to put in a book. I'd never been to Bunker Hill or the site of the Boston Tea Party.

Cheryl was at the front door. She told me she'd left her notebook at school and needed the English assignment. I knew there was more to this visit, because there had been several times she hadn't handed in the homework.

I'd never seen her wearing the blue, tight shorts she had on, which hugged her buttocks. She sat down in the kitchen, but then we decided to go into the backyard and sit on the lounges, which had gone unused all winter. I made some lemonade and brought the pitcher and two paper cups outside. I dropped a few lemons on the floor and found her smooth, muscular legs staring at me as I rose from picking them up. The ice cooled my hands, and I took a cube and rubbed it against my face.

We sat at the table in back of the house, and for five minutes, neither of us said a word. She finished drinking the lemonade and placed her cup on the white, round table between us. I went to pour her more, but she waved me off. I placed my cup on top of the large rust stain, which had formed from exposure to the winter weather.

The sun was still high in the sky, and the green meadows extended for miles. Other than a few scattered clouds, only a panorama of blue existed above us. Several hummingbirds skirted across the yard. There was the occasional sound of a dog barking or a bird chirping, but otherwise we sat in silence. It seemed like midday, although it probably was around five thirty. My father wouldn't be home for two hours, and none of the neighbors seemed to be around either.

It was the silence that made me feel that if something were to happen, it was up to me. I got a brief respite when my four-year-old neighbor, Dominick, came by with his dog and said, "Bonjour, Roy."

But the reprieve was short-lived as his sister screamed, "Dominique, *viens voir*," and he scampered off across the field to his house.

Other than the first time we went to Strasbourg and danced, we had mainly been friends—going to the art museum, driving her *velo*, and taking long walks. Beads of perspiration formed on my brow.

She sat up in the chaise lounge, and I gazed at her thighs. She stepped back inside the kitchen, and I walked behind her. She saw a magazine on the floor and picked it up, revealing the cheeks of her buttocks under her shorts.

She walked into the living room and bent over to place the magazine on the cheap wooden table and picked up another one. The curtains were open in the front of our small house. There were two cottages directly across the street, but the shades were closed. She sat down on our couch, crossing her legs, and started to read the magazine.

I sat beside her and put my arm around her shoulder. She just sat there, reading. I was about to release my arm and give up. It was just as well, since I didn't have any more idea what was going through her head than usual, and I was afraid of what could happen. Suddenly she turned and kissed me forcefully, as though she were on a train. I kissed her back. Although I didn't understand her, she was beautiful, and I was flattered she was attracted to me. She increased the pressure of her arm around me and hugged me more affectionately than anyone had in my life. I got up and closed the curtains. Why now? I wondered. Was she impressed with that presentation I gave? Was it because she realized our time together was ending?

I returned to the couch and went to kiss her again, but she stood up. She told me she came over to say good-bye. "I got a job at the United Nations this summer, and I'm leaving tomorrow," she said.

I felt as though I'd been shot with a stun gun. "I don't know what to say," I said.

She sat down and put her arm around me and said she was really going to miss me, but I didn't believe her. "I didn't know who you were for a long time, and I'm proud to know you," she said. She had a funny way of showing it.

She said she had my address and would write to me. Within five minutes, she was gone. I took the next bus to the gym, then ran up and down the stands twenty-five times until I almost collapsed. I took a twenty-minute shower and returned home to fall asleep on my bed without taking my clothes off or brushing my teeth. I received one letter from her, which I answered, but never saw her again.

* * * *

The day for the trial grew closer, and the weather became humid. Now I would arrive at school dressed in a short-sleeved shirt and Levi's jeans; I once again looked like an American. I asked my father if I could return home at the end of the school year, so I could take chemistry in summer school to prepare for a premed program in college.

"I'm glad to hear that you're thinking ahead about what direction you want for yourself, Roy. The trouble is that the timing isn't right for leaving early. We have a trial. I'd like to go along with your plan, but I don't see how you can go back home until this trial is over," he said and picked up his pen and started writing.

"We don't need to go through with the trial. I'm fine about what happened, and LePerrier doesn't bother me anymore. I know you respect the law as a tool for solving problems and righting wrongs, but you don't have to settle every argument in life in a court," I said.

My father put his pen down. "I agree, but it's important to do what you say you're going to do. It will set you apart," he said.

Even then I had to admit to myself that his point was well-taken. He snuck these pearls of fatherly wisdom into unusual places. They would pop into my mind years later at strange times, undisguised as the gems they were. However, my sixteen-year-old self also wanted to see his viewpoint as excessive vindictiveness, because it interfered with my plans. He buzzed his secretary, my signal that I was dismissed.

The start of the trial had been postponed until July 10, then rescheduled for July 31. The soldiers were to start returning home on July 1. By the time the fifteenth of July rolled around, the base would be a ghost town. During the month of June, in the courtyard between classes, I chose a different part of the inside of the school wall every day and, when no one was looking, pressed the cool concrete with my hands. Somehow the cold touch grounded me. I knew that when my classmates returned in September, I would no longer be a part of the team. I wondered if my name would ever come up, and if my classmates would remember me.

No ceremony marked the end of the year, which went out with a whimper. There was no final assembly or class meeting or time when everyone in the class went out to Chez Richert in the town center and had lunch together. It was a huge disappointment to me. Everybody just said *salut*. The girls kissed me on both cheeks. Georgette said, "*Tu as envie de bien faire*." Even Robert LePerrier waved from across the yard. We all said good-bye on the long-awaited June 27. As I walked under that gate and three flags for the last time, I looked up at a cloudless, blue sky, as I had when I was anticipating going to play baseball in the little league. But I was also leaving something behind…something important.

As July 1 neared, the reservists sat in the canteen, making plans for a reunion at Cape Cod at the end of summer. They raised their fingers, indicating the number of days remaining.

I sat listening as I nursed a vanilla milkshake so large it looked like an oversized vat of popcorn. I read the *Stars and Stripes* and listened to Frank Sinatra over the loudspeaker as I sipped the drink intermittently for over an hour through a pudgy straw.

I received a letter from Julie, who was excited to be accepted at Northwestern and would be going to Chicago the end of August. She wanted to know if I'd be home before then. She signed the letter "Love, Julie." As I read it for the third time, the disc jockey announced a newly released song. "You Belong to Me" by the Duprees about a girl going off on vacation to Africa and her boyfriend anxiously awaiting her return. I placed the letter next to my mirror in my room and looked at it constantly. Every time I heard the song, I thought of her.

Dad brought me *The Sound and the Fury* from the library when he heard William Faulkner died in the beginning of July. He told me Faulkner was America's greatest writer and had won the Nobel Prize. I tried to read the book, but gave up after ten pages. It made no sense, and the author was clearly an idiot or someone with a mental disorder. I returned it to the library and took out *Babbitt* by Sinclair Lewis, which I could understand. It never crossed my mind why Faulkner won that prize.

I sat in the library during the day, reading while sipping lemonade. When I repeated my request to my father to go home and start summer school, he said we both had more important business than my summer school or his legal work. There was a bad man to punish, someone who had escaped justice.

My father was as busy as I was idle. His office was responsible for processing each reservist's paperwork back to the United States and was chaotic from early morning until dinnertime. In addition he wrote letters to several branches of the United States government and was met by nothing but apathy. Although he used every connection he could muster, none of the newspapers were interested in writing articles about ex-Nazis. His letters to the French government, translated and sent out by the French attaché, were disregarded. M. Creteuil tried to persuade him to reconsider abandoning the trial. I was healthy, his time in France had elapsed, and there was no interest anymore in such matters. His arguments fell on deaf ears; he didn't know my dad.

Every afternoon I'd wander down to the airstrip and watch a planeload of men head back to the States—or Stateside, as they liked to say. After the planes took off, I walked over to the gymnasium, which felt like an abandoned warehouse as the sound of my bouncing basketball reverberated through the cavernous building.

My father took me to Paris for a weekend in mid-July. When we were outside the Luxembourg Gardens, he went into a store to get a Perrier. An overweight American wearing a Stetson hat with an enormous cigar dangling from his mouth grabbed me by the arm. He almost fried my eyes with his cigar as he asked if I knew the location of the Champs-Elysées, but he pronounced Champs like "champions." I pretended I didn't understand English and walked away. Now I thought I knew what people meant by the phrase, "the ugly American."

I loved being in Paris and wondered why we'd never come before. We went to the Louvre, and I saw the small picture of a lady everyone was making such a federal case over. She was kind of a homely woman, but she did have a great smile.

The next weekend, we went into the big gambling casino in Monte Carlo. My father lost a hundred dollars in ten minutes on the slot machines. I thought about how upset my friends became when they lost ten dollars after a whole evening of cards.

"That's why I don't gamble, and neither should you," he told me. "It's not worth it to work hard to make money and then just lose it like that."

We spent the afternoon lying inside a poolside *tente*, which we rented at our hotel. I walked to the edge of the cliffs and gazed out at the blue Mediterranean. The sun sparkled off the water as boats sprinkled the sea's surface. There were only sailboats and yachts—no commercial barges or tugboats like in Boston harbor. We sat at a table and had a seafood salad with *moules* and mustard.

"This is how rich people live," my father said.

I was determined to come back to Monte Carlo and Paris many times. In later years, I realized that my father never presented himself to me as rich, even though he paid for my entire education, left me no debt, and bought me a car when I graduated medical school.

The next week, I was reading *Babbitt* in my living room around ten in the morning when I heard a knock at the front door. Two of my classmates were at my doorstep, perched on their motorbikes. How did they know I was still here? Bertrand waved his hand. "*Viens*, we're taking you to the *piscine* in Saverne."

I got on the back of Bertrand's bike. It was a more powerful motorcycle than Cheryl's, but Bertrand was more careful. I envisioned surviving the rugby ordeal only to get badly injured or killed in a motorcycle accident.

We drove to the Saverne municipal pool and spent the day swimming and lounging around. At lunchtime we went into the town and bought large baguettes full of ham, brie cheese, and spicy French mustard. There were pretty girls at the pool whom my friends knew, but who went to a different school. They were leaving to go to the ocean in Normandy the following week and stay for a month. Everyone went to the seashore for the entire month of August in France. How could their parents take that much time off work? Dad never took more than two weeks.

Another morning, my dad drove me to the pool, but my friends weren't there, as their families had gone off on holiday. I didn't want to go alone, so I didn't return. It was time for the trial to begin anyway.

*   *   *   *

It started the last day of July and took place in an old building in Sarrebourg, which was the nearest courthouse to the school. They couldn't use Strasbourg as a venue because it was in Alsace, and the school where everything happened was in Moselle, a part of Lorraine.

The courthouse had Corinthian columns and was the largest building in the municipality. It was one of the few buildings made of red brick I'd seen in France. It sat atop a gentle, sloping hill with a large lawn and many oak trees, which gave a feeling of coolness and shade as my father and I walked up the broad, sand-colored steps.

I wore my only tie and jacket, which my dad had bought when Alexandre's of England visited the base. Going to court was not an everyday thing for me, as it was for my father, and I was very nervous. My stomach churned the moment I entered the old building, and I felt nauseated. I looked around for a WC in case I'd have to throw up. Fortunately I started feeling better as I sat down beside Dad and looked at him. He seemed completely calm and content to let M. Creteuil take care of us.

After we took our seats in the first of ten rows, I leaned forward on the firm wooden railing, which separated us from the judges in front, as though we were livestock in a pen with room for about thirty pigs. I started asking my father questions about trials, but he raised his hand, and I quieted down.

I strained to recognize the artists whose pictures covered the high ceilings but couldn't. One was of a group of men standing around a desk, reading from a piece of parchment. They had white wigs on their heads. Cheryl would have known, and at that moment, I missed her.

M. Creteuil, dressed in a black robe, shook hands with both of us and actually appeared enthusiastic about the whole thing for the first time. But when he walked away, my father told me that as recently as two days ago our attorney had tried to persuade him to call the whole thing off.

Jean-Claude and Robert LePerrier walked into the room, accompanied by a large, balding man dressed in a black robe like M. Creteuil. However, this man's robe was frayed on the edges and appeared too tight. He had an unpleasant expression, as though he would be impatient…but maybe he was just uncomfortable in his tight clothes.

Dan Connolly was not there. My father had to persuade him to return to the United States in the middle of July, since his training camp was already underway. When he had arrived in France, Dan's highest priority was to make sure he would be home by mid-July to fight for his job. But Dan felt that he had to see the trial through, so he had called his coach and told him he would possibly be a month late for his training camp. My father told Dan that he had already helped us more than we could ever have expected, and that he had to go back. Dan finally agreed, but he was really upset. It was the only time I ever heard him talk back to my father.

After what seemed like I had sat for a long time in that front row next to my father and M. Creteuil, three judges in black robes entered from a door in the front of the room and sat behind podiums elevated in the front of the room on a stage. The judge sitting in the middle seemed to be in charge. He was about Dad's age. The two others were younger, but it was hard to tell how old they were. Remembering Perry Mason from television, I asked my father where the jury was. He told me that since the case wasn't a felony in France, there would be no jury.

The first judge, whose chair was slightly higher than the other two, took control. This judge spoke slowly and explained the rules like one of those rare teachers who were concerned about people understanding them. Listening to him gave me a sense of control, and my stomach quieted down. We would get justice, despite the language and cultural differences. But the other two judges spoke quickly and slurred their words, so I could understand only about 80 percent of what they said. My father brought Suzie, and she translated everything for him. I tried to listen to her, but it was too hard, so I just depended on myself.

The trial started, and M. Creteuil took about five minutes to state our case. I was surprised at how well I understood him. The judge read from Dr. Cook's report about my injury. He used the phrase "near-fatal accident." I looked up at the dome of the room and kept my eyes fixated there for several seconds. I'd heard the phrase *presque disparu* several times in the courtyard but hadn't realized they were talking about me. But it was true—when a person died, they disappeared. I wondered at that moment how something that obvious was so hard to accept, and how death gave me such an eerie feeling. I remembered the two dreams right after I'd returned to the *lycée* after my hospitalization—dreams in which I was invisible. In both of these dreams, my classmates would talk about me, but couldn't see or hear me when I tried to speak, and I'd felt so frustrated. Our attorney also used the phrase *presque tombé*, and I visualized a white, rectangular tombstone with my name carved on it next to my mother's on a field of grass, and my father holding flowers and staring at the stones for a long time.

The physical education teacher, M. Richard, was barely recognizable in his plaid sports jacket. It must have pained him to wear those clothes on a humid summer day in a room without air-conditioning. I turned around and saw my English teacher in the back row. M. Richard gestured as usual as he described Robert LePerrier delivering the blows that caused my problem. He added that he'd witnessed Robert LePerrier tripping me in a basketball game a month before the rugby incident.

Jules Falkstein described the soup incident in the cafeteria, as well as the basketball game incident. He mentioned his own experience with Robert LePerrier. As he stepped down from the witness stand, he looked over at me. I knew I would miss "*le Premier*." Maybe we could stay in touch somehow.

It was time for lunch, and we went with M. Creteuil to a *brasserie,* in Sarrebourg. As we ate our meal in the restaurant, I knew I was going to miss the hot onion soup with cheese when I went back home.

"I'm glad your appetite has come back. When we get home, there's a great French restaurant in Copley Square I can take you to," my father said. I guess it had registered with him that I felt ill earlier in the morning, although he hadn't mentioned anything. Maybe there were a lot of my problems he just didn't want to deal with. But I was excited, because we never went out to restaurants in Boston.

"We're going to start doing a lot of things differently," he went on, as he spread butter on his oversized slice of French bread. He and M. Creteuil discussed the trial, and Suzie helped out with a few words. I did process that Robert LePerrier would be called to testify in the afternoon.

We finished our meal and walked across the large square and up the long lawn to the courthouse. How did people get dressed up in these hot clothes every day? The tie choked me, and I wanted to tear it off and open the top button of my shirt, then run under the hoses that two men were using to water the grass. It was the kind of afternoon meant more for frolicking outside than sitting in a stifling courtroom. I wondered at that moment whether adults felt that frustration a lot. We reached our seats and were in them less than a minute when the judges entered the room and called the meeting to order.

Robert LePerrier lumbered up to the witness chair. He kept his eyes on the floor as he was sworn in. His hair was even shorter than his usual crew cut, but he'd regained most of his weight. His face was tinged with its usual red. I felt a wave of nausea and feared I'd lose the onion soup I had enjoyed so much, but then my stomach settled down, and I wiped the perspiration off my brow and thought about whether the ordeal of this trial was worth it. I was being detained in France, missing summer school, and subjecting myself to emotional torture so that my father could teach some guy a lesson. By the time my mind returned to the courtroom, Robert had begun his testimony.

M. Creteuil asked about the incidents where Robert was accused of harming me.

"All of those things were accidents," Robert said. "I didn't have anything to do with this injury to his hand, and in rugby, it's legal to try to kick the ball from someone's grasp if they don't release it." He said he'd always been a competitive player and did nothing against the rules. I leaned forward in my chair, impressed at how much he sounded like a mature young adult. It didn't occur to me how much he must have been coached. Also I had no way of knowing he'd threatened his father with the exposure of M. LePerrier's relationship to Klaus Barbie in the courtroom. I only found out about it so much later, when we met in Paris.

M. Creteuil followed the judges and asked Robert, "Why is it none of the witnesses viewed any of these occurrences as accidental?"

"That was their opinion," Robert said. He looked around the room at his father, who looked back in agreement.

"Do you want to tell us about the fight you had with Abdelak Bonnini on the day after the basketball game?"

He said the Algerian was always starting trouble. "If you check his record at school, he has more *mauvais points* than the rest of the class combined," Robert said. He stared at M. Creteuil.

"Is that because he's Algerian that he's got those *mauvais points*?" M. Creteuil asked.

Robert did not answer.

M. Creteuil then asked him why he referred to Abdelak as "the Algerian."

"I didn't mention his nationality when I asked you about the fight," M. Creteuil observed.

Robert was silent again.

M. Creteuil then asked Robert if he targeted me because I was Jewish. I wondered where he got that question. Wasn't it enough to show Robert was anti-American? Maybe he was trying to throw him off balance.

Robert sat up straight in his chair. The question obviously caught him by surprise. "I didn't know he was Jewish. Harrison isn't a Jewish name," he said. I wondered how he'd known that.

"Why would you care whether it was a Jewish name or not?" M. Creteuil asked.

Robert didn't answer. He looked as if he were frustrated, as though there was something he wanted to say but couldn't. It must have been the stuff about his father.

If M. Creteuil lacked enthusiasm, it wasn't showing. He asked, "If Harrison isn't a Jewish name, then what would be an example of a Jewish name?"

Robert didn't answer that question either. He looked as though he were about to explode. His ruddy face became the color of the inside of a watermelon. I was just wondering why the judges weren't forcing him to answer these questions when the first judge advised him gently that even though he was a minor, he was a witness and had to answer.

Suddenly Robert turned his head to seek out his father. He then looked back at M. Creteuil. The attorney stood there and folded his arms in front of his chest.

At least six people coughed or cleared their throats.

M. Creteuil gently turned his eyes to the judge—the first judge.

The judge told Robert, "*Jeune homme, vous devez repondre a la question tout de suite.*"

Robert LePerrier continued to look around the room. He shifted around in his chair. He looked as though he were searching out someone to rescue him. I wondered whom he thought that would be.

Robert never forgot that moment; he told me later he felt as though someone had squeezed his throat, and he couldn't breathe. He wanted to tell the judge he'd never meant to harm me, that he was only acting out his father's hatred of Americans. But he couldn't get himself to say it. He asked for water. He started to cough. His mother looked down at her lap.

The judge asked if Robert was feeling ill.

He drank the water and continued to cough. M. Creteuil stood there as though he had an eternity.

When Robert finally stopped, M. Creteuil repeated, "How did you find out that it wasn't a Jewish name?"

"I asked my father," Robert said and resumed his original position against the back of the chair.

"Why did you ask the question in the first place? Why was it not sufficient to know that he was an American?" our lawyer asked.

"I just thought he might be Jewish," Robert whispered. I had to lean forward to hear him.

The stenographer asked him to repeat his answer. The people in the gallery turned to one another.

"*Qu'est-ce qu'il a dit?*" the man behind me asked the woman next to him.

"Why did you think that?" asked the attorney. He was standing about three feet away from the teenager, and he backed away another three feet.

"He just looks like it," Robert said.

"What does a Jewish person look like?" M. Creteuil asked immediately.

Robert was sweating. He finally said, "My dad told me Jews have special features."

"Do you know what those features are?" M. Creteuil asked.

"I don't remember." Robert took his hands and made a gesture as though he was pushing something away.

"Do you know any Jewish people?" M. Creteuil asked.

"No!" Robert yelled. I sat upright when he raised his voice. I'd never heard him yell. While it jolted me, it wasn't nearly as scary as when my father did it.

"What else did he tell you about Jews?" M. Creteuil asked. M. LePerrier's attorney stood up and hollered it was irrelevant.

"I want to show this boy's actions were motivated by anti-Semitism as well as anti-Americanism," M. Creteuil said to the judge.

"If it was an accident, it's all irrelevant," said M. LePerrier's attorney.

But M. Creteuil responded by saying if Robert LePerrier had never met a Jew, he must have gotten his information from someone else. "No one is born an anti-Semite," M. Creteuil said to the judges.

The judge overruled the objection.

"What has your father said to you about Jews?" he asked the boy.

"He said that they are greedy and want to control everything," Robert said in a loud, clear voice.

"Did he give you any examples?"

"No." He wrung his hands.

"What does he say about Americans?" M. Creteuil asked in his soft voice.

"They are stupid, spoiled, and have too much money."

"Anything else?"

"No."

I sighed and took a deep breath as Robert LePerrier stepped down. The whole thing was so embarrassing. He walked to his chair with his head down, then put his hands over his face.

That night in our cottage, Dad said, "Roy, you won a victory over Robert LePerrier. A pained or anxious expression is often the entire triumph one gets, but it can be savored."

I told him, "Actually, I felt like I already won a long time ago by the way my classmates responded after my injury. What you're calling a victory may just be a high for you and a strain for me."

I don't think he paid any attention to that. He started in immediately with the need to focus on preparing me for my cross-examination the next day.

But I was determined to tell him how I felt about sacrificing my summer to satisfy his vindictiveness. "That kid was demolished up there today. What more do you want?" I asked.

He didn't even seem to hear me, so I told him, "Listen, Dad, I'm just going to tell the truth on the witness stand."

"The truth isn't good enough, because attorneys seek to twist the facts to suit their side's benefit. The other attorney will try to minimize what LePerrier did to you."

I didn't ask him why he was in a profession where people would try to bend the truth, but I later learned that, in some ways, the law was best suited for crooks.

"He's going to present these attacks as a series of accidents and coincidences, 'boys will be boys,' and so on," my father said, as he grabbed me by the bicep muscle. It was the first time he could see how much my muscle had grown, and he released it with much more respect than he seized it.

Just when I thought my father was totally out of touch with me, he pushed a button that got me completely in line with his way of thinking.

"Well, you want to nail his father for what he did to Jean Moulin, don't you?" he asked.

With the mention of Moulin's name, I became quiet. I walked to the kitchen window and watched the sunset. It was almost a quarter to ten. "When we get home, the sun will never set this late, will it?" I asked.

My dad didn't answer. He just stared off into space. There was no one behind his glasses for five minutes. I thought about my friends going to the beaches, driving around in cars while I was stuck here until our trial ended. That night I dreamed of Robert LePerrier's father torturing Jean Moulin, and Moulin staring at him with those big, black eyes.

I walked up to take the witness chair the next afternoon. The large attorney, in the frayed, dark robe, stood two feet away and looked at me as though I would be the first course in a long-delayed meal. He was the only overweight Frenchman I'd seen in France. There were cigarette stains on his fingernails, and he gave off a pungent garlic odor.

My tongue stuck to my teeth, and I felt as though the roof of my mouth had been scalded with a hot potato. It was like the time I ventured across Checkpoint Charlie into East Berlin. This time, though, I had a new symptom: both my ears began to shriek. It was a loud, whistling sensation, like the sound a teakettle makes as the water boils. The noise interfered with my ability to understand the lawyer, who spoke rapidly in a foreign language. At first I thought I might be having a stroke, like my grandmother, who had complained of that very symptom a week before her life-ending catastrophe.

"Why did you never complain to the school authorities?" the man asked me. He continued to hover around me like a bumblebee, and I turned my head toward the judges and motioned for some relief.

"Can he step back a little?" I asked.

The judge told me the attorney was under no obligation to back up. He told me to answer the question—and he didn't say it as nicely as he had to Robert.

"I'm not a tattletale," I said.

The attorney backed up but frowned, causing the area under his chin and his cheeks to shake like Jell-O. He held a copy of my report card and read that the *proviseur* had characterized me with the words *eleve turbulent*.

"Why would he write that about you?" he asked, as he stared at me.

"I don't know why the principal would call me unruly," I said. I told the court I only got two *mauvais points* all year, and those were for speaking English with Cheryl in the courtyard.

"Several of the teachers have said you haven't made any effort," the attorney said.

"I did my best. It's a hard school for foreigners," I said. My head was up high now that the ringing in my ears was abating, but I was confused and disturbed that he would have my record without my permission.

"Well, maybe you provoked more people at the school than you realized. If you bothered the teachers, don't you think it's possible you could have irked some of the students too?" the lawyer asked.

"By doing what?" I asked. I told him I never said much in class and certainly never bothered Robert LePerrier. My father always told me to be respectful to adults, but with this attorney, Dad had told me not to be overly cooperative. It was a strange message from him, but I was enjoying following it more than I expected.

The LePerriers' attorney continued. "You insulted his mother. You went into her class and didn't take it seriously."

I told him that whatever I did in his mother's class wouldn't have satisfied her, and my class involvement didn't justify his kicking me in the chest and putting me in the hospital. Even then I realized this guy couldn't be much of a lawyer to ask me these kinds of questions, which would allow me to respond so forcefully.

M. Creteuil stood up and objected that the attorney was harassing me and should stick to asking me questions. I really didn't mind, because if the attorney asked me questions, I might be forced to answer yes or no.

M. LePerrier's attorney said he was just giving a profile of me to put the whole matter in context. The judge allowed him to continue.

The man read the art teacher's comments, as well as those of the history teacher from the first term. They both used the identical comment, "*N'a fait aucun effort.*" Another teacher commented that the class was "too strong" for me. The lawyer looked at me as though I were a convicted felon. He asked me why the man would say that. I swallowed hard and felt my cheeks burning as he read further from the report card as though he were reciting from an important document.

"*Ne peut s'appliquer aux méthodes de travail du lycée,*" were the words of that huge, ranting foghorn of a physics teacher who didn't think I could keep up with his class. Of course he was right, but it hurt to hear it trumpeted unnecessarily in front of all these people. What did he expect me to do? It was a miracle I didn't suffer hearing damage in his class.

Fortunately I looked at my father, and he smiled at me. Because Dad didn't mind my poor performance, I sat back and looked the attorney in the eye. The man started to speak, but then stopped and said, "Scratch that." This happened twice before he asked his next question: "Exactly what did Robert do to bother you during study halls and breaks in the courtyard?"

I answered, "Nothing."

"*Rien*," the attorney repeated. "*Absolument rien*. Don't you feel you're making too much of this whole thing?" He held his palms up and spread them apart with an oily smile to imply he was resting his case.

"Has Robert LePerrier spoken to you even once during his months at the school?" he asked me.

"No," I answered.

"So why do you think he had any interest in you? You present things as though he seeks you out to torture you. Aren't you being a little bit paranoid?"

It was the first time I'd heard the French word for "paranoid," and I told him I didn't know what it meant. He had it translated into English, but I still didn't like the sound of the word. Even later, when I knew its precise meaning, I liked it even less. I felt its main use was to make a person feel uncomfortable about being sensitive, as many people could be if you picked the wrong subject.

I said nothing.

The man yelled "*Alors!*" as he turned his head to the gallery as if to say, "Well, what are you waiting for?"

Then it hit me, and I sat up in my chair straight as a telephone pole. I said, "Wait! I remember after my report on Jean Moulin, Robert came up to me in the courtyard to ask if he could borrow one of my books on him." I felt relieved and told them I'd forgotten.

The attorney stepped back two steps and cleared his throat twice as he glanced at Jean-Claude LePerrier, who turned around and faced the back of the room.

"Why were you doing a report on Moulin?" the man asked in a whisper. I told him I'd become interested in him during the year.

"That will be all," the attorney said. His eye twitched as he stepped away. I realized I'd said something powerful in introducing the name of Jean Moulin into the courtroom, but I didn't immediately understand why, and that frustrated me.

M. Creteuil stepped back up to redirect questions to me but gave me ten feet of space. His black robe glistened and looked freshly pressed. I felt I had as much room around me as a marble on an empty ballroom floor. I took a deep breath; it would be easier answering his questions.

"How did you become involved in doing a report on Jean Moulin?" he asked me.

I said both Dan Connolly and my father had learned about him from investigating Klaus Barbie.

The attorney asked how Barbie came to interest them.

"I told him Barbie worked with M. LePerrier during the last world war."

"Do you know what M. Barbie and M. LePerrier did together?" M. Creteuil asked.

The opposing attorney jumped to his feet and interrupted, claiming M. LePerrier's activities during the past world war were irrelevant to this case. The man's voice was piercing, and my ears started ringing like a telephone again.

The judge allowed the question, since it stemmed from a question M. LePerrier's attorney himself had asked me.

"I'm not sure, but supposedly they tortured Jean Moulin," I said.

The noise in the small, half-filled gallery became appreciable as people began talking, shifting their positions and causing chairs to scrape against the floor. Two or three people exited; however, they returned immediately. I wondered where they went.

The LePerriers' attorney interrupted again and demanded to know about the significance of this line of questioning.

M. Creteuil said, "LePerrier's history of working with Barbie indicates his Nazi sympathies and supports the notion that his son's actions could have been motivated by anti-Semitism."

The courtroom buzzed again. The first judge banged his gavel on the table, and the place became silent. It was the first time one of the judges had done that, and it jarred me; it must have had the same effect on many others. He said Jean Moulin wasn't a Jew, and bringing up war crimes went beyond the scope of his court.

"Such a matter will have to be referred to the commission on war crimes," he said.

The second judge joined in by saying he wouldn't allow this court to be used as a forum for information that sensitive.

Jean-Claude LePerrier spoke very fast to his attorney. M. LePerrier's attorney raised his hand and asked the judge for a recess.

"We need to have a meeting with the two attorneys in our chambers anyway," the first judge said.

Because it was late afternoon, the judges decided to break until the next day. I was disappointed, since I was beginning to feel confident. I knew a lot about Jean Moulin and wanted to repeat my lecture, which I still knew by heart. I viewed it as an opportunity and didn't realize that to the others in the courtroom, the whole subject might have been a festering wound. In those days, if I wanted to show off, I didn't care what my audience wanted.

M. Creteuil and my father stood outside the courthouse under the trees as our lawyer explained his strategy, which I didn't understand. It looked as though it was going to rain any minute. My father smiled at M. Creteuil and told him he was meaner than he'd realized.

The French attorney laughed and said he liked to have people underestimate him. While I believed him, he certainly didn't set up his office in a way that supported underestimation.

My father slapped him on the back, and I saw his face relax. "The only reservation I had about you was I thought you would be too nice," he said.

The next morning, M. Creteuil had a meeting with the judges and M. LePerrier's lawyer. M. Creteuil told them he had new information to present from Dan Connolly. He handed the judge several old photographs in a large manila envelope postmarked from Paris and sent by M. LePerrier's niece. The packet showed that M. LePerrier was Guillaume Sendef, a scientist known to have worked with Klaus Barbie and who was suspected of participating in the torture of Moulin.

The photographs revealed two birthmarks on M. LePerrier's cheek and lower chin, which he still had. So many years later, during our conversation outside the Moulin memorial in Paris, Robert told me that the group who provided his father with a new identity in 1946 offered to pay for their removal, but he had never taken advantage of their gift.

The judge asked how Dan knew M. LePerrier's relative, and M. Creteuil explained how they met. The judge thought for about ten seconds, then said the war crimes court would be interested in seeing the pictures and talking to Isabelle.

"We would like to enter it into this trial here," M. Creteuil persisted.

The judge agreed that M. LePerrier should have to answer for harming Moulin, but felt his courtroom wasn't the place. "I'm sorry, but that won't be possible," he said.

The meeting ended, and we began the third day of the trial. The rain made a steady patter on the roof, and moisture clouded the large windows on the side of the courtroom through which I'd viewed the extensive lawn and oak trees the past two days.

Despite my father's efforts, there were no representatives of the French press, and the *International News Tribune* had shown no interest either. He'd pleaded with the editor of the *Stars and Stripes*, who finally relented and assigned a reporter. My father introduced me to him on the first day, but the man wasn't interested in the trial. He spent only half of the time in the courtroom and didn't take any notes.

Jean-Claude LePerrier took the stand late in the morning. By then the rain had stopped, and the sun was high in the sky. Even with the shade of all the trees that draped over the old building, everyone was fanning themselves with papers. Two large fans were also in perpetual motion in the back of the courtroom. They looked like propellers on a helicopter and produced a continuous hum, which I tried to ignore.

During the break, I heard people talking about their beach houses in Brittany and Normandy while smoking Gitane cigarettes on the steps of the courthouse. By afternoon the judges removed their black robes and worked in their shirts. While food wasn't allowed, the judges made an exception, and each of them sipped Orangina, the soft drink I'd seen advertised in every village between the base and Strasbourg.

M. Creteuil asked M. LePerrier his position on foreigners and Jews, and asked him to describe any discussions he'd had with his son about such matters.

He said he was a man of science; he held no prejudices and judged each situation on its own merits. He added he was grateful to the United States for rescuing France from the Germans.

"But you fought for the side of Germany," M. Creteuil prodded him.

The first judge banged the gavel and glared at our lawyer. "Please remember, M. Creteuil, what I told you in our meeting *a huis clos*," he said.

But M. Creteuil kept bringing up Barbie over and over again. He had an inexhaustible number of arrows in his quiver.

"I had to work for Barbie," M. LePerrier said.

The judge then stood up and said he would declare a mistrial if anything more about Klaus Barbie was brought up.

"But we are trying to show that this boy's actions are based on anti-Semitism," said M. Creteuil.

"You are trying the man for his son's actions, not for his," the judge said.

M. Creteuil asked another question that I don't remember…but what I distinctly recall was M. LePerrier clutching his chest. Then things became blurry for me. I only remember him appearing pale, as though all the blood had drained from his face, and he forgot the question he'd been asked. I knew he wasn't faking it, although he had every reason to.

"Are you in pain?" the first judge asked.

"My chest is killing me," M. LePerrier replied weakly.

The judge asked if it had started suddenly.

M. LePerrier said it was hurting a bit yesterday and this morning a little more, but now it was torturing him.

"I don't have any more questions," said M. Creteuil.

The judge said court was dismissed, and at that point, I became really distressed, because I figured if this man was seriously ill, the trial could be delayed indefinitely. With my father's compulsion about seeing this thing through, I pictured myself a member of the *classe de première* at the *lycée* next month. As we walked out of the courthouse, M. Creteuil told my father the judges would let us know when we would resume within forty-eight hours.

My father thought M. LePerrier was faking the whole thing, which came as no surprise. He was irate that the judges would let him get away with it. M. Creteuil said they didn't want to discuss war crimes; they just wanted to get away on their family vacations to the coast as much as everyone else.

After we got home, I couldn't bear to watch my father pacing, so I lay down and put a damp washcloth on my forehead. I didn't belong in France anymore and needed to move on. Sometimes finishing off the details of a job was the most difficult part. When I got up, Dad was sitting in the backyard and had already had two beers. I didn't even know we had any in the house. It turned out he got them from Captain Brooks; fortunately the captain didn't have the cigarettes my father requested.

Our state of uncertainty was aggravated the next day when M. Creteuil called to tell us Jean-Claude LePerrier might have had a heart attack, and the trial would have to be postponed indefinitely. But what were we supposed to do, wait until August was over? It had thirty-one days! I would die of boredom.

"How could they just shut down the country?" my father asked.

M. Creteuil shrugged and said we had a victory either way. I failed to understand what he meant. However, within twenty-four hours, we learned it hadn't been a heart attack, but the shingles. M. Creteuil told my father M. LePerrier had blisters all over the left side of his chest. But my misery ended, since the judges had ruled the trial was over. I felt like a stallion allowed to gallop in the meadow after having been cooped up in a barn all winter.

Jean-Claude LePerrier would have to perform one thousand hours of community service at American and Jewish institutions in France. His case would also be turned over to the French War Crimes Commission.

My father told me he might need to come back, but I wouldn't have to. We drove to Strasbourg that evening and had dinner in a five-star restaurant. We took our time eating, just like French people. I was shocked my father split a bottle of wine with me; he'd never encouraged me to drink. The owners had to tell us to leave when they closed at 11:00 PM.

We had no way of knowing about the stormy conversation that took place in the LePerriers' living room two evenings later after Jean Claude returned from the hospital. I only learned the details thirty-seven years later, during my conversations with Robert in the Tuillerie gardens and outside the Louvre. Robert's recollection of detail jarred me as it dwarfed my own sketchy recall of the trial. But he told me it had been the turning point in his life, so I could see how it wedged in his memory.

Robert told me his sister Jeanne was so frightened by the noises coming from their living room that evening that she cringed under her blankets for over an hour, as he confronted his father again about Jean Moulin. He described the exchange verbatim after all those years and I recorded the conversation in my brain exactly as he recounted it to me.

"What did you personally do to Moulin?" Robert asked, as he sat down opposite his father, who was lying on the living room couch.

His father told him he was a scientist and had nothing to do with the torture of Jean Moulin.

Robert turned to his mother and asked her why they never told him they changed their names. They both told him he wouldn't understand.

"Who turned Moulin over to the gestapo on June 21, 1943, in Caluire, outside of Lyon?" asked Robert. He remembered what I'd said in my lecture and what he had read from the book I lent him.

His father told him it was Maurice Parron. When he mentioned that name, Robert remembered that his mother, who was sitting across from her husband in a large easy chair, gasped, "You mean the assistant chief of police in Paris?"

After my conversation with Robert, I read about a former assistant chief of police in Paris who had been murdered for atrocities he'd committed during the war.

At this point, Robert's father grabbed his chest, as he had done in the courtroom, and castigated Robert for asking all these questions. "Can't you see I'm in pain?" he whimpered.

Robert asked his father what questions they asked Moulin when they were torturing him.

His father said he didn't remember, because when Klaus Barbie tortured someone, the torture was more important than the questions. "Even with children and women, he would just beat them before anyone could answer," he said. It annoyed Robert that his father's voice was so flat and factual and betrayed no emotion whatsoever. If M. LePerrier felt disgust for what he and Barbie had done, it was buried deep.

Robert's next question to his father impressed me. I'd never thought of him as smart, although the teachers at the school seemed to have a high regard for his abilities, at least before the incident with me. He asked his father, "Why did you always say that Barbie was so efficient if he never cared about answers?"

"The real goal of torture is to break someone's spirit," M. LePerrier said and turned his head away. His answer chilled Robert at the time—and me as well, later.

"It was at this point," Robert told me, "that my father seemed as though he had heard his own words for the first time."

Robert went on and asked his father, "Why didn't you ever try to stop Barbie?"

"Do you realize how naive it is to think that a mere scientist could have stopped Klaus Barbie from doing what he did?" But when M. LePerrier said that, he looked as though he realized how shallow his words sounded.

"If you were a scientist, why were you working in a prison with Barbie? Why didn't they have you doing experiments someplace?" Robert asked.

His father asked, "How do you know all those things? Suddenly, you're a student of history! I've always viewed you as a clumsy oaf."

"Why didn't you defect like Barbie if you were such a prominent scientist?"

His father's face became red, and his eyes glared. M. LePerrier's unemotional demeanor evaporated. He sat up on the couch, and his voice became clearer and louder.

"Barbie didn't defect. The United States government paid for him to escape to South America, something they refused to do for me, because I'm not a rocket scientist or a spy." Jean-Claude LePerrier pounded his two hands against the coffee table in front of the couch, almost shattering the glass. "Those Americans paid for all those other scientists to come to the United States."

His father said the United States not only paid for Barbie's escape, but also told the French government they didn't know where he was.

"Klaus called me up about six months afterward and had a good laugh. But he was plenty scared, believe me, even though he would never admit it," he said. So the reason M. LePerrier hated Americans and infected his son with his contempt was because the United States wouldn't lift a finger for him, but had protected Barbie. "Klaus gloated that I wasn't important enough for the U.S. to be interested in me. After that time, I've had a disgust for Americans," he said. He told Robert he was more valuable than an informant like Klaus Barbie and could have helped the United States discover new drugs and advanced medicine. "All the Americans care about is beating the Russians," he said.

He went into how Barbie boasted about traveling via a clandestine line, called the "ratline" and run by a Yugoslavian priest, through Genoa to South America. It allowed ex-Nazis to escape prosecution in Europe. "The United States government paid for Barbie to use it," he said.

For me, that was the most shocking part of the conversation. I had read about the federal government paying for ex-Nazis to come to the United States, but I hadn't realized we'd actually supported Klaus Barbie.

Later, M. LePerrier told Robert, "It's an odd thing, but that trial was what caused me to realize at last that I'd worked with a monster. I'd never thought twice about it, and as a result, I had become one myself."

When he finished his thousand hours of service, M. LePerrier continued to serve as a volunteer. Robert came to work for him at the pharmaceutical company, but after six months, he decided he could help people more by becoming a physician. His father encouraged Robert and told him, "Becoming a doctor is the greatest contribution you could make to people's lives, Son. I hope you will be able to undo some of the harm that I myself have done by misusing my scientific training."

At the *lycee*, I had never seen any hint that Robert had feelings. He told me that the whole episode with me was the start of his becoming a human being himself. Unfortunately, at that point, Robert stopped his story, because he had an engagement that evening. He said he would try to stay in touch with me.

* * * *

Two days after our trial ended, we drove five hours to Paris through the flat, green countryside. Now that I knew I was going home, I loved France again and enjoyed the freedom of the sunny, warm summer air. My father would be dropping off his Peugeot there and taking delivery of a new, navy blue Mercedes-Benz 220SE.

We spent two days in Paris, which was packed with sightseers in the middle of August, but not very many Parisians, because they were all away *en vacances.* Several American tourists, who must have assumed I was French by the way I was dressed, blurted questions at me, assuming I'd understand. I feigned a French accent and asked them to speak slower, but instead they spoke louder. When I didn't answer fast enough, they scowled, just as people did when I worked as a waiter at a hotel in Boston a few years later to help my aunt, who was the general manager. I knew those people I waited on made two assumptions about me: first, I was stupid, and second, I came from a low socioeconomic background.

My father brought his Peugeot to a parking garage, but the attendant refused him entry, claiming the lot was full. But when we drove around the corner, then I drove the car in and made the same request in French, he not only allowed the Peugeot, but also the Mercedes-Benz, which my father had just bought that day.

Later that afternoon, we stood on top of the Eiffel Tower. Heights scared me, so I backed away from the protective barrier.

"Everybody has something that they are afraid of. Don't worry about it," my father said, as he put his hand on my shoulder. He told me about the two times he parachuted from an airplane at ten thousand feet during World War II. He told me people sometimes broke their legs or got caught in trees. "When you land in one of those parachutes, you're going much faster than it looks," he said.

I told him about Jean Moulin parachuting on a freezing winter night to enter France after his meeting in England with de Gaulle. My father said he must have had ice in his veins. So I suggested we go to Pere Lachaise cemetery and visit Moulin's grave. Although my father didn't appear excited, we took the Métro to the burial ground.

"It is the closest I'll ever get to Jean Moulin," I said as we labored up all the stairs of the Métro station at the cemetery stop. I was beginning to realize one of the reasons there were no fat Parisians—the countless steps in the subway system.

Because there was every size and shape gravestone in the expansive cemetery, it took time to find the grave. Although Moulin's tomb was set off from the others, there were no other visitors. As I stood ten feet away from his burial place, picturing him moving through his abbreviated life, my hero seemed so close, yet so far away. My father paced around, looking at his watch. For once he was waiting for me. After we spent half an hour there, we went back to our hotel. The next day, I'd be going home.

* * * *

Orly Field looked so different to me from that cold December morning when I was thrust out of the womb of that warm airplane into this freezing and strange country that I'd learned to love—a country of bread, wine, croissants, and museums. This time people were walking around in shirtsleeves, and the sun lit up the concourses and waiting rooms. I could understand every word spoken in the lounges and could read the newspapers and signs on the walls. I had a new life full of optimism and hope.

There were young people everywhere—Americans and Europeans preparing to travel, their eyes wide with expectation as they clutched their belongings. I heard the phrase *Etats Unis* at least once a minute. But my good mood evaporated when I picked up an issue of *Paris Match* and learned Marilyn Monroe had committed suicide.

"Why would a beautiful woman like that kill herself?" I asked as I handed my father the magazine. I held the conviction that just as doctors would never become ill, famous, rich people were happier than everyone else, because they had what everyone wanted. He told me it was old news and happened a week ago.

"This is a weekly magazine," he said, as he tapped his finger on my article.

When I told him I didn't see it reported in the *Stars and Stripes*, he said it probably wasn't in the sports section, and maybe I should expand my horizons now that I was a man of the world.

"There may be more to this whole thing," my father whispered. But when I asked what he meant, he told me to forget it.

The afternoon flew by; it was time to leave. As the passengers walked out the door to board the plane, Dad kissed me on the cheek and told me he'd see me in a week.

"I hope you don't have any trouble with the new Mercedes," I said.

He told me he had to drive it to Bordeaux to put it on the ship, then fly back to Strasbourg. "You'll get to Joyce's before I get back to the cottage," he said. I felt bad he'd have to make that long drive alone and sleep in that shack by himself. But my excitement about going back overwhelmed my guilt at leaving him. I gave him a hug, and he squeezed me back. When I got onto the plane, I was able to see him from my seat. He didn't leave until the plane took off.

Unlike my flight over, this trip would take place during daylight. I sat in a window seat near the back, reading *Paris Match*. But I couldn't concentrate on the magazine, because I was too excited. When I got back to school, people would besiege me in the cafeteria, and I would tell them about my experiences in France and Germany while they stood around and listened with bated breath. The American students would be like my French classmates had been during my first week at the *lycée*.

The plane glided over the green French countryside. The stewardess must have thought I was a native, because she gave me a menu in French. I wanted her to continue to think that, so I covered up *The Tin Drum* under a napkin on my lap. Picking up the book caused me to think about the mayor, the German-British man, and how he'd influenced me. I wanted to speak foreign languages, as he did.

I was too keyed up to concentrate on anything, so I just stared out the window. The green countryside went on forever. I could see horses and cows below me. Then, abruptly, the land was gone, and we were over water. I strained to see the earth, which had disappeared without warning. These sudden changes always jolted me more than I expected. I walked to another part of the plane, but could only see water. So I returned to my seat and sat silently for fifteen minutes, then picked up the book and read for half an hour before falling asleep in the warmth of the afternoon sunlight.

HOME AGAIN

The plane glided over Boston Harbor and landed in the midst of a pelting summer rainstorm. By the time I made it through customs, it was dark. I don't even think they checked my bags; they just let me through. Aunt Joyce and my fourteen-year-old cousin, Jonathan, were waiting outside. She looked a little older; there were a few more lines on her forehead. I wondered if she'd been fighting with Mitty.

"You look wonderful! Wow, I can't believe how much you've grown!" she said as she kissed me hard on the cheek. What was it with relatives' obsession with height? She pulled out her handkerchief and wiped the lipstick off me.

"Did you have a good time?" Jonathan asked.

"It was amazing," I said. It was a good way of putting a positive light on the trip without having to go into too many explanations with my family.

We drove through the same Callahan Tunnel we had navigated in the predawn cold in December. However, in this direction it was named the Sumner Tunnel. How often I'd pictured this moment during my initial weeks in France. I stared at the dirty, streaked walls of the passageway, which had been so brightly illuminated when I left for France. We were through before I knew it and into the north end of Boston. I wondered how many people went back and forth through this tunnel every day without giving it a thought, other than scowling over the toll.

Each bridge along the Charles was a little different. Why hadn't I noticed that before? Joyce blurted out how well Jonathan did in summer camp. "They're asking him back next year as a junior counselor," she said.

I looked over at Jonathan's kind, simple face and felt a lot older all of a sudden. I patted him on the shoulder and said, "Way to go."

She told me she and her husband had a great summer and just got back from the Hamptons. "Would you like to go back there for Labor Day?" she asked me. I told her I would if it was OK with my father.

Then I looked at the green Fenway as we moved away from the Charles. It was a pleasure just to recognize this large road with grass on both sides, which I knew led to the Museum of Fine Arts and the Gardner Museum.

We arrived at Sal's, an Italian restaurant not far from my house on Route 9, the main highway west of Boston, where three of my friends had taken me for a farewell lunch before my departure. Pizza was one of the things I'd dreamed about in France; it had been my only disappointment in Italy. The pizza over there was so much blander and less crispy than our pizza in America. Ours was so much better that it made me wonder if Italian Americans invented it.

One of my classmates was sitting at a table with several people I didn't know. The second he saw me, he bounded over to our table. He seemed excited to see me, even though we didn't know each other very well.

"Roy, how are you? I heard you were coming home soon," he said. He told me he loved the article I wrote in the *Gazette* about Berlin. "Those photographs were great. Everyone was talking about it," he said. The other boys came over and asked about my year. The waiter was standing behind them for five minutes until Jonathan complained he was hungry, so they went back to their table.

The next morning, I woke up at eleven in the large guest bedroom on the second floor of my aunt's house. It took me five minutes to realize where I was. But I just lay back and luxuriated in the big room, safe within the boundaries of the United States. The room was all mine, and the house was silent. No Germans or Russians could get me. I felt free, with the whole day in front of me to do whatever I wanted.

I went to the window and stared at the trees and watched the cars speeding by on Commonwealth Avenue. I turned on the television and watched a soap opera for fifteen minutes. Then I put on my cousin's bathrobe and wandered down the spiral staircase into the kitchen.

The morning's newspaper ran a story about Marilyn Monroe's death, even though it was old news.

"I wonder if there was foul play," said Joyce, as we sat in the spacious kitchen around the breakfast table.

Mitty sighed. "Why do you always think the worst?"

Joyce picked up the paper again. "She wasn't a very good actress," she said bitterly.

"Maybe you're envious, because she didn't have to be a good actress," he said, as he strode across the kitchen to take the garbage out.

"I'm not envious of someone who dies of a drug overdose," Joyce said, as she slammed down the newspaper and stomped out of the room.

"She was a good actress," I said. I told them we saw *The Misfits* at the base theater just a week ago, and I thought Marilyn was great, but Joyce wasn't listening and Mitty was outside.

I sat at the coffee table and picked the newspaper off the floor. It thundered outside as Jon grabbed the front page out of my hand and started reading about the fallen movie star. I called the high school and was told my guidance counselor wouldn't be back until after Labor Day. I'd have to wait until school started to discuss college applications.

The next week, we drove to the airport to pick up my father. It was raining again as we drove to my house. The water was dripping from the gutters onto the front yard. A lightning bolt cast the street into an eerie sheen.

I'd never seen our floors so polished and the rugs so freshly vacuumed. As I walked from room to room, my house was like a mansion. I felt rich as I lay down on one of the two beds in my room, kicked off my shoes, and pulled my beret over my face. After five minutes, I took it off and stared at the high ceiling and lush lawns across the street through my drenched window.

I felt kind of restless, so I sat at the large mahogany piano in my room and played "Heart and Soul" three times, then went down to the back porch and listened to the summer rain pelting the roof. I watched the waving of leaves and branches of the trees in the warm, humid wind.

I decided to call up Julie. She told me she was thrilled to hear from me, but would only be available the next day, because she'd be leaving for college. She gave me directions as though she expected me to drive to her house. Fortunately she lived within walking distance, as I wasn't about to ask my dad or even a friend for a ride.

Although it was late August, the weather was cool. I was going to wear my beret, but thought better of it; maybe it was too much. So I wore a blue and red jersey that I bought in Paris on the Champs-Elysées, along with blue jeans and my brown, zippered shoes from Chausettes Michel, which I had to clean with a brush. I never used to think about what I wore, as long as it fit and was clean. I wasn't really a slob, just clueless.

Julie was wearing shorts and a white blouse. She appeared as beautiful as I remembered her. She came running out her front door, kissed me on the cheek, and escorted me into her two-story, wooden, Cape Cod house. Their sprinklers watered the grass and flowers on their perfectly landscaped front yard. The kiss on the cheek should have been a tip-off as to how she viewed me, but as I said, I was inexperienced.

Her mom was standing in the electrical kitchen when we came in. For the last seven months, I'd been living in a country where the kitchens were different. In Alsace, our kitchen had a refrigerator and an electrical light switch. Here in the United States, Julie's kitchen was much more endowed than our own. She was so lucky to have a mom in her kitchen as well. Julie's mom was an older version of Julie, but her face was saddened by time. I refused the offer of a drink, although I was thirsty. I wouldn't have used their bathroom either, no matter how badly I had to go. I just was uncomfortable using other people's bathrooms, because I was afraid the toilet wouldn't work, or I'd break it or something.

Her mom asked me where I was going to college. I told her I was going to start my senior year in high school, if they'd promote me. I didn't mean for it to come out that way, but didn't know how much credit I would receive for the past year.

"I have to get back to my travel preparations," Julie's mom said as she wished me good luck and looked as though she were trying to figure out what the hell I was doing there. Maybe she was used to seeing college guys coming over to see Julie.

Julie brought me down into their basement and told me she'd just gotten back from Israel and would've liked to spend more time there. She asked if I'd enjoyed the French school.

"It was a great experience," I said. It was a good way of letting people know they could ask more if they wanted, but absolved them if they didn't. I figured she would want to know more than Jonathan, but I was wrong. She pulled out her yearbook, and we studied it for twenty minutes until the phone rang, and her mother called out to her. Although there was an extension in the basement, Julie took the call upstairs.

After about five minutes, I stood up and looked at her record collection. She had the Beach Boys and Elvis Presley, and also jazz albums like Count Basie, Duke Ellington, and Miles Davis. After I perused them all, I walked to the bottom of the stairs and could hear her laughing. She was in no hurry to get off and come back down. I was about to leave when she finally returned.

She said she was sorry, but said the call had to do with college. But I told her I wanted to leave. It wasn't so much that I was angry or disappointed, but it was the beginning of my being able to see reality—something that had previously evaded me. I could feel a part of me protesting about how she was ignoring me. Even though I knew she had a right to make whoever was on that telephone upstairs more important than I, part of me rebelled. Although it was a part of my mind that I hadn't heard much from, I sensed it was my friend, an ally making its way closer to the surface.

"I'm sorry," she said and looked as if she meant it.

It was the first time I'd seen Julie upset, but thanks to Cheryl, I had experience with girls being distressed and knew it wasn't the end of the world. I told her not to worry—my dad just wanted me to go down to Cape Cod with him later that day...which was almost the truth.

I gave her a hug as I opened the front door and wished her a good year at college.

"Please don't be angry," she yelled again. I turned around slowly. I studied her pretty features for a moment and shook my head. "I'm not. I just have other stuff to do," I said.

I walked home feeling disappointment...and something else, something new. I lay down on my bed, staring at the ceiling, but after an hour, I sprung up from the bed like a phoenix and found Dad in the living room. I told him I wanted to buy some record albums.

He jumped up out of his chair and put the Maimonides book on the ottoman. "Let's go," he said. He startled me, because he usually made me wait at least two days before responding to my requests.

We drove to Newton Centre and arrived just as the owner was about to close the record store. He asked us to come tomorrow, but my dad told him we were going away and would make it worth his while if he would keep the place open a few more minutes. I bought two Beach Boys albums, two by Elvis Presley, and one by the Four Seasons. "We should get a new phonograph as long as we're here," my father said. I spent the evening listening to my records and dancing around my room.

The next day, we went down the Cape for Labor Day. We stayed at the same hotel we had visited with my mom every summer when I was little. We walked the half mile to the beach and listened to the Red Sox. But Mom wasn't with us, and it made the experience bittersweet, which was probably why we'd never gone back there since she died. The frustration of not being able to bring her back weighed on my shoulders, but only to a point. Normally we'd have sat staring at the ocean like two robots, but we laughed and talked about France and cheered for the Sox. When we got home at the end of the weekend, school was ready to begin.

* * * *

I paused when I reached the school grounds, because I felt so excited to see the wide, green fields and the modern buildings connected by a system of walkways. My homeroom teacher asked if I'd had a nice time in France. "I enjoyed your article in the newspaper about Berlin last year," she said. I wondered how many people had read it until almost every student in the class stopped at my desk and welcomed me.

After school the cross-country team did a two-and-a-half-mile practice run on the campus of a nearby junior college. Although I was in my usual position after the first lap, I passed seven teammates on the second lap and ended the run in second place, only ten yards behind the first man.

The head of the foreign language department met with me to decide if I could be in the French honors class. I thought they'd be thrilled to have me there after all my experiences from the previous year, but I was in for a surprise. During a five-minute interview, the man tried to trick me with confusing phrases and obscure words. He asked nothing about my year abroad and warned me the class was an all-star team comprised of National Honors students. He was French himself and sounded like the *proviseur* or *censeur*. "If you can't cut it, we'll ship you back to Curriculum I," he warned me. Just as my father had tried to reassure the *proviseur*, I told him I'd make it.

The second day, I had to meet with my guidance counselor during lunch. Based upon his recommendations, I wrote to eight colleges for applications, which I filled out a week later, the day they arrived. I asked Dad for checks to enclose with the forms.

"Why are you applying to such mediocre schools?" he asked as he signed the checks with his blue fountain pen.

I told him I had mainly Cs from my sophomore year and no record from last year. "My guidance counselor told me to apply only to safety schools," I said.

My father insisted I could do better. "You're not the same student as in your sophomore year," he said, as he leaned against the refrigerator. "Those Cs were because you didn't believe in yourself even though you said it was just bad luck," he said.

During my next meeting with the guidance counselor, I mentioned my father's encouragement, but he still thought I should stick to security schools.

"However, your development augurs well for your performance in college," he said, as he gave me a gentle pat on the back.

I was in the cafeteria during lunchtime during my second week of school. I went to exit through the back door to go for my daily walk on the grounds. I felt exhilarated to go for a stroll on the expansive green grass and think about my future, which would never have occurred to me the past year. As I approached the door, I saw a boy commanding David Haskins to pick napkins up off the floor.

I'd known David since seventh grade. There was something wrong with him—actually, a few things—but I wouldn't have been able to put a name on it back then. He probably had cerebral palsy, and while he did well in school, he couldn't speak correctly and had some type of problem with his affect. We all liked him and accepted him. But here was this guy, treating David as though he didn't understand him.

It was very loud in the room, and the place we were standing was near the place students dropped off their trays, which made crashing noises every two seconds as they banged against the trash conveyor. I looked at this bullying boy, whom I'd seen before but not often, and he glared at me, as though I'd insulted his mother. I told him David didn't mean any harm and was just a little different. He said something back to me, but the noise was so loud I couldn't hear, so I asked him to repeat it. He said something else, but I couldn't hear that any better than the first thing he said, so I asked him to repeat himself again.

The boy then said, "If you say that again, I will beat your head in."

This time, despite the racket, I heard him and looked him in the eyes. He was a little bigger than I and had a masked look to his face. I could see he wasn't afraid of me, but that was probably why he made that comment in the first place.

"Don't talk to me like that," I said. I didn't yell it, but I didn't whisper or stutter either. I used my eyes like beams and stared back at him. I must have known that anyone who would pick on Haskins couldn't be that tough, and his expression had to be a facade.

The boy strode up to me, his fists clenched. His eyes were as cold as a wolf's. His sleeves were rolled up, and he had a haircut that was swirled back on the sides and probably came together in the back, like the feathers of a duck. He didn't hesitate to try to grab me by the collar. But my right arm, which had been working for months with Dan Connolly and with Nicky the boxer, had a mind of its own. I've heard people say that it was their fingers that did something, not them, and others have argued in response that those people are making a nonsensical, irresponsible statement. But I could no more have stopped the trajectory of that right cross than I could have stopped a Mack truck. Nicky had always told me it was my worst punch, that I should only use it as a last resort, and that my left jab was so much quicker and dependable and more damaging.

Nonetheless that punch landed almost before I threw it. It settled in the boy's left cheekbone. His hands were not even up to protect himself. It felt like the time I hit a ball over the left fielder's head in the Babe Ruth League, even though I had just tried to meet the ball. The ball never went that far when I tried to hit it as far as I could.

The boy fell backward against a large wooden table, which sagged and knocked over three empty chairs, but he didn't fall. One of the chairs banged into a girl who was sitting at another table, talking to her friends and she screamed. A few milk cartons spilled onto the floor. The noise of the furniture crashing was deafening and resulted in a stampede of students. I could see everything unfolding as though it were in slow motion.

The impact of the boy against the table caused a switchblade to fall from his pocket. Before he realized what had happened, one of the football players picked it up and closed it, but made no attempt to break up the fight. The boy's look of coldness was replaced with one of surprise and bewilderment, but his confusion didn't stop him from rushing at me. At this point, my memory of boxing strategy failed. Nicky and I had worked a lot on the heavy bag, but there hadn't been anyone for me to spar with, and I had little experience in defending myself. I must have used my left jab, which Dan had told me was my fastest punch by far.

By now a hundred students were screaming in the corner of the cafeteria. I heard my name more times in one minute than in the twelve previous years I'd been going to school. I, who had lamented that no one noticed me, realized again that attention wasn't such a great thing. Suddenly I felt myself being dragged from behind by someone much stronger.

A young teacher with a crew cut and a plaid sports jacket ripped my French shirt, the one I'd bought on the Champs-Elysées. He glared at me with more hatred than the boy who'd fought with me. I, who had hit this boy because he wasn't giving me respect, was getting even less from this teacher. He pulled me outside and slammed me against the glass wall of the cafeteria, as if I were a criminal who'd been apprehended after an exhausting chase. He could have learned a lot from Dan Connolly about how to break up a fight. My back burned, and an electric shock ran down my right leg. For the first time, I realized my right hand was throbbing.

I think if he had handcuffs, he wouldn't have hesitated to apply them. He held me against the wall by pressing his hand against my chest, and I was beginning to feel like Jean Valjean, the character from *Les Misérables* who was sentenced to twenty years in prison for stealing a loaf of bread. Then an older man appeared and said he'd take over. I felt relieved, since anybody would be better than this vigilante.

"What's the story, son?" the new man asked me. He folded his hands in front of his chest as the younger teacher went inside the cafeteria. Before I could answer, he scratched his head and asked if we knew each other. I realized he was Coach Prescott, who drove me to my doctor's office when I had my bad nosebleed last year. I reminded him of the incident.

"It looks like you've got another one, but this one isn't as bad," he said as he dabbed my nose with Kleenex. I put my finger on my nose and discovered blood.

He told me I was the last guy he would have expected to find in this situation, adding that someone could have killed me or I could have been expelled. He leaned his left hand against the glass wall of the cafeteria. He didn't seem angry, which was a nice change from his predecessor, who could have been a Marine drill sergeant.

After a minute I blurted, "You're supposed to stand up to tyrants. Otherwise they'll take away your freedom." He grinned and asked me who had given me that advice.

"Someone who did it," I said.

Coach Prescott told me there were other ways of standing up for myself. "I'm sure your friend picked his tyrants more carefully than you," he said. He told me it was my good luck that he happened to be supervising the cafeteria that day, something he did only once every three weeks.

I often wondered later whether that fight was a good thing for me or not. The coach had asked if I wanted to throw all my hard work away, but none of it would have meant much if I couldn't stand up for myself. I told Coach Prescott I'd be able to walk away next time, and he asked me what the difference would be then.

"Now I'm sick of it," I said, quoting Dan Connolly.

Three days after the fight, David Haskins came to my homeroom with a box of freshly baked brownies, which I shared with my classmates. Some of my classmates were acting as though they were in awe of me, holding open the door, getting a chair for me, asking me if I needed anything. But several girls looked at me after that day as though they wanted nothing to do with me. All I wanted was to blend back into the anonymity I had bemoaned before leaving for France. It wasn't totally possible; it was hard for people to forget violent experiences. I also never understood afterward why the boy I'd fought with never seemed unfriendly when we'd cross paths in the corridors.

That evening, even before my father had a chance to read his mail, he noticed the gauze in my nose and asked what happened. When I explained, he looked relieved and said he was wondering what I was doing with all my anger about Robert LePerrier. I felt thankful, as I'd expected a version of the luncheonette threat.

The first few weeks in honors French, the teacher called on everyone but me. I thought he was avoiding me, but during the third week, one of the students read, "*la voiture utilize gas-oil*," from an article in *Paris Match* that the teacher had brought in.

"*Qu'est-ce que ca veut dire, gas-oil?*" the teacher asked in his Parisian French. I had learned he'd been a member of the resistance during the war.

"I don't know what *gas-oil* is," the student answered in perfect, but heavily accented, French.

"*Est-ce qu'il y a quelqu'un qui sait la reponse?*" the teacher asked as he surveyed the class.

When everyone was silent, I answered that *gas-oil* was diesel oil. I'd seen it advertised in every gas station in France. Nobody said a word, but from my seat in the second row, I could feel my classmates' eyes burning into my neck. The teacher didn't look at me, but muttered a two-syllable "*Oui*" under his breath. The next day, he told us to open our book of short stories by Guy de Maupassant.

"*Est-ce que vous pouvez lire pour nous aujourd' hui M. Harrison?*" he asked. I felt I was back in the *lycée*, as he pronounced my last name just as everyone had the previous year. I read the portion of a short story about a young man walking along the Seine smoking a cigar, feeling exhilarated with the beauty of the spring afternoon. Unfortunately he suddenly developed a cold and retreated to his bed in depression. Jules Falkstein had read that very passage in our French literature class, and I tried to duplicate his accent. After I finished, the class was silent. The teacher moved on to another subject. But now I was a player on a team; it was one of the feelings I'd been searching for.

Toward the middle of September, I received a large envelope from Harvard University. I asked my dad if he'd sent for it. He glanced at his mail while sipping coffee and didn't answer directly. "I think you should give Harvard a crack," he said without looking over at me.

I couldn't believe how deluded he was. I told him I had a cumulative C+ average, and that only National Honor Society members applied to Harvard. I continued to mechanically place dishes into the dishwasher, stunned by his grandiosity. But he just smiled, took a deep gulp of his coffee, and walked to the window, staring into the twilight.

He finally said those honors students hadn't spent their junior year in a French *lycée*, didn't speak French, and didn't know what I did about the crisis in Germany. I told him other students had their own unusual experiences, which were equally impressive as mine.

"I haven't earned Harvard," I said.

My father sat down at the kitchen table. He said, "Who says?" and told me I had become an A student, and that was what I would be in college. "If I thought a safety school was the best you could do, I wouldn't encourage you to venture in over your head," he said.

But from where did he get that I was an A student? It was only four weeks into the year. He claimed to have seen the grades on a few of my tests on the kitchen counter. Somehow he knew I'd changed, but he never told me how. Maybe somehow he sensed that I no longer felt like a victim who would be receiving Cs from teachers who sought to limit my future options.

Even though I was convinced he was deceiving himself about Harvard, part of me wanted to believe he was right, as he'd been about so many other things. So I struggled with the complicated application and planned to take it to the mailbox in the morning. But at dawn, it was nowhere to be found, and I nearly went into a panic until I discovered my father's note saying he would mail it. He must have had radar for that thing, since he never turned on my light.

"How is Marcel feeling today?" the football coach said as he viewed Mickey and me in the locker room, as we prepared to go out for cross-country practice.

We both turned around, looking for whomever he was addressing, but it was me. He sometimes called me Marcel after that. Maybe he thought I would know about Marcel Cerdan from my year in France, but no one had talked about him or his girlfriend, Edith Piaf, despite my efforts to repeatedly bring up her name. I didn't really learn about the French boxer until I saw the movie *Raging Bull* years later. Thankfully the name never caught on. I would not have wanted to have to try to live up to a name like that. I didn't have the skills or the inclination.

About thirty seconds later, Mickey and I walked to the swinging door and waited to push it. Before we had the chance, it swung open, and two huge football players in shoulder pads, helmets, and cleats prepared to enter. We stood to the side as usual, but instead of marching through, the players stepped back. "After you," one of them said. He didn't smile, but there was something positive in his eyes.

"Respect is the most positive of feelings between two people," my father said when I told him about the incident. He told me I'd only get esteem from others if I appeared to have it already.

After dinner Dad complemented me on my roast beef and asparagus. I had steamed them longer than usual. I told him Babe Ruth loved asparagus just to throw him a little off balance. But my father was interested in Babe and asked me how I knew that.

"I read it in a book," I said, adding that he said his only problem with asparagus was it odorized his urine.

"Babe Ruth would have said it made his piss stink," my father said. I wondered for a split second if my father might have actually met Babe Ruth, but it was impossible. We both laughed for a minute, then he leaned back in his chair, put his arms over his head, and stretched. He told me he was in the midst of a tough trial and was going to turn in early. Before he left to go up the stairs, he told me that Willy Brandt would be in Cambridge next week to present two lectures at Harvard. "He's invited us to come hear him speak," he said.

"I'd love to go to the lecture," I said, not realizing how pivotal a decision I'd made.

* * * *

It was a warm October evening, and the leaves had turned red and orange. It was still light when my dad and I arrived in Cambridge. My father said I should be hearing from Harvard soon about an interview.

I didn't know why he was persisting in his fantasy. Maybe because he had had to go to night school, he wanted me to satisfy his dreams of getting into a top school. But it was enough for me to fulfill my own ambitions. Fortunately I was finished with the tedious application. The writing sample had been a particular pain.

A lengthy queue of students and adults awaited us as we crossed the campus and approached the amphitheater where the mayor would speak. I asked my dad if the adults were Harvard faculty and he answered that people from the community would also be interested in this lecture. There wasn't space for everyone to be admitted, but my father walked to the head of the line and showed a piece of paper to the man collecting tickets, and we were ushered to two seats near the front of the hall. By ten minutes before the lecture, the room was full, and people straddled the back of the room and sat on the floor, covering the sidewalls.

I remember thinking what a compliment it was to attract a standing-room audience, and I could tell my father was excited about seeing the mayor. "Everyone wants to know about the Berlin wall," he said. Maybe that was true of his friends, but in the months since I'd returned, not one person had asked me about Europe, not even my teachers. But there was no arguing that the mayor had become a famous man because of the crisis.

The president of Harvard introduced Mayor Brandt and mentioned this was the second of a series of two talks. They were called the Gustav Pollak lectures, and the title was "the ordeal of coexistence." The mayor appeared exactly as he had on March 31, the anniversary of his escape from Germany in 1933. He stood up and scanned the room, then gave his presentation.

He spoke in perfect English for forty-five minutes. I understood a lot of what he said, because to me it was pictures, not a bunch of concepts. As he spoke, I visualized the evening in Alsace when we first met. It was the same day Cheryl became sick, and I had decided I wanted to be a physician after looking at the competence and concern on Dr Ksarjian's face. I felt the intensity of the bright light in the room and all the people staring at the speaker.

After the presentation, twenty people lined up to ask questions, some of whom wanted autographs, while two or three security people stood nearby. Had it been the nineties instead of the sixties, there would probably be triple that amount and several police officers. When the mayor finished with the line, he walked over to shake our hands enthusiastically. The next day, he would be on his way to Washington to meet with President Kennedy. He introduced us to the president of Harvard. Some people were looking at us, probably wondering whom we knew, but we didn't know anybody except the speaker.

About three weeks after the talk, the issue of missiles and Cuba was splattered across the front pages of the newspapers. My father said, "This time, I'm glad my unit won't be reactivated. Let someone else get into a war with Russia over the missiles. No doubt Mayor Brandt has heard from President Kennedy about what may be in store for Berlin if we attack Cuba. He told me for the first time that JFK was a very courageous guy.

I no longer needed to ask him what the connection was between Cuba and Berlin. I read the *Boston Globe* every day and focused on anything to do with Germany, Berlin, and Communism. I read about the Cuban missile crisis, but none of my classmates ever discussed it.

* * * *

Three days after the lecture at Harvard, I was sitting in a cove in one of the walls near the cafeteria, looking over the summer school catalog. I knew I'd have to take chemistry there to be prepared for a premedical curriculum in college. I'd been hoping to take it last summer, but our trial had taken care of that.

It was the same cove where the three girls had spoken with me almost a year ago. When I looked up from the catalog, a girl with dirty-blond hair and hazel eyes was standing in front of me. She must have been waiting for me to pause from my reading.

She was holding books in front of her chest. Her name was Sarah Fox; I knew it from a class we had together sophomore year. She had a perfectly straight nose and the most beautiful mouth I'd ever seen. Why hadn't I thought about her before? She was wearing a white blouse and a navy blue skirt with matching dark blue stockings that came up to her knees.

"I saw you the other night at the lecture in the Sanders Theatre," she said. She didn't address me by my name. I asked her what she was doing there.

She said she went with her parents. "I saw you with your father," she said. I got nervous and almost made a joke. I was going to say he was my older brother. I would've actually said it the past year, when I wouldn't have been so aware of how idiotic it sounded.

Then she smiled for the first time. "It seems as though you know the mayor personally," she said.

I told her I'd met him three times. She told me her father belonged to the Harvard alumni club. "My parents have a season ticket for those lectures," she said. At this point, she sat down on the ledge near me and placed her pile of books between us, running her hand through her hair. I couldn't believe that she did that; it seemed like such an intimate gesture. No girl from the high school had ever done anything like that with me before, and I worried that my fear would show.

Her cheeks flushed a little. I could feel my heart speed up and felt nervous, as I had with Cheryl.

Sarah and I had passed in the hallways many times, and I'd never given her a conscious thought. While she was nice-looking and very cool, none of the other guys mentioned her either. We spent forty minutes sitting there and talking, and I started to simultaneously calm down and get more excited. If I'd never gone to

France, I'd never have had the slightest interest in that lecture. My father was right about opportunities not always coming in wrapping paper.

She must have perceived me in a different light after seeing me in Cambridge, and because she looked at me differently, it changed how I viewed her. The transformation took a second. If I hadn't gone to Cambridge to see the mayor, we never would have registered on each other's radar screens and would have walked past each other for another year.

A week later, Mickey and I were sitting on the same wall where I'd announced my move to Europe a year ago. Sarah pulled up in front of us in a green 1959 Bonneville convertible. She was wearing a white sweater, and her hair was tied up in a ponytail. She offered us a ride.

When she leaned over and opened the car door, Mickey said he was busy and walked away, but I hopped in. She was wearing the same dark skirt with navy blue socks that came up to her knees. Her skirt rested at midthigh as she drove the car. I tried not to stare at her legs, but it was an exercise in futility. She accelerated, and I loosened my collar a little, surprised at how fast she drove. She asked me if I wanted to go to an ice cream parlor.

"Is Bowman's OK?" she asked before I had the chance to answer her first question. I said it was fine.

We both ordered sundaes, and she grabbed the check, saying it was her treat, since she invited me. But I refused and plunked down a dollar for the sundaes and thirty cents for the waiter. I thought I was being a man.

After we ate the ice cream, she asked if I'd like to play golf.

I took the opportunity to look intently at her. "You mean you golf?" I asked. I couldn't imagine ever becoming interested in that game, which I didn't even consider a sport. It was something businessmen did so they could make money. At least that's what my father said.

"I go every weekend," she said, looking at me with those unwavering hazel eyes. She played at Wright's Course, where we ran our cross-country home meets. I didn't know the difference in those days between a public course like Wright's and private ones or country clubs, and what all that meant to golfers.

That night I didn't go to bed until one, because I couldn't stop thinking about Sarah, and I woke up at six. My father and I were downstairs in the morning together for the first time I could remember. He picked up on my mood swing and asked if I'd met a girl or something.

The first time Sarah and I played golf, I brought my uncle's clubs, because my father didn't own any. Mitty tried to give me pointers, but he raced through his explanations, and I remembered nothing. When I went to tee off with a putter,

Sarah pulled the driver out of my bag. I don't remember what she said, but we ended up on the driving range, where she showed me how to hold the club. It was embarrassing and distracting to learn from a girl.

She had on no makeup and wore an engineer's cap, with her hair tucked under. She smelled like distant flowers. The pleasant expression on her face wasn't a smile; it was something else, something more, and something real. She looked like someone who had a plan and was following it. I didn't feel as if I were in outer space, as I had with Cheryl. I just felt safe, as if I wouldn't be alone anymore. Before she dropped me off, I asked if she wanted to go to a movie Saturday night, but she invited me to dinner at her house. It was just as well, since I didn't have my driver's license and would have had to ask my father to chaperone us.

I got up early on Saturday, since there was no getting back to sleep, and watched cartoons, as I had when I was a little boy. I remembered envying my friends who told me that whenever they got up on Saturday, their younger brother or sister was up before them, watching cartoons. I always felt cheated being an only child.

The day crept as though the hands of the clock were glued together. I finally went for a long run, which calmed me down. We drove to Sarah's around five in my father's Mercedes, which he'd picked up the previous day at the docks in East Boston.

Her family lived in a colonial, three-story house in a leafy neighborhood of similar houses with manicured lawns. "This is a Boston high society neighborhood," my father remarked. He started talking about Boston Brahmins as we pulled up to her house. I'd heard the word in connection with tennis clubs we weren't allowed in, but didn't ask what it meant.

The house stood atop a hill like a fortress, with a view of the reservoir. My father wondered why Sarah went to my school, because her home seemed too far away for her to be a student there. "She must have some special permit or something," he said.

"Do you want to come in?" I asked. I immediately regretted it, but fortunately he refused.

"This is your show," he said. It was his new strategy regarding me. As tough and controlling as my father was with all the things he forced me to do, now he seemed to know when to let go. He'd grown up a lot in the past year. The exception was his Harvard obsession, but nobody was perfect; I too held out hopes, although I'd never tell him. He waited in the navy 220SE sedan as I climbed the never-ending stairs and rang the bell. I paced the wide brick terrace and took in the reservoir, which shimmered in the late afternoon, as my shortness of breath dissipated.

I was about to ring a second time when Sarah opened the door. She was wearing a pale blue shirt and khaki pants with a kerchief over her neck. She wore only a slight touch of lipstick. As soon as I saw her, my anxiety evaporated, despite the magnificence of her family's property. She introduced me to her parents in the sprawling living room, which looked out on the reservoir and displayed about ten pictures that could have been in the Boston Museum of Fine Arts.

Her brother, a sophomore at Dartmouth, was away, but I met her younger sister, who attended private school, and who didn't hesitate to tell me that all their neighbors did too.

Sarah's father offered me a Coke. I was glad I'd started shining my shoes in France, something I never did before, as his glance took in my feet. I wonder if he checked me for a manicure, although I would've thought he was checking out my watch if he looked at my hands. "How does your dad like that Mercedes?" he asked.

I told him he'd only had it for a day; I didn't mention that it jerked switching gears. Our Ford gave a much smoother ride. Mr. Fox brushed some dust off his white slacks and asked if my father was a career military man.

"He's an attorney with Schuster and Shatten," I answered and threw my shoulders back.

"I know Dale Shatten," he said as he unbuttoned his red cashmere cardigan. He was about my father's height, but must have weighed fifteen pounds less and looked about ten years younger. He had on the same kind of shoes the golfers wore up at Wright's.

He asked how we knew the mayor. "He's a real hero of mine," he said.

I explained how I'd met him and said I'd been to his house.

"So you went to the mayor's official mansion?" Mr. Fox interrupted, appearing impressed for the first time.

I told him the mayor didn't live in a mansion, but in a two-story duplex in a modest neighborhood. "There's a beautiful lake right behind his house," I said. I didn't usually use the word "modest," but my father had emphasized it after our visit, and it had stuck. I wanted to tell Mr. Fox he had a much nicer place than the mayor, but didn't. Fortunately obsequiousness wasn't one of my character defects. Some things were always OK with me.

"What part of Berlin does he live in?" Mr. Fox asked.

"It's called Am Schlachtensee," I said.

He told me he was stationed there during the Berlin airlift. "Do you know about that?" he tested me, as he looked over at his wife who'd just entered the room.

"June of 1948 to May of 1949," I answered. The mayor had explained the airlift the afternoon I'd been at his home. It was one of the things I remembered from that crazy day, when I'd feared being ensnared behind the iron curtain. The mayor had told me that years from now, people would confuse the Berlin airlift with the Berlin crisis, which was what they were going through now. The airlift involved flying food and supplies into West Berlin, where the Soviets had blocked all surface traffic, whereas the crisis concerned the cold war tensions in East Berlin and the building of the wall. Both times it was the United States to the rescue—the first time with airplanes, the second with troops, including my father.

Mr. Fox turned on the living room lamp, even though it was still high noon outside. What an odd thing to do. I remember wondering if he was having vision problems.

He asked my opinion about the mayor's suggestion of risking a peaceful coexistence with the Soviet Union.

I fished for some recollection. When I couldn't come up with anything, he said, "Don't worry about it. The mayor was just testing the waters."

Sarah's mother called us to dinner in the oversized, eighteenth-century dining room.

"Where do you live?" She smiled as she looked intently at me. She looked as if she could have been in a fashion magazine, with every blond hair in place and a perfectly fitting beige pantsuit.

I gave her a general description, but she wanted my precise street address. She looked serious as she asked about my plans for college, career, and other future endeavors.

I told them I'd switched from journalism to medicine as I tasted the fresh-fruit cocktail. Then Sarah said her first words all evening: she said she wanted to be an editor for a magazine.

"Sarah has written several articles for the *Newton Voice*," her mother said. I could tell Ms. Fox was proud even before she placed the scrapbook containing ten articles in my hands and moved the fruit plate I was enjoying so much out of my reach.

Sarah's writing was laced with humor and dealt with politics, opera, and golf. She seemed to have nicknames of her own for certain people and places, but hers poked fun, compared to mine, which were more affectionate. One of her articles was a satire about her dad's country club.

"Would you like to go with me sometime to the club?" her father asked me. He said Sarah wouldn't come. While I was relieved and flattered that maybe he liked me a little, I wondered out loud why Sarah didn't go.

He seemed to feel he was her spokesperson. "She doesn't like the people there, as her article suggests," he said, as he raised his nose. Sarah just stared at her dad.

After dinner she asked if I wanted to go to the movies. Her dad jammed his hand into his shirt pocket and pulled out his keys before I could answer.

Three days later, I saw her in the school corridor and invited her over to dinner Friday night, since I wanted her to meet my father. She asked if I'd want help cooking, but I told her just to show up.

But she surprised me by arriving half an hour early with a chocolate cake she must have picked up in a bakery. She put on one of my mother's aprons she found in the pantry closet. I walked into the living room and stared at my mother's picture. She would have something to say about all this, but she just looked still on the wall. While I was relieved my time alone was coming to an end, the picture exerted a pull. I had to pry myself away to return to the kitchen, and when I walked back into the room, Sarah had removed the apron.

I warned Sarah about my father not communicating before his drinks, but he walked into the kitchen and greeted her, chatting for at least fifteen minutes. We sat over dinner for an hour and a half rather than our usual fifteen minutes as my father and Sarah disagreed about Eleanor Roosevelt, who had died of some blood disease in the past few days.

The next morning, my father told me I'd picked a winner. He certainly hadn't said that with Cheryl or Julie, although he didn't know either of them. "Sometimes it's hard even finding the wrong person," he said. He told me one of his clients gave him two opera tickets, and Sarah had said she liked opera. "Why don't you use them?" he said.

My father was generous with his Mercedes once I harpooned the elusive driver's license. His only question now was whether I was having a good time. It was what would have been important to my mother.

The night of the opera, the weather had turned cold, and I wore my overcoat over the suit I'd only worn for the trial. I drove to Sarah's to pick her up, thinking about how much my life had changed. First it was golf, now opera…interests I never thought I would pursue in a million years. Opera was for old people from Europe who liked to eat borscht, which I found revolting.

Ms. Fox answered the door dressed in an expensive red business suit. I guess she must have had a job, something unusual for women in those days, especially for people with the kind of money they had. Sarah wore a fancy, dark blue dress. The two of them looked like sisters; I hadn't appreciated how beautiful her mother was.

I felt grown up driving the car to downtown Boston at night, getting a ticket, and parking it in the underground garage. Three dollars seemed a lot to have to pay for parking, but my father had given me ten.

The opera was *Aida*, and it was boring. But there wasn't an empty seat in the auditorium, even though it was the middle of the week. At the end, Sarah stood up like everyone else and applauded for ten minutes, although I couldn't understand why. It was only because I wanted to be with her so much that I agreed to a second opera a few weeks later. But as I watched *La Bohème*, tears ran down my face as the heroine died of tuberculosis. Then I was hooked.

When Sarah got dressed up, she looked five years older. Men of all ages stared at her, not only when we walked in, but during intermission. She downplayed herself at school, and I wondered why but was grateful at the same time. I asked myself at least five times during the evening if this was all a dream. It never occurred to me that she could break up with me, as I always worried about Cheryl.

I walked her up to her door, and she turned around to say good night. I went to kiss her for the first time, and she put both arms around my neck and kissed me on the mouth. The next week, she came over to my house after school and suggested that we get onto my bed and make out; there were no games as there had been with Cheryl. Then we spent the rest of the afternoon listening to music. I didn't ask where she'd got her experience for a long time.

One weekend we explored the north end of Boston, while on another we were out in the Berkshires. On the way back, I said I would never have gone to that lecture in Cambridge if I hadn't spent the year in France.

"My parents forced me to go," Sarah said. "I really had no interest in Berlin until I met you."

"Do you think we would have found each other if you hadn't seen me at that lecture?" I asked.

"I don't know," she said. We drove in silence for the next five minutes. She slipped her hand into mine and squeezed it. We didn't want to talk about roads that weren't taken. Life was too short.

* * * *

I received a letter from Harvard early in November requesting an interview. I called my dad at his office. I could picture him sitting back in his swivel chair, watching a large, white steamer come into the harbor, as he said he told me so as though I'd already been admitted. I knew he'd take the day off to drive me into Cambridge, even though I could have driven myself or taken the MTA. We met Dr. Bromley from admissions, a friendly man with none of the airs I expected from Harvard.

He called in Dr. Roger, a professor of French literature. We spoke for thirty minutes in French, while my father and Dr. Bromley listened. I really don't know how much my father or Dr. Bromley were able to understand, but it was a different conversation than the one I'd had with the teacher in high school. I told him about my report on Jean Moulin, and he became excited, since he knew more about him than I. He had met Moulin's sister, Laure, who my history teacher told me was off-limits. She never told me exactly why but I assumed it was because of privacy issues, or maybe the subject of her brother was too painful. I would have traveled to any part of France to meet her. Dr. Roger said people accused Moulin of being a Communist because he befriended Russia. But Moulin had felt they were the only country with the military might to stop Germany. "When they signed that nonaggression pact, he was really frustrated," he said.

As the meeting drew to a close, Dr. Bromley said that they didn't accept students with my average. To be honest, I felt relieved, because I didn't know if I could compete there and didn't feel I deserved it. I felt as though I was a guest in a ritzy hotel, where I could never afford to pay, but I was there because someone invited me. I wouldn't have wanted to eat the food.

But he wasn't through talking. He told me my year in France had done a lot for me. He said the university was interested in attracting people with diversified experiences, especially if they would share them with the academic community. I didn't believe it—I wondered why no one at my high school besides Sarah was interested in my experiences, including the honors French class.

"Being a long-distance runner makes a statement about your perseverance also," he said. It was the first time anyone had expressed any admiration over my cross-country running. I always felt that the people at school viewed us as a bunch of gluttons for punishment. He shocked me by saying I would be given every consideration.

A month later, on the first Friday in December, I walked home during the first snowstorm of the season. It was that fifteen-minute period, particular to that time of year, when the sky changed from brightness to total darkness in fifteen minutes. I came home later than usual because of indoor track practice. A thin envelope from Harvard University awaited me. I'd heard thin envelopes were bad omens.

I paced around the house for fifteen minutes before I ripped the envelope open. They couldn't rule on my acceptance, but were giving me a favorable indication. They placed me on the waiting list, and I'd be informed within three months. The improvement in my grades had to be sustained. I called Dad, who said I'd get in. He said they were just covering themselves because it might look too easy if they just admitted me.

The next evening, Sarah and her family invited my father and me to the Union Oyster House, the oldest seafood restaurant in Boston. I met her brother for the first time. The governor came into the restaurant while we were there. Sarah's dad knew him and introduced him to my father and me. The governor asked my father, "How do I know your name?" The answer had something to do with someone in the registry of motor vehicles.

We all went to the Boston Garden nearby to see the game between the Celtics and San Francisco. Sarah's parents had seats at the floor level, directly behind the Celtics bench. I loved the atmosphere and realized how much I'd missed it when I had been away.

The Celtics players received thunderous applause during the introductions, while the crowd greeted San Francisco as if they were a potpourri of the Ten Most Wanted list. I'd never seen the players so closely. I stood up in my chair and looked around, hoping to find anyone in the crowd I knew. I would have settled for an enemy.

As the two centers, Wilt Chamberlain and Bill Russell, stepped into the center of the court for the jump ball, it occurred to me that it had been a year since the night I'd flown to Europe, feeling so alone and scared about my future. If I hadn't gone, none of this would be part of my life. I grabbed Sarah's hand and held on to it. The referee threw the ball up, and the centers jumped. The game was under way.

EPILOGUE

▼

Monday, July 19, 1999

I spent much of the time on the flight back from Paris thinking about John F. Kennedy Jr. and my conversation with Dr. Robert LePerrier. He told me he'd become closer to his father after the ordeal, which had transformed his dad. Was it the trial, the community service, or the pain of the shingles? I wondered. Although M. LePerrier had to do a thousand hours of community service based upon our trial, he was acquitted in the war crimes trial because his sister, Isabelle's mother, died before the case came to trial. So despite the photographs, his identity as Sendef could not be confirmed without witnesses.

I had heard in the late eighties about the Ryan Report, which exposed our government's deception of France regarding our knowledge of the whereabouts of Klaus Barbie and our arrangements to relocate him to South America. It didn't jibe with my concept of how our government operated. After hearing the same story in so much more detail from Robert's perspective, I could never dismiss it again.

It was very early in the morning by the time I arrived home. My kids and a friend who had spent the night formed a semicircle around the television set in our family room. Dressed in their soccer uniforms, they were always up at the crack of dawn during the summer.

They were watching an episode of *The Lone Ranger*, a rerun from the fifties. Although I had slept little, I was too stimulated to feel tired, so I joined them. I didn't want to disturb Sarah, who was a light sleeper once she solved or surrendered to her crossword puzzle and called it a night.

I recalled *The Lone Ranger* from my childhood. Actually, I remembered the commercial for Cheerios more than the actual program. They would always interrupt the episode to bring a message of interest and importance...but of importance to whom?

As I watched with the kids, I couldn't help but be aware of the masked man's soothing voice. I could appreciate his skillfulness with his guns using either hand, even though he didn't kill anyone. He preferred to shoot weapons out of opponents' hands. He outsmarted villains, using disguises and strategy rather than force. In the end, he helped a confused young man find direction in his life. As he sped away on his white horse, he left behind a silver bullet, a calling card. While he wore a mask, never mentioned his name, and didn't expect any gratitude or recognition, everyone knew him.

Although none of these things had registered when I watched the program as a child, I recognized that I received my own silver bullet years ago. I revisited three of my heroes, Jean Moulin, Willy Brandt, and Dan Connolly. These men's courage came from a place I couldn't imagine. All three were now gone; the German-British man died in 1992.

Like many stories, this one is bittersweet. Attorney Dan Connolly, father of a one-year-old son, died at the age of thirty-three from a brain tumor. Many years ago, I read an article in the *Boston Globe* when I was visiting for a school reunion. I called the reporter from the *Globe*, and the man spent twenty minutes on the phone with me. He had known Dan and his family well. Despite the reporter's congeniality and helpfulness, I hardly slept for two weeks after that conversation.

I had to make another trip to Boston a few years ago when Dad passed away from lung cancer. He quit smoking when I was twelve, two weeks after I had used a pencil to squish a package of his Camels. Unfortunately I had been too late. I remember standing on the platform at the large synagogue packed with people from the temple—military members, attorneys, relatives, and friends. Many people were there whom I'd never seen before.

The eulogy was difficult; my mind went blank in the middle. But I was able to say how right he'd been about so many things, and how his actions transformed my life. I felt comforted from knowing I'd delivered the message to him personally.

Had he pulled any strings to get me into college? If he had, he wouldn't have told me. Maybe that was why the Lone Ranger, who operated the same way, made me feel so nostalgic. My mom was a distant memory. Once in a while, there would be a longing for something unattainable that sat within my consciousness but beyond my grasp. At moments when I was able to visualize it, I had overwhelming feelings of wistfulness. Most of the time, however, it was hazy. No amount of money, power, attention from other people, or accomplishment would help me to satisfy it.

My favorite author, William Faulkner, said the past is still with us; in fact, it is not even really past. I knew I must live with this feeling and not try too hard to gratify it with external accomplishments, because it was just a part of who I was. I was usually successful in focusing on everything I had.

I left the children to their television and walked upstairs. The sun was reflecting off the windows, forcing me to open my eyes. Maybe Sarah would be up by now.

978-0-595-36104-5
0-595-36104-8

Printed in the United States
54986LVS00003B/259-294